TEXAS Lilies

samantha christy

Books Publishing Group

Saint Johns, FL 32259

Copyright © 2021 by Samantha Christy

This is a work of fiction. Names, characters, places and incidents are either the product of the author's imagination or are used fictitiously, and any resemblance to actual persons, living or dead, business establishments, events or locales is entirely coincidental.

Cover designed by Letitia Hasser | RBA Designs

Cover model photo by WANDER AGUIAR

Cover model – Andrew Biernat

TEXAS *Lilies*

Samantha Christy

CHAPTER ONE

Aaron

"You have a ghost in your lodge," Mr. Hudson says, tying his horse to the post out front.

I stop what I'm doing and turn. This isn't the first time I've heard that; last week, a wedding guest said the same thing. "The hunting lodge is a hundred years old. There's bound to be creaky stairs and unoiled doors."

"Whatever you say." He climbs the porch stairs. "But Hank swears he saw someone late last night."

"There are eight of you staying here this weekend. Someone probably got up for a snack."

He shakes his head. "Six of us were at the bar you recommended. He and Kora stayed behind for some alone time." He motions to his colleague. "Hank, get over here. Tell Aaron what you saw last night."

Hank strides over and joins us on the porch, pulling a piece of straw from his mouth. I try not to laugh at these northerners who come here for a weekend and think they're cowboys. "Saw a damn ghost."

I open the door and lead them inside. We stand in the grand foyer. "You saw a ghost," I say dryly. "In your room while you and your lady were…"

"Getting frisky. Damn right I did. But not in my room." He nods at the living room to his right. "We were on the couch, you know, taking advantage of this place while everyone was away."

I glance at the couch and turn up my nose. I make a mental note to pull out the steam cleaner after they leave.

"We'd lit a fire and turned off all the lights. Saw something walk right through the main area."

"Did Kora see it too?" I ask.

"She was busy," he deadpans, earning him a congratulatory pat on the back from his boss.

"And what did this ghost look like?"

"I don't know, man. I was too busy at the time to take notes, and I wasn't about to stop what I was doing and freak out Kora."

"But was it like a person? A floating sheet? A shadow?"

He thinks on it as he looks toward the back hallway. "A person, I guess. A shadow, but with definition, you know?"

"And what did it do?"

"It didn't do nothing. It just came and went."

"Thanks, Hank," Mr. Hudson says, dismissing him. "You can go pack up now. We need to be out of here by one for our flight." He pulls an envelope from his pocket and hands it to me. "This weekend was spectacular. Everything we needed for my team to blow off steam and regroup for our upcoming project."

I wave the envelope away. "You don't have to. Really."

"Take it, Aaron. You more than earned it. This place—the food, the trails, the history. Hell, even the ghost. You've really got something here."

"Thank you." I tuck the money into my back pocket. "I'd be most grateful if you'd spread the word to anyone who needs a similar getaway. We're still getting started."

"You wouldn't know the operation hasn't been running for years. This place is run like a well-oiled machine."

"I appreciate the vote of confidence."

I don't tell him Friday's catering order was almost late, and my cleaning lady quit yesterday with zero notice. Well-oiled machine, my ass. Some days I feel I'm hanging on by a thread. Maybe I do deserve the tip. Cleaning all eight rooms while they were on their ride yesterday had been no easy feat.

I'll split it with Lora, Joe, and Luca. Lora is my events planner, Joe is our cook, and Luca is one of the assistant horse trainers here at Devil's Horn Ranch. He helps me run horse tours, in addition to all his other responsibilities. Mrs. Garcia would have gotten a cut, too, had she not bailed on me. I guess I can't blame her. Her sister is very ill, and she went to be by her side in New Mexico. Still, it leaves me in a bind. Even the temp service I called couldn't get anyone out here. Looks like laundry and toilet scrubbing is how I'm going to spend my Sunday.

The good thing is we don't have more guests coming in for ten days. Or maybe it's a bad thing, but it gives me time to find a new housekeeper. Not many people can afford to work part time on such an irregular schedule. The hunting lodge is barely breaking even. But I'm determined to make it work. Like Mr. Hudson said, we've got something here, and damned if I'm going to let Gavin or my parents see me fail.

After the eight guests are picked up by the airport shuttle, I get busy cleaning. I start by sweeping downstairs. Dirt gets tracked in from the trails, and I'm not about to let these floors get mucked up; I installed them myself. In fact, I almost single-handedly fixed up this lodge. It's why I thought I should be the one to try to make something of it.

The loud music blaring from the sound system I put in helps pass the time. Someone taps my shoulder, and I jump. It's my cousin Maddox. I pull the remote from my pocket and mute the song.

He laughs. "Didn't mean to startle you. You'd think I was the boogeyman, based on your reaction."

"Guess I was into the music. What's up?"

"Andie wanted me to invite you for supper."

It's one o'clock in the afternoon, and I recently had a sandwich, but my stomach growls just thinking about the meals his wife cooks. "I've never been one to turn down an invitation to the McBrides'. What time?"

"Seven?"

"I'll be there."

He glances at the mop in my hands. "Where's Mrs. Garcia?"

"You're looking at her."

He chuckles.

"What's so funny?"

"You're learning what it's like to run things."

"*You're* the one who runs things, Maddox."

"That's bullshit and you know it. From day one, the hunting lodge has been your project, Aaron. I have to admit, I had my doubts. But I've read the guestbook comments. There hasn't been a single negative word from anyone. No complaints that I'm aware of. Luca says he's making bank on tips. I'd say you're doing one hell of a job."

"Thanks." I point to the vacuum cleaner. "If you're done pumping my ego and have nothing else to do, feel free to help."

He backs away. "Sorry. Andie's expecting a few mares to foal this afternoon, so I'm on diaper duty."

"I'm not sure how you do it."

"Change diapers?"

"No, raise a kid while you run the ranch and she does her vet stuff."

He heads for the door. "It takes a village, man." He waves casually over his shoulder and leaves.

He's right, and Devil's Horn Ranch is like a village. Almost thirty people work here, and most of them live on the property. Two small houses are occupied by Mickey, the head horse trainer, and Miguel, the barn manager. Owen, the ranch manager, lives in a small log cabin on the outskirts of DHR. The others either reside in the small apartments behind the arena or the bunkhouse. Me—I built my own cabin out by the ridges the property was named after.

I've spent summers here since I was fifteen. When I decided to go to college in Texas, I came here over every break. I slept in the bunkhouse and earned wages for being a ranch hand. Saved every penny to put into building my one-bedroom cabin. I finally finished it shortly after I graduated last year.

Gavin McBride, Maddox's dad and my uncle, agreed to let me fix up the old lodge and try making it into a business. Although we still call it the hunting lodge, it doesn't get rented out to hunters. We do have a few thousand acres of hunting ground, but it's been deemed too much of a liability to have drunken hunters stay here. With Lora's help, we rent it out for parties, business meetings, and weddings. Most people stay for long weekends to enjoy the property, which is well over ten thousand acres. We've got some of the best horse trails around, not to mention the Fort Worth nightlife, which is only a limo ride away.

Six hours later, my hands raw from washing, scrubbing, and laundering, I return to my cabin to shower before hopping onto my ATV for the trip to the main house.

After pulling up to Maddox's, I'm waved at by no less than five barn workers and ranch hands. When I'm not doing lodge business, I'm usually here, helping mend fences or bailing hay. To them, I'm one of the guys, just like Maddox wants us to be.

Andie is coming out of the south stable. She bounces over to me, clearly elated.

"I'm guessing you birthed a horse today?" I say.

She smiles big. "Two of them. Two healthy foals. I'd say that makes for a good Sunday."

My eyes flicker to her hands. "You will be washing up before cooking supper, yes?"

Laughter follows me up the porch steps. "Already did. Anyway, I'm not cooking. Maddox is making his famous short ribs."

My mouth waters. If there's one thing my cousin does well, it's cooking short ribs.

Andie scoops up her daughter, who is playing on the living room floor. Viv squeals as her mother twirls her around the room. Andie holds the baby out to me. "Can you take her for a minute?"

I balance her on my hip. "How old is she now?"

"Six months yesterday," Andie says, heading across the room to join Maddox in the kitchen.

I peer down at the small human. "You're a big girl now, aren't you?"

She babbles.

Andie sets the table and puts Viv into her highchair. During supper, she spoon-feeds her orange and green goop from a jar.

"I'm thinking of staying at the lodge for a few nights," I say.

"Something wrong with your cabin?" Maddox asks. "Your toilet broken?"

"Nothing like that. The cabin's great. But several people in the last few groups at the lodge have claimed a ghost is there."

Andie freezes, the spoon halfway to Vivian's lips. "A ghost. Really?"

Maddox's head bobs up and down repeatedly. "You could use it as a hook to get more business. Haunted hunting lodge. People love that shit."

Andie gives him a biting glare.

He looks guilty. "Sorry, babe. I meant people love that stuff."

"I'm not buying it. I'm going to stay there a few nights and see what's up. I'm sure it's a creaky step. Maybe shadows made by the stained-glass window I installed over the front door."

"You're staying there *alone*?" Andie asks.

"Last time I checked, I was a grown man."

Andie studies me. "I wouldn't do it, even for money. A hundred-year-old building in the middle of nowhere? Nobody will hear if you scream."

I roll my eyes. "There's no ghost, Andie. I just want to get to the bottom of why people might think there is."

She points her fork at me. "There's a lot of history here, Aaron. You've seen the graveyard beyond the ridge. We've told you the stories Maddox's grandmother passed down to us." She turns to her daughter. "Your namesake knew everything about this place. One day we'll tell *you* all about it."

"Want company?" Maddox asks.

"Oh, no," Andie says. "You're not leaving us alone here if there's a ghost on the ranch."

He looks amused. "You don't really believe in that shi—uh, *stuff*, do you, babe?"

"Like I said, there's a lot of history on this ranch."

"Could be my grandmother," Maddox says.

She shakes her head. "If Vivian were going to haunt anything, I guarantee you it would be this house or maybe the stables. She barely went into that old lodge."

"You're probably right. Could be that some hunter died there years before she bought the place."

I snicker. "Jesus, you two are way too gullible. There's no ghost."

"Guess you'll know soon enough," Maddox says. "Might want to keep your gun handy."

Andie narrows her eyes. "Will a bullet hurt a ghost?"

"Fair point," he says. "Might want to try garlic or a pointy stake through the heart."

"Those are for vampires."

I clear the dishes and wash up. "Thanks for dinner. I'll see you in the morning… if I survive the night." I cackle a spooky laugh and kiss Viv's soft curls before leaving.

Maddox says, "If I don't hear from you by nine, I'll send a search party."

"Ha-ha." I grab my cowboy hat and put it on, then leave.

At my cabin, I get a book, a six-pack of Coke, and some snacks, then start for the lodge. Before I get too far, I decide to go back and find my gun.

Once inside the lodge, I contemplate locking the doors. But here on the ranch, we never lock doors, so I decide against it. I can hear Andie saying, "Ghosts don't use doors."

There's a logical explanation for what people have seen. There always is.

I take the sodas from the plastic rings and place them in two rows on the left side of the refrigerator, then check the expiration dates on the yogurt and stack them according to freshness. Being raised by a woman who owns a restaurant, it was ingrained in me to organize a kitchen properly.

It's late, and I had a long day, but I'm determined to stay up as long as I can. I take my book into the living room and open it to the dog-eared page. I'm not sure how much I read, however, because I'm concentrating on every little sound. It's windy outside, which isn't helping.

I trace a banging noise to the screen door I hadn't latched right. A window rattles in one of the guest rooms, and I mentally put it on my list of things to fix.

I settle back down to read, my eyelids growing heavy.

The next thing I know, the lodge is illuminated by the morning sun. Damn. I didn't even make it to midnight. I rub my eyes and go to the kitchen for a soda to help wake me up.

I know how I organized the cans last night—two rows of three—but one of them is missing. Not one from the front either; one from the back. As if someone didn't want anyone to notice a can was gone. A yogurt is missing, too.

There's no ghost at the lodge. It's a goddamn thief.

CHAPTER TWO

Deryn

Three weeks ago...

I gaze at the old lodge, only it's not so old anymore. It doesn't look lived in necessarily, but changes have been made. There are no cars around, unless you count the old junkers off to one side that we used to get stoned in while looking at the stars until dawn. That is, until some guy named Matteo put the fear of God in us and banished us from the property. I was sixteen. Life was good then.

There aren't any horses either. No signs of life. I hide in the trees a good hundred feet away. I can see the renovations from here. The stained-glass window over the entry doors—new. The railing around the front porch—fixed and painted. The grounds— immaculate, with the exception of the old cars.

I pull a protein bar out of my backpack and watch. My ass hurts after a few hours of sitting on the ground. I get up and haul my pack onto my aching back. I'll come back tomorrow at a different time.

Until then, I pass the hours like I always do. Walking. Scavenging. Sleeping. Staying out of the way. I never hitchhike, though it would be pretty safe to do around here. This is a small town. But I can't risk being recognized, even though I'm not from here. It's close enough to Fort Worth so it's not completely off the map but far enough away to be separate from big city life. The kind of place people never lock their doors. It's what I'm counting on. It'll be the perfect place—as long as nobody lives there.

The next day at dawn, I wake, roll up my sleeping bag, collect my things, pull my baseball cap down low on my forehead, and return to the tree line to observe the lodge.

I watch for an entire week. A small group of people stayed for the weekend. A pretty blonde woman greeted them. Some guy with black hair peeking out from under his cowboy hat led six people on horses away and came back two hours later. An older black man came and went around mealtimes. Whenever the people left, a heavy-set Mexican lady went in the back door with cleaning supplies.

Realization dawns. It's being used as a hotel. Some sort of dude ranch. I sit on the ground with a thump. Well, this ruins my plans.

I observe the lodge for two more days before I boldly decide to go inside and check it out. I've learned people rarely come here unless guests are expected. The problem is, I'll never know when that might be, but it's barely after dawn. I take a calculated risk that nobody will arrive anytime soon. I can be in and out before anyone is the wiser, and if someone shows up, there are places to hide. It's a big lodge. I know because my friends and I trespassed a time or two back then.

I take one last look around and listen. No engines. No sounds of horses in the distance. Nothing but birds waking with their morning songs.

I leave my stuff camouflaged under a bush and fly across the yard so fast, my hat flies off. I backtrack to retrieve it before settling against the side of the house near a hedge. I sit for a moment, making sure I wasn't seen, as I catch my breath, then slink around to the back door. Just as I suspected—unlocked.

I walk in, my heart beating out of my chest, the sound of blood rushing through my ears. I know what I'm doing is wrong, but what choice do I have?

"Hello?" I whisper, then louder, "Anyone here?" I keep one hand on the door handle, ready to bolt.

When nobody replies, I finally breathe, but I don't let my guard down. Someone could arrive at any time. I run through the place and count ten bedrooms, each with an en suite bath. A rec room. A huge kitchen and dining area. An office. A smaller bedroom off the mudroom. Several large gathering areas. And the grand foyer. The foyer is the room I remember best. The staircase curves at the base and then after seven or eight steps splits off in either direction the rest of the way up. There is a second staircase off the kitchen that goes up to the hallway left of the guest rooms.

The whole place has been completely refurbished. It's a mansion if ever I saw one. But none of what I see excites me until I find a doorway at the end of the right upper hallway that leads to an attic. The stairs are creaky and dusty. At the top and to the left, lean large pictures of men who must have lived back in the eighteen hundreds. It's creepy the way they stare at me. There's an old bookcase, miscellaneous furniture, and several mattresses. Mattresses! I haven't slept on one of those in a while.

I go over and sit on one, dust rising as I sink into it. I cough and then straighten. What if someone came in the house while I was coming upstairs? I bolt to a large octagonally shaped window with a view out back and then to another overlooking the front yard. The attic is massive. Dust motes dance in the light from the east window. That window is huge—big enough for a person to climb through. I cross the floor on light feet, happy the floorboards aren't as creaky as the stairs. I stand in the center of the attic until I'm sure I don't hear anyone below. It's completely quiet. I could stay here until I figure something else out.

I hear a noise in the distance and race back to the south window. There's a small cabin maybe a quarter mile away but in clear view, especially from up here. The guy with the black hair, who was giving the horse tour, is wielding a chainsaw. He's cutting a downed tree into sections. After a while, he takes off his cowboy hat, wipes his brow, and then, oh my… he removes his shirt. He picks up a smaller piece of wood and whacks it in half with an axe. I'm not sure how long I watch, but by the time he's finished, he must have a cord of wood lying there. Why would one person need so much? Does the cabin not have electricity?

He disappears for a minute, then returns riding an ATV, hops off, and throws the split wood in back. Then he gets back on and, oh Lord, he's coming toward the lodge.

My heart pounds. No time to clear the house and make it to the woods. I'm stuck here.

I drop down and watch him by peering over the windowsill. He's still shirtless. When he comes closer, I can almost see sweat rolling down his torso as it glistens from the manual labor. He must be the caretaker of this place. How did I not see the cabin with all my reconnaissance?

He comes so close he disappears from view. I sit quietly and listen. There are a few vents in the floor, making it easier for me to hear what's going on below. The back door opens and closes. I hear footsteps and other noises, which I assume is him stacking the wood. He makes three more trips in and out, then drives away. He goes back to the cabin, puts his shirt back on, gets on the ATV, and leaves.

He delivered wood. Does that mean new guests will be arriving? I think it's Wednesday. Sometimes I don't know what day it is unless I go into town and visit a store. Last week, guests arrived on Friday. Could I stay here with other people in the house? They do come and go, and with these vents, I can hear a lot.

Yes. I can do this. It's better than camping, especially when it rains.

But I have a lot of work to do if people will arrive tomorrow. I need to get my things. Clean the mattress. Find some food—I'm running out, and I vow to make my remaining supply last as long as I can.

I race down both sets of stairs, run to where I hid my pack, cross back to the lodge, and return to the attic, making note of which stairs creak. I'll mark the ones that do. I'll find some old clothing upstairs—something to place on the steps that make noise.

I hide my stuff behind the bookcase. Not that it looks like anyone comes up here, which is what I'm counting on. I look at the old mattresses again. I can't risk coughing or sneezing. I'm going to have to clean one of them.

In the kitchen, I find a utility closet with lots of cleaning supplies. I gather what I need, along with a handheld vacuum. It'll make noise, but I'll be careful.

Back in the attic, I peek out all the windows, then cringe when I turn on the vacuum. I know it can't be very loud, but right now it sounds like buzzsaw. I run it for about fifteen seconds, then stop and look out the windows again. It's not very efficient doing it this way but necessary.

Satisfied I have an acceptable mattress, I turn my attention to the old chair in the corner. I drag it over by the window. This will be a nice place to read. There's a whole wall of books down in the rec room. I even have a flashlight in my pack. I'll be able to read at night. I glance at the south window. I wonder if he'll be able to see the glow of my light from his cabin.

There are lots of old drapes lying around. I'll figure out how to tack them over the windows at night. In fact, I see an ancient parlor lamp on its side. Maybe all it needs is a lightbulb. Surely they have extras in their supply closet.

I make sure the coast is clear and take the cleaning supplies downstairs. I open one supply closet; spa-like toiletries line the shelves. Soft cotton towels, pillows, duvets, silk sheets. Do they keep track of what they have? There's so much, I decide to take a chance. I take a pillow and towel. If I don't hear anyone complaining about them being gone, I'll try for more.

There's a box labeled Lost and Found. Things left by guests, I assume. Inside it are Dopp kits, various tubes of lipstick and makeup, several articles of clothing, an e-reader, and a few pairs of shoes. Each is labeled with a room number and date. Nothing is dated before September of last year. I surmise if the older items haven't been claimed by now, they never will be. It's not like stealing. I'll bring them back when I move on. It will be nice to have some new things until then. And an e-reader! Oh, yes. Even the charging cord is with it. I hope the attic has electricity.

The next closet has paper products. I eye the toilet paper. What if I have to pee in the middle of the night? It's not like being outside where you can just up and go.

I dart into the bathroom attached to the small vacant bedroom off the kitchen. I quickly use it, not knowing when I'll be able to again. It's rare I get to use a real toilet unless Mr. Choi, the nice man who owns the corner store I frequent, lets me use his. He feels sorry for me because I pay using my Lone Star Card, which is just a fancy title for food stamps.

Before I go back upstairs, I take a look in the refrigerator and pantry. Although there are currently no guests, there is no shortage of food. With my gut full of guilt, I take a few bottles of water from the back, an older-looking brick of cheese, and some crackers that have been opened but are nearing expiration.

In the attic, I pull my notebook from my pack and start a list.

2 water bottles

Brick of cheese

Half-box of crackers

Someday I'll pay for everything I take.

CHAPTER THREE

Aaron

My phone rings. It's Andie. "Oh, good," she says. "You're still alive. The ghost didn't kill you."

"Very funny, and it's not a ghost."

"You figured out the mystery?"

"It's no mystery. It's a thief. Found some food missing."

"You took inventory of the food?"

"No, but I know what was there."

"Maybe you're imagining things."

I start to question myself. Did I drink the Coke and eat the yogurt? I remember being dog-tired, but what if I came in for a midnight snack?

"Maddox wanted me to tell you it's all-hands-on-deck. With the new stable going up, he wants everyone to rotate the horses in and out of the pastures. He doesn't want them stressing because of the noise, and there will be a lot of it today."

"Want me to see if Quinn can help?"

She hesitates. She likes Quinn, but she hates his family. Namely his uncle, who kidnapped her briefly over seven years ago. Jon is still in prison for that and a slew of other offenses.

"Forget it."

"It's fine. Ask him. Maddox and Owen will appreciate all the help they can get."

Quinn Thompson is my best friend. Has been since I was sent down here when I was a delinquent fifteen-year-old. His family, or what remains of it, wanted him to follow in his grandfather's footsteps and become an oil and land tycoon. He wants nothing to do with it. He'd be happy being a ranch hand. Although he has access to millions in a trust fund, he never touches it. Calls it blood money.

An hour later, Quinn and I meet at the main ranch. The others are leading horses out of the stables. Maddox has a huge smile on his face. He's waited years for this. Saved every penny for the expansion. His father owns this place, and Maddox is determined to see it flourish. He's become quite the businessman. It's a far cry from his last gig as a bartender in New York City. But now he's just as much at home sitting in a saddle as anyone else on this ranch.

"Aaron, you, Quinn, and Luca take those horses in paddock ten to pasture two. Keep an eye on Mr. Kalik's mare—she's a feisty one."

"You got it." I carry a saddle over to paddock ten and pick a horse to ride. I have my favorites. Most of the horses here are boarded by paying customers, but several are owned by the ranch. Reuben neighs when he sees me coming. He's one of Maddox's. He named him after his favorite sandwich at my mom's restaurant, where he used to work. "Hey, Reuben. Let's you and I lead this bunch outta here. What do you say?" I turn to Quinn. "He says yes."

Quinn shakes his head. He doesn't believe horses understand people. I do. It's one thing Andie and I have in common.

We spend the afternoon with the horses in the pasture. Ordinarily, we'd leave them to their own resources, but with so many out here at one time, we could be asking for trouble when they're used to being in their stalls. Not to mention we have customers who keep valuable stallions and broodmares here. We can't risk anything happening to them if one of the others becomes unruly.

Andie makes the rounds between pastures, seeing if we're having any trouble and bringing us drinks and snacks.

It's early April, a beautiful time to be in Texas. Warm days, cool nights. The rainy days of late April and May haven't started.

Even this far from the action, we can still hear some of the construction. Maddox worked it out so there would only be occasional days with heavy construction going on. He'll do anything to make Devil's Horn Ranch the most desirable place to board and train horses, not to mention the best place to work.

"Want to go out tonight?" Quinn asks.

"Can't. Busy."

His eyebrows shoot up. "Is there something you're not telling me? You're never busy." He stares me down. "Who is she?"

"There is no she. I'm busy with things at the lodge."

"Such as?"

I think of the missing Coke and how stupid I'd feel if I was the one who drank it, so I don't bring it up. "There are some things that need fixing before the next group comes in."

"Need help?"

"Nah. I've got it covered."

"Friday, then? Head into town for some action?"

"Sure. Friday."

At six o'clock, we take the horses back. The frame of the new stable is up. They got a lot done in one day. I smile, knowing my small stake in the ranch will someday pay off big time.

At home, I shower and make dinner, then head to the lodge just after sundown. I'm torn between a desire to catch the perpetrator and an urge to deter him. I decide to lock the doors as a test. I thought about it a lot today. If I wasn't imagining it, and someone really did come in and take those things, it could have been stoners. Kids are known to hang out on the airstrip at the north end of the property. I should know; I was one of them back in the day.

Then again, what would stoners want with one Coke and a cup of yogurt? Seems like there are more valuable things around here. Namely liquor. But if they are in and out quickly, they might not know about the booze.

I peruse the liquor cabinet we keep stocked for guests. I take two bottles, whiskey and tequila, and place them smack in the center of the kitchen island. I leave on the light over the stove. Anyone looking in through the window in the back door will clearly see the bottles.

Before leaving the kitchen, I do a little purging from the pantry. Call it my mother's influence, but I always check expiration dates. There's a loaf of bread about to go bad and a half-full bag of chips that didn't get sealed properly and are stale. I toss them in the trash. There are three jars of peanut butter; two are unopened. The third is half-full but still good, so I put it back. Everything else is in order. I neatly stack some vegetable cans and close the door.

I settle on the couch with my book. My head bobs as I try to keep my eyes open. I turn on the TV, but I'm not much for watching mindless television, and it almost puts me to sleep. I get up and walk around. I shoot a game of pool. Then I realize the thief won't come in if they can see or hear me, so I go back to my book.

Seven hours later, I wake up, my back sore from a second night on the couch. I jump up and race to the kitchen. The bottles are still on the counter. And they're intact. I'm not sure why I feel a twinge of disappointment. Maybe I wanted to catch him after all.

I open the refrigerator. All five Cokes are still there. Could be I *was* imagining things. I close the door. This is stupid. Those guests were hearing things that clearly weren't there.

I glance at the trash on my way out. What I put there last night is gone.

Son of a bitch! The loaf of bread is no longer there. Dude came right through a locked door and stole old bread from the trash can. In the pantry, a jar of peanut butter is missing—the open jar. If you're going to steal, why not take a new one? I scan the rest of the shelves, fairly sure a can of vegetables is missing. What kind, I can't remember.

I check the doors—still locked. But how hard is it to pick an old lock like this one? I sit at the kitchen table. I might be able to understand the bread and peanut butter. When you're high and have the munchies, you'll eat almost anything. But a can of vegetables? Doesn't make sense.

My third night at the lodge, I get more creative, determined to catch the delinquents. I've seen enough movies to know how to do this. Before dark, I close and latch all the windows, then I walk the perimeter. There's no way anyone is climbing in through any of the windows; they're too high off the ground. Then I attach a string of bells to the handle of every door to the outside. Even if they get through the lock, they won't know about the bells. They'll be busted before they get two steps inside, and I'll be ready and waiting. I'm quick. They won't get far.

Just for good measure, I install a video camera I borrowed from Maddox. He bought it when one of the horses kept escaping his stall. I can't find a good place to hide it in the kitchen, so I tuck it into an artificial flower arrangement in the front hall.

I finish the book at three o'clock in the morning. Still nothing. Then I must drift off, because I'm startled awake by what I think is a toilet flushing. It's just shy of seven a.m. I hop up, grab my gun, and check every bathroom in the house—all twelve of them. The toilet in guest suite four is running. Great. I wonder how long it's been doing that. The water bill will be higher than normal; I don't think anyone has stayed in this suite for weeks. I jiggle the handle and it stops. I must have dreamed about hearing a flush.

When I get a text from Maddox, I rub my eyes. Working on four hours of sleep today will be difficult, but I promised I'd be over there first thing to help with the new stable. He's got us doing everything but the engineering and structural stuff. Today is sanding or painting—I forget which. I don't mind, though. Every ounce of sweat I put into this place is an investment.

I go to the fridge for a bottle of water. What I see stuns me. Or rather what I don't see. I'm as sure as shit there were seven cups of yogurt. After the first night, I counted everything. Yet there are only six.

I check all three doors to the outside. Still locked. I open one, knowing the jangling bells would have woken a bear in hibernation.

My heart pounds. The yogurt, the toilet— "Jesus Christ," I whisper, looking at the ceiling. "They're in the fucking house."

CHAPTER FOUR

Devyn

It's not hard to be invisible. I've gotten pretty good at it over the past few years. You just have to watch people. They all have routines. The people who stay at the lodge—they're predictable. Breakfast is at eight thirty, then out for a riding lesson. Lunch is usually at one, sometimes here, oftentimes not. Then some group activity or more riding. Dinner at six, followed by drinking, rec room games, and then bed.

I typically have the run of the house from about two to six in the morning. That's when I grab food and maybe a fresh towel. I use the bathroom. If there's an open guest room, I shower—even when guests are staying here. They assume it's another guest. I was even spotted by a delivery person the other day. He thought I was part of the group. And if the guests catch me milling about, they'd assume I'm an employee.

Yup, they're predictable. Until last night. I don't know why Black-haired Guy is staying here. I knew he was here the night before last; I heard him playing pool. I figured maybe his girlfriend kicked him out, even though I haven't seen a woman near his place. What I didn't count on was him being here again last night. Could be he has a bug infestation in his cabin or something. Has he been staying here longer, and I simply didn't know? I thought I saw him leave, but he must have come back in when I was putting up the window coverings.

I've been complacent. For three weeks, I've assumed if there are no guests here, the lodge is vacant. I have to be more careful because I was almost caught this morning.

He's gone now. Drove off on his ATV a while ago in the direction of the main ranch. I assume that means he won't be back for a while, so I descend the stairs, being sure to skip the creaky steps. I crack the attic door open and sit on the bottom step, listening for several minutes, as I always do, before stepping through. When I'm sure nobody is around, I go to the first floor. I'm on a mission. I swear I heard sleigh bells yesterday and again this morning when Black-haired Guy was here.

It doesn't take me long to see the string of bells attached to every outside door handle. I throw my head back and sigh. Does this mean I have to leave? Coming and going will be way more complicated now. I jingle them a bit. They're annoying. And loud. Why would he put these here? You'd think the guests would complain.

Wait a minute. This could work in my favor. *They're loud.* I'll hear them through the upstairs vents like I did earlier. Maybe I can stay a while longer. I like it here. I'll be more diligent about knowing exactly when people are here.

As I'm downstairs, I look through the refrigerator and the pantry again, hoping it's been stocked for an upcoming event. It hasn't.

I'm almost out of the bread and peanut butter I took the other day. I eye the yogurt, thinking I might be able to get away with one more. I reach around and take one from the back. People never notice when you pull from the back.

I get my small notepad and pen from my back pocket and open it to the third page. The list is getting longer by the day. I add to it.

1 cup yogurt

I look at the sleigh bells once more. Then I dare to do something I wouldn't normally do. I take a bath bomb from the supply closet and run upstairs to guest suite four (the closest one to the attic) and fill the tub. The bells will alert me and give me plenty of time to get upstairs. I can even leave the water in the tub if I have to. I mean, how many times do people really go into bathrooms anyway? Especially in unoccupied hotel rooms.

For the next thirty minutes, I enjoy something I haven't done in well over two years: a soak in hot water. I think back. Did I ever take baths? It's funny what becomes a guilty pleasure when life is so different.

I brought clothes into the tub with me. They were in desperate need of washing. I make quick work of laundering, wringing, then hanging them over the side. After, I rest my head against a soft towel and let the bath salts soothe me. I'll bet there is a lot of dirt and grime coming off me right now. All I've been able to manage are quick showers. This is a real treat. I rarely get to wash both my hair and body; it's usually one or the other. In and out in thirty seconds. It's all I allow myself. I've become very efficient at speedy showers.

I find myself relaxing for the first time in a long while, but that doesn't mean I let my mind wander. Thinking can be dangerous. Thinking of the past is heartbreaking. Thinking of the future is pointless. I live in this one moment in time. Because if I've learned anything over the past years, it's that these moments are few and far between.

Not wanting to push my luck, I step out of the tub and pull the plug. Drying off, I watch the water swirl down the drain. It leaves a dirty ring. Oh, jeez. I rub it off with the towel, leaving the tub as I found it.

I catch a glimpse of myself in the full-length mirror on the back of the door. It's something I try not to do often. The girl I see is nothing like the woman I'd hoped to grow into. She's dirty, even though her body has been cleansed. She's skinny, even though she eats several times a day. She's pathetic, even though… Well, there is no even though. She's just pathetic.

My good mood ruined, I gather my wet clothes and take them and the soiled towel with me to the attic. I'll throw the towel in with the guest laundry the next time people are here.

Sleigh bells ring in the distance. I lie down on my mattress, thinking of my perfect timing. I hear voices. It's not Black-haired Guy. I peek out the window and smile. It's the delivery van from a supermarket. Food! Tonight I'll eat well. Food always gets delivered a day before an event, and I've learned the chef is a different person from the food delivery guy, so the chef doesn't miss jars of this and boxes of that. Oh, I love food delivery day.

I can only hope *he* doesn't stay here again tonight. I'll have to be super careful if he does. I'm light on my feet. Socks, not shoes. Never shoes.

I peel back the foil on the yogurt and try to enjoy my breakfast. Still hungry, I fish a granola bar from my pack. It doesn't satisfy me either. Crap, I know what this means. I'll get my period soon, and I'm low on supplies. I'll have to make another trip to town, but not today. Today I'm finishing the Nicole Snow novel

I've been immersed in. Thank God for this e-reader. There must be more than a hundred books on it. And I'm pretty sure I go through a book a day. It's a great way to pass the time.

My eyes close, and I drift off, dreaming of perfectly proportioned alpha males and happy endings—things I can only have in my dreams. Because people like me don't deserve them.

CHAPTER FIVE

Aaron

Squatter. We've got a fucking squatter. Or squatters, plural. Who the hell knows?

I dip my roller into the paint and slather it on the wood, my mind not at all on the task at hand. It's got to be only one. How could multiple people be so quiet? And the amount of food taken could hardly sustain several of them.

Let's think about this. What exactly am I dealing with here? How long has he been there? A few weeks? A month? I think back to the first time someone mentioned the ghost. Yeah, almost four weeks. How in the hell has a bum been living in the lodge for four weeks without being caught? And where?

Of course—the attic. I haven't been up there since Dad and I moved the last of those old portraits out of the main hall. That was more than seven years ago. It's got to be dirty as shit. My eyebrows go up. But there are mattresses, if I recall correctly. I suppose living in a dusty attic is better than sleeping under a bridge. It'll get hot as hell up there in a month—dude picked the best time of year to become a low-life, criminal, trespassing squatter. Wait, can I even call him a squatter? Maybe it only applies to vacant houses. What do you call someone who lives in an occupied one?

"Something on your mind?"

I jump, startled. Maddox is appraising my work. I'm being anything but efficient. I've been painting the same place over and over. "Just tired."

"Ghostbusting keeping you up at night?" He chuckles.

I contemplate telling him about the uninvited visitor but decide against it. I can deal with it myself. Maddox doesn't have to know every single thing that happens on the ranch. It is partly mine, however small the part is. "Don't you have better things to do than stand here, watching me paint? Like maybe pick up a damn brush?"

"I did. Painted the whole east wall."

"That's the smallest one."

"Yeah, well, at least it's done. I'm taking a break to check on Vivian." He almost pinches his fingers together, leaving a small space between his thumb and forefinger. "She's this close to sitting up on her own. Man, she's growing up fast. Need anything from the house?"

"Coffee."

"You got it." He turns to Owen, who's down a ways on my left. "For you, too?"

"You musta been readin' my mind, McBride," Owen says with his heavy southern drawl.

Owen is the ranch manager. He basically runs everything around here. He pays the bills, maintains supplies, and supervises the workers. He recently took over the job from a guy named Matteo, who was the nicest Mexican immigrant you'd ever meet.

After thirty years in Texas, twenty-two of them spent here on Devil's Horn Ranch, Matteo left to go back home to take care of his severely ill mother.

Owen was Matteo's assistant for eight years. He slipped right into the job without missing a beat. He's firm but fair. Nice but commanding. He knows Maddox is the "real" boss around here, even though he doesn't carry the title and has far less experience. The best part about Owen is that he's not beneath doing the jobs the rest of us do. He'll clean up a pile of horse shit rather than walk past it. I admire that in a person of authority.

"Andie told me about your ghost," Owen says, slathering on paint. "You believe in that crap?"

"There's no ghost. And no, I don't believe in them. The lodge is old, is all."

"Uh-huh," he mumbles. "That why you can barely hold a paint roller or balance on your ladder?"

If he were anyone else, I'd tell him to fuck off. But it's Owen. I just shake my head and get back to work.

After a long day, a shower, and a change of clothes, I return to the lodge, peering up at the window in the attic along the way. There's a clear shot from it to my cabin. Has the fucker been watching me come and go? Is he looking at me right now? I should have stormed up into the attic this morning and tossed his ass out, but where's the fun in that? I'd rather get him when he doesn't see it coming.

It never even dawned on me until this second to call the police. Could be that a part of me thinks this is all in my head, or maybe one of the guys is pulling a prank. I wouldn't put it past them. Last year, Zac got the others good. He kept playing a sound bite of a sick horse in the middle of the night. Had the guys out searching the stables night after night. When they finally caught on, they practically tarred and feathered him. Ever since, it's been a competition to see who can out-prank him.

I enter the back door to the resounding greeting of the bells. I throw them in the trash, along with the others. Supplies are stacked on the counter. The pantry is full from the delivery for tomorrow's arrival. Oh, this is good. It's a veritable smorgasbord. No way will he be able to resist this. I glance at the ceiling. What does he do when guests are here?

I yawn twice, then slap my cheeks. I cannot be tired tonight. I open the fridge and pull out a Coke. My eyes are drawn to the yogurt. Five of them now, not counting the new, unopened packs. It's definitely not in my head.

But it still could be Zac or one of the others messing with me. *Ghost*, I think and snicker. That would be damn clever of them, and if it turns out to be one of the guys, I'll have to come up with something exceptionally good to get them back.

I go to the living room, sit, and try to keep myself awake. My mind immediately goes to thoughts of Cameron. God, I miss him. The guilt creeps up, as it always does when I think of him. I get out my phone and look at pictures of the two of us in college. Then my head falls back on the couch cushion as I relive that horrible night for the thousandth time.

I hear a noise. Could be the wind against one of the shutters, but it could also be the squatter. I straighten and listen again, glad for the distraction. I take hold of my gun. Is he watching me now? My eyes wander to the grand foyer, where I can see the bottom of the staircase. Is he standing at the top behind the wall, spying on me? Waiting for me to fall asleep so he can steal more food?

If I'm being honest, I'm a little freaked out. It's dark outside. Quiet. There's nobody around for miles. What if the guy is a psycho? He could kill me and dice me into pieces, and no one would know until Lora shows up to greet our guests.

I'm being ridiculous. If there really is someone in the attic, he obviously knows I've been here. He's had plenty of opportunities to take me out. Whoever's up there is used to having people around. We've had several groups of guests over the past month. That's a lot of tiptoeing and light-footing. I'm kind of amazed he's been able to pull it off. Part of me wants to meet the guy who's been so stealthy.

I yawn again, despite being fully caffeinated. I glance at my book on the coffee table. Can't do it—I'll fall asleep for sure. I look at the large TV hanging on the wall, half expecting to see movement behind me reflected on the dark screen. I whip around and see nothing.

I have a plan to catch him in the act, but it's only ten o'clock. If he knows I'm here, he'll wait until I'm asleep.

I play on my phone for a few hours, have another Coke and a snack. I pretend to call it a night. I could take one of the guest rooms, but I've been in the living room for three nights. He'll be expecting it.

I get pillows and a blanket from the supply room and take them to the couch, counting the steps it takes me to get there. I take stock of my surroundings. I need to be able to navigate this place in the dark. The coffee table is in front of the couch. There are two more couches flanking this one, with about two feet between them. It's about three steps to the edge of the couch. Behind this couch is a table with a lamp—best be careful not to knock it over. Then it's almost a clear shot through the foyer and into the kitchen. I'll have to be careful not to run into the round table in the middle of the grand hall or catch my foot on any of the rugs.

I turn off the light, lie back, and put my legs up, careful to keep my filthy shoes dangling off the couch. I could remove them, but catching a thief in bare feet is not manly at all. I rest the gun on my chest.

It's hard not to fall asleep. The only thing that keeps me awake is thinking back to first semester sophomore year. How stupid I was back then. How invincible we thought we were at nineteen. We couldn't have been more wrong. If I had only said no. If I had only put a stop to things. But that's how things were done. They were done to me, and I was passing the torch. It had been like that for years. Generations even.

My eyes flood and my pillow becomes damp as I think about everything that happened. The camaraderie. The elation. The king-of-the-world feeling.

The stunned silence. The sirens. The out-of-body experience. It couldn't be happening to me. Us.

The sheer devastation.

I blow out a deep breath, pull my phone under the blanket so it doesn't light up the room, and check the time. Twelve thirty. I've been lying here for two hours. I worry that maybe I'm too late. Could the squatter have already raided the kitchen? After sitting up, I become acutely aware of the cloying darkness. Not one shadow falls across the living room floor. I can't see a single tree branch outside the window. There's no moon tonight. I may have my work cut out for me.

I grope my way to the kitchen, careful not to make a sound. The toe of my boot meets the bottom step in the foyer, but I'm walking in slow, methodical steps, so there's no noise. I alter my course slightly and complete my journey. I'd previously pulled out a kitchen chair and positioned it so I'd be facing the pantry to my left and the refrigerator dead-on. I even tested the chair to make sure it wouldn't creak when I sat.

I wait, my ass hurting from the hard wooden surface. I don't dare check the time. My phone would illuminate the room. My guess is it's been an hour. I obsessively trace the outline of my gun on the table in front of me.

Something is happening. It's subtle, but I hear it. Not footsteps, though. Breathing. Hard, fast breathing. Like someone is afraid.

I remain perfectly still, trying to control my own breaths so he doesn't hear me.

Minutes pass. I'm not sure how many. I only hear the breathing. It's coming from the entry to the back stairs. He hasn't moved. How long is he going to stay there? Maybe he knows I'm here and doesn't know what to do. Even though it's pitch black, I sense slight movement as he crosses the room. There's no sound. Even his breathing has become silent.

He's almost to the fridge. As soon as he opens it, the room will light up, and he'll see me. I quietly raise my gun and point. He hesitates. Did I make a sound?

I sense him cringing as the door to the refrigerator opens. I tense as a small sliver of light slices the cabinets and counter to the left. I can't see him yet, only his silhouette. He glances aside, but I'm not in the path of the light yet. He's small. Good. He'll be easy to take. The fridge door opens more—not all the way, just enough for him to see inside. He reaches in and takes a few things. Now's my chance. His hands are full. The refrigerator door closes, and I stand, the chair falling backward behind me.

I hear a gasp, followed by glass shattering on the floor, then hurried footsteps. A pained scream echoes in the kitchen. When my shoes crunch glass, I understand why. I flip on the light in time to catch a glimpse of him fleeing the room, running for the front door.

"Stop!" I race after him, seeing bloody footprints dot the foyer. He doesn't stop. I cock the gun. "Stop or I'll shoot!"

He puts his arms up and turns. I'm stunned. He's a *she*. A goddamn beautiful she.

CHAPTER SIX

Devyn

I may have lost a few brain cells over my lifetime, but I'm not stupid. When someone points a gun at you and threatens to shoot, you stop.

My hands are in the air. Black-haired Guy is staring at me with a slack jaw after flipping on a light. I eye the barrel of the gun. I'm caught, and knowing what could happen next brings back terrible memories. I shake uncontrollably.

He sees my reaction and puts down the gun. I bolt to the door. I don't care that all my stuff is two floors up.

"Wait!"

He comes after me, but I'm almost to the door. An overhead light turns on. I flinch and try the handle, but it's locked. It takes a few seconds to unlock it, but that's enough time for him to grab my arm. Instinctively, I push him away. He goes for my other arm. Not happening. I cock my arm back, bend it, and give him an elbow in the face.

He backs away. "Oh, shit." He touches his face, then examines the blood on his hand. He tackles me. My knee comes up and connects with his crotch, but off-center. He doubles over but stays on top of me. He flips me face down and pulls my arms behind my back. He holds me in place, his knee in my back, droplets of his blood splattering a few inches from my face.

"Calm the fuck down," he says. "I'm not going to hurt you."

"Then let me go."

"You'll run."

"I won't get very far without shoes." It's a lie. I'd run like hell, cut up feet or not.

He stays on me but eases the pressure on my wrists. "No, I suspect you won't. And you must have stuff in the attic. What about that?"

"I've gotten by on less."

"Who are you?"

"No one."

"What are you doing here?"

"Nothing."

"You're stealing from us."

"I wasn't. I mean, I was, but I was going to pay you back when I could. I promise."

He laughs disingenuously. "So you're an *honest* thief."

"I'm telling the truth. It's all there in the notepad in my back pocket."

His weight shifts off me momentarily. He releases one of my hands and goes for the notebook. I hear him page through it. "You kept track of everything you took?"

"So I can pay it back someday."

He's quiet for a beat. "All this probably adds up to less than a hundred bucks. If you're so desperate, why didn't you take the electronics? The artwork?"

"Because I'm not a criminal." Another lie.

His weight shifts again. "Your foot is bleeding."

"So's your face."

"When I get off you, you're going to follow me to the kitchen, and we'll get cleaned up, okay?"

"You mean before you call the police?"

"I'm not going to call anyone."

"Why wouldn't you? I've been stealing. I've been sleeping in your attic for—"

"About a month."

I strain my neck to look back at him. "You knew? All this time?"

"Not until a few days ago. Guests told me they saw a ghost. I guess you weren't as invisible as you thought."

"You stayed here in hopes of seeing a ghost?"

"Listen, my knees are starting to hurt, and my cheek is swelling. Mind if we continue this conversation in the kitchen?"

He gets off me but keeps a hand firmly on my upper arm. What can I do? My foot is killing me, and all my stuff is upstairs. I try to take a step. Pain sears through my foot, and I almost fall down.

He suddenly sweeps me up in his arms and carries me back through the house. I can almost see a purple bruise spreading across his cheek. I resist the urge to wipe the blood oozing from his wound.

He gazes down at me. "We're quite the pair."

I'm set upon a chair. He rights the one that fell over and puts my hurt foot on it.

"Stay," he commands, as if I'm a dog. He turns on another light, reaches under the sink, and pulls out a first-aid kit. He uses tweezers to remove a small shard of glass from the pad of my foot. Then he cleans the wound, wraps my foot in gauze, and sweeps up the broken glass. "Don't walk in here without shoes until I can run a vacuum."

"Why are you being so nice to me?"

He crouches down and views his reflection in the stainless-steel four-slice toaster. "I probably shouldn't be. I'm going to have one hell of a shiner. Where did you learn to defend yourself like that?"

I shrug.

He sits. "We have ourselves a bit of a situation."

"What are you going to do about it?"

He motions to the ceiling. "I'm curious how you lived here and got by so long without being noticed. Show me."

"Show you what?"

"Your hiding place in the attic."

"If I show you, you'll let me go?"

"Yup."

"Just like that?"

"Yes."

"It's your house. You can go where you want."

He inclines his head to the back stairway. "You first."

I hesitate. I'm weary of men who bark directions at me. Most of them have ulterior motives. What if he gets me up to the attic and rapes me? I look up at him. He doesn't seem the rapey type, though, and I've seen plenty of them. He seems... compassionate. Though it's funny to think that after he chased me down with a gun.

"I'm not going to hurt you, uh... what's your name?"

"Does it matter?"

"We've known each other for ten minutes. It's awkward not knowing who I'm talking to."

"We don't *know* each other," I say aggressively.

"You're right, we don't. But even strangers introduce themselves. I'm Aaron Pearce."

"Devyn."

"Devyn what?"

"Just Devyn."

"Well, Devyn Just Devyn, it's nice to meet you. I'd have preferred we meet under different circumstances, but you have to admit it might be a funny story someday."

"I doubt it."

"Why?"

I wave my arm. "Because this is your life, *Aaron Pearce*. You work in this mansion. On this incredible ranch. You have a place to call home. I'm assuming you have friends here. Maybe you're even happy. So while this may be funny to you, it's not from where I stand."

He sighs, clearly feeling guilty. "You have a point. You wouldn't be here doing what you've been doing if you weren't down on your luck. So, the attic?"

"You should tend to your face first."

"And leave you alone? Not likely."

"Then let me do it. Hand me the first-aid kit, a wet rag, and something cold from the freezer—a bag of peas would be best."

"Seems like you've done this before."

"Are you going to let me help or not?" I ask. He gathers the things I requested. I clean him up, butterfly-bandage the gash, and hand him the peas. "Hold this on your cheek, twenty minutes on and twenty minutes off to control the swelling."

"Are you a nurse or something?"

"I'm not anything."

He looks at me like he feels sorry for me. He wouldn't look at me this way if he knew the truth. He stands. "Like I said, you first."

I get up and hobble across the room using only the toes on my left foot. I flip on the stairway light, something I've never done before. It feels strange. He follows me upstairs, down the second-floor hallway, past guest suite four, and then up the attic stairs. At the top, he glances around.

I point. "I keep my stuff behind the bookcase."

He keeps me in his sights, but I doubt he sees me as a flight risk anymore after seeing the laceration on my foot. He checks out my backpack. It's open and all my food is lined up on the old trunk next to it. I'd become complacent. I should have kept everything together, in case I needed to make a fast getaway.

He picks up the remaining two granola bars and examines them. What's he looking for? He surveys the rest of it: a few cans of tuna, some soda, packets of cheese and crackers. He picks up the empty bag of bread. "You took this from the trash."

"It was still good."

"Some of this stuff isn't from here. Where did you get it?"

"Public assistance."

"As in food stamps?"

"They call it a Lone Star Card, but yeah, basically."

"If you can get public assistance, why not stay in a shelter?"

My foot throbs. I sit on the mattress. "I tried someplace like that; didn't work out. And the women's shelter in town is full."

"But you must get this Lone Star Card from someone."

"The state, but not for long. I only got three months' worth, since I'm considered an able-bodied adult. There's only a month of benefits left. I've been rationing. It's why I had to take some of your food."

Curiosity crosses his face. "What happened two months ago that made you seek public assistance?"

I don't answer.

"Fine. Tell me how you went undetected up here."

I explain about the drapes I hung over the windows at night so nobody would see the light. How I snuck down to use the shower or the bathroom.

He notices a bucket in the corner. Thank God it's empty. "For emergencies?"

I nod in shame.

"Jesus, Devyn. What happened to you?"

"You said if I showed you, you'd let me go. Are we finished here?"

"Where will you go? You're injured. I cleaned your foot, but it could get infected without proper care."

"I know how to care for a cut. I'm not stupid."

"I never said you were. In fact, I'd say you were pretty smart to pull this off. But why not get a job at Target or Wendy's? Surely they'd hire you."

"I can't."

"Why not?"

"I have my reasons."

"Fair enough."

I hobble over and put the food away, roll up my sleeping bag, and gingerly stuff my injured foot into my tennis shoe. I sling my pack on my back and hop on one foot down the stairs. He follows.

"This is ridiculous," he says back in the kitchen. "It's two o'clock in the morning. I'd be a dick if I turned you out right now."

"Yet you're thinking you'd be crazy to let me stay the night."

He narrows his eyes as if I've read his mind. "You've been here for a month. If you were going to trash the place or try and hurt me, you'd have already done it. The guests won't arrive until after noon." He motions to the small bedroom off the kitchen. "Use that room. Sleep in a bed. Take a shower without worrying about someone finding you and calling the police. In the morning, I'll send you on your way with food and supplies."

I wonder about his ulterior motives.

He notices my suspicion. "I'm just being human, Devyn. Anyone would do the same."

"I stole from you. Anyone would *not* do the same."

"Well, I guess I'm not anyone. So you'll stay the night?"

"Only if you'll let me pay you back when I can."

"Sure. Whatever you want."

"Will you be staying here or going back to your cabin?" I glance away. I basically just admitted I've been watching him.

"If it's all the same to you, I'll sleep where I've been sleeping all week. Don't worry, there's a lock on the bedroom door."

"Okay."

"Wait." He walks to the refrigerator and takes out two individual cups of chocolate mousse. They look expensive. I would never take things like that. He holds one out to me. "I don't know about you, but I'm starving." He pushes the decadent dessert into my hand. "On the house. It's been a long night."

He opens a drawer, pulls out two spoons, and hands me one. We sit in silence and eat. This has got to be the weirdest night of my life.

CHAPTER SEVEN

Aaron

My alarm goes off at six a.m. I wanted to wake up before Devyn. I suspect she'll run out of here and never look back, even after my promise of sending her with supplies. There's something about her. She's sad. Lost, yet somehow strong.

I sent a text to Andie, knowing she's probably up with Vivian by now. She replies immediately. I go to the kitchen and quietly start breakfast. I wonder how long it's been since Devyn had a hot meal. I'm no chef, but I can make a decent omelet.

As suspected, she emerges by six thirty. She stops in the doorway, pack on her back.

I put down the spatula. "You were going to leave without saying goodbye? That's not very nice."

"Figured you didn't need the hassle." Her eyes close, and she inhales. "Oh, that smell."

"Sit. I made omelets, sausage, and toast."

She removes her pack. So it *has* been a long time since she's eaten a real meal. "Thank you."

Devyn eats more than I do, and that's saying something. We're still at the table when the back door opens and Andie walks in. Devyn immediately goes on high alert.

I maintain a relaxed air. "Andie, this is Devyn. She's a friend of mine. We were making breakfast and a jar broke, and she cut her foot. Can you take a peek?"

"Of course."

Devyn reaches for her pack. "It's not necessary."

"She's a doctor," I say. "A veterinarian. But she takes care of everyone on the ranch with minor injuries. Let her check it out as a favor to me."

"I promise to be gentle," Andie says.

Devyn hesitates, then removes her shoe and sock.

Andie takes the chair between us, lifts Devyn's foot into her lap, and removes the blood-stained gauze. "That's a pretty nasty gash." After opening the doctor's bag she uses for fixing humans, she gets out large Q-tip like swabs, coats one in brown liquid, and rubs it across the wound. "I could throw a stitch or two in it. Might make it heal quicker."

"That's okay. I'll be fine."

"How about some skin glue, then? Either way, you should try and stay off your feet for a day or two to let the healing process begin."

"Skin glue would be great. Thank you."

Andie does her thing and then wraps the foot like the professional she is. "There. All done."

"Thanks for coming over so quickly," I say, getting up and opening the door for her.

Andie understands it's an invitation for her to leave. She glances at my cheek. "You sure you don't want me to have a look at that, too?" She looks between Devyn and me. I know she's wondering what's going on. I can almost guarantee she'll talk to Maddox about the girl at the lodge. I'm going to have a lot of explaining to do later.

"Some other time."

She steps outside. "Oh, wait. Devyn, are you the new housekeeper? Maddox mentioned Aaron was in need of someone. Aaron here is a trooper. He thinks nothing is too mundane a task for him, and he'll do anything to keep this place running, but we all know he sucks at hospital corners." She giggles.

Devyn is caught off guard. "I… uh…"

"Yes, she is. She arrived early. Hitched a ride from Dallas with one of Wyatt Jenkins' ranch hands. I heard the truck from my cabin, and figured I'd run over and give her a good ol' Devil's Horn Ranch welcome with some down-home cooking."

Andie eyes me curiously. I should have shut up after *yes*.

"Okay then," she says. "Devyn, nice to have you on board. See you around."

Devyn taps her foot. "Thanks again for this."

"Don't let Aaron work you too hard today. Rest that foot."

"Yes, ma'am."

"It's Andie."

Devyn nods shyly.

After Andie leaves, I turn to Devyn. "I apologize for all that. I didn't know what to say."

"You didn't think you'd have some explaining to do about having a woman here at the crack of dawn?"

"I didn't think. I only wanted her to patch you up properly."

She stands and picks up her pack. "I should go."

It pains me to watch her limp to the door. "What the hell. You need a job. The lodge needs a housekeeper. So let's just make it official. You can stay in the room you used last night. It's not a full-time job yet, but it'll be enough to get you by until you find your footing. What do you say?"

I'm brilliant. Or Andie is. It's the perfect solution. And I will no longer have to make beds and mop floors.

Her expression immediately dulls my elation. "I can't."

"Why not?"

"For the same reason I can't work at Target or Wendy's."

"You never told me why that is."

"I should go. Thank you for the offer and breakfast and… everything."

I can tell she doesn't want to go. She walks out the door with her head hung low. She turns back once and smiles before slowly moving into the trees. I imagine that's where she cased the place. It'd be where I would have done it. It kills me to think of her sleeping on the streets. No matter who she is or what happened to her, nobody should have to be without a warm bed and a place to call home.

Maybe she doesn't want to be found. Oh, shit. Is someone after her? Maybe she doesn't want to get a job because then someone would be able to track her down.

I run after her. "Devyn!"

She turns on her good foot and waits for me to speak.

"It's not much work. Making beds, doing laundry, mopping floors, dusting, cleaning bathrooms. It's not glamorous, but it's easy, and it's only three or four days a week. Not even full days at that. Fifteen hours a week. Twenty tops. You can stay here. Room and board for your work. There's always plenty of food. Good food. Joe makes fantastic meals. You're welcome to all the leftovers." I chuckle. "But you already know that. No paperwork. Nothing official. You don't even have to give me your last name."

"Are you for real?"

"I'm for real offering you this deal. Cleaning for room and board. No strings."

"Why?"

"Because you've had some bad breaks, but I can tell you're a good person."

"You don't know that. I could be a grifter, a con artist. A… murderer."

"I'll bet you the notebook in your pocket you're none of those. I'm willing to take the chance. Are you?"

She looks down. "I have three changes of clothes, and none of them are nice. You wouldn't want me around your guests."

I look her over. "You may be the same size as Andie. I'm sure she'd be happy to let you borrow an outfit or two."

"I don't like handouts."

"What do you call public assistance?"

She grimaces and starts to walk away.

"Wait. I'm sorry, that was mean. Please. Stop."

She does.

"I'll give you money to buy clothes."

Her expression sours even more. "What don't you understand about me not liking handouts?"

"It wouldn't be a handout. You'll be working for me."

"I'd be working for the lodge for room and board. Taking care of me personally is not part of the deal."

I try not to smile. "So we have a deal?" She's still hesitant, but I get an idea. "Check the lost and found. People leave all kinds of clothes here. I'm sure you can find something acceptable."

Looking guilty, she reaches into her pack. "I almost forgot to return this. It's from the lost and found." She hands me an e-reader.

"Keep it for now. If the owner ever comes back for it, I'll know where it is." I leave, saying over my shoulder, "You coming?"

She gazes at the lodge, clearly deep in thought. Then she follows me.

CHAPTER EIGHT

Devyn

After washing my clothes and taking the longest shower I can remember, I lie on the bed and put my foot up. I pull a clean shirt over my face and inhale the fresh scent. This almost feels normal. As normal as anything has felt in well over two years.

Why is Aaron helping me? I stole from him. Hit him. Yet here I am in a room of my own in a place I can call home—for now anyway.

He had work to do. Said he'd meet me back here at eleven before the guests arrive this afternoon. I have a little time, so I explore the lodge. I've done it before, but never without looking over my shoulder, and not without the constant pounding of my heart. It's strange what a change of perspective can do.

This place is amazing. The intricate woodwork on the stairway spindles alone is a testament to how well the place is maintained. There are ornate area rugs in each room. Books line the walls of the library. Someone even took the time to organize them alphabetically by author name.

The large front porch has six rocking chairs. I sink into the cushions of one and imagine myself relaxing out here with a cold lemonade at sunset. Maybe something stronger. I glance at the rocker next to me and picture Aaron. I think of his black hair and how it looks good even when it's messy and matted from his cowboy hat. His inviting smile isn't judgmental in the least. I frown and get up. It would be judgmental if he knew me.

Back inside, I tour the guest rooms. Incredible photos hang on the walls. Each room has a different set, and I get the idea they're all pictures of the ranch. In one room, the series of photos depicts individual parts of a horse: a hoof, a mane, a muzzle. In another, a stable door, tack, an empty stall, and the Devil's Horn Ranch brand. Another has different photos of riding trails.

I've never been into horses, but these pictures make me want to learn about them and the ranch.

Someone clears their throat. I'm startled, and I feel the urge to run. Then I realize I don't have to.

"My dad took those," Aaron says.

"All of them?"

"He's a photographer," he says proudly.

I swallow. It must be nice to have a relationship with a parent. "He's very talented. These are breathtaking."

"Thanks. Unfortunately, I didn't inherit his eye for beauty—well, in scenery anyway." His gaze travels across my face, and my cheeks heat. "Looks like you've already taken the tour. Are there any questions?"

I walk around the guest bed and pull up the duvet. Andie was right. Aaron does not know how to make a proper bed. I quickly straighten the flat sheet and replace the duvet. Then I plump the pillows and place a decorative throw from one of the chairs on the bed.

Aaron stands back and watches. I see the smile, and it makes me smile back. I wonder how long it's been since I've done that.

"Wow," he says.

"It's all about the pillows."

"Not what I meant, but yeah, the bed looks great." He's still looking at me. I wait to feel uncomfortable. I'm used to being invisible. For years, nobody noticed me, and those who did, I didn't want to. But the feeling never comes.

Do I want him to notice me?

"Why don't you give me the rundown?" I say.

"It's not too complicated, and you don't have to do anything until tomorrow. Everything's clean and ready for guests—unless you want to do the pillow thing in the other guest rooms. Your job is to make beds and clean bathrooms when the guests are out for their morning excursions. Only change the sheets if they are clearly dirty, otherwise just switch them out between guests. The mattress pads, too." His nose turns up. "It's disgusting when hotels don't wash the mattress pads."

"Change the mattress pads. Got it."

"There's a large commercial washer and dryer in the laundry room near the kitchen, along with a smaller one for single loads of sheets or clothes. You can use that one for your personal stuff, too. You have the run of the place when the guests aren't here. Feel free to use what you want. Play pool. Enjoy the grounds. Even ride a horse if you want."

"I've never ridden one."

His head tilts. "Are you from Texas?"

"Yes. And no. But mostly yes."

"That's not cryptic at all." He laughs but doesn't pry, which I appreciate. "I'll teach you how to ride if you want."

"I probably shouldn't with my foot."

"Later then. The invitation stands."

"What else do I have to do?"

"The guests are shuttled from the airport and usually arrive between noon and three. Lora Belmont is my events planner. She greets them most times. She also has another job, so when there are conflicts, I do it. She'll show them to their rooms, give them the schedule of events, and tell them how things work. Basically they can treat the lodge like home during their stay. Grab a drink from the fridge when they need one, get an extra towel from the supply closet—you know, like you did."

I flush, still not believing I did those things and ended up with a job.

"You're not their servant or their butler. If they have an issue, they'll call Lora or me. If a guest becomes unruly or belligerent toward you, call me." He pulls out his phone. "Let me give you my number."

"I don't have a phone."

He sighs. "I thought as much. I didn't see one when you gave me a tour of the attic." He pulls a phone from his pocket and hands it to me. "It's been programmed with every number you might need."

I wave it off. "I don't take—"

"Handouts. I know. But as an employee, you have to be able to get in touch with me. What if a pipe bursts, and the lodge floods? Or the washing machine stops working right before guests arrive. This is business, not personal. Okay?"

I reluctantly take it and set it on the table. It's not just a phone. It's an iPhone. "Exactly what is your job here? Caretaker of the lodge? It seems like there's more to it."

"There is. You could say I'm part owner of the ranch." He chuckles. "A very small part."

"What does that mean?"

"My uncle owns this place. He inherited it eight years ago when his mom died. Damn—that was a lot of drama. If you're ever bored and want to hear a good story, ask me about it. Anyway, Gavin, my uncle, is Maddox's dad."

"Maddox?"

"Andie's husband. Maddox is Gavin's proxy, I'd guess you call him. He's the one who lives in the big house and signs all the paychecks. He's part owner, too, only he has a bigger part. My uncle made a deal with him back then, the same one he made with me. For every year he works at Devil's Horn Ranch, he gets one percent ownership. On his next anniversary, he'll own eight percent."

"How much do you own?"

He looks embarrassed. "One. But don't laugh. I do a hell of a lot for that. I work my ass off because with one percent ownership comes one percent of the bills. This is a big place—lots of moving parts—but one day, it'll all be worth it."

"I wasn't laughing. One percent of something is a hell of a lot better than zero percent of nothing." He looks guilty, so I add, "Don't feel sorry for me, Aaron."

"I don't. Well, maybe I do a little. It's kind of hard not to. You're young and living out of a backpack and sleeping on fifty-year-old mattresses. God knows where you slept before. But that's all behind you now. I promise I'll try and stop feeling sorry for you. How old are you, anyway?"

"Twenty-two."

"I'm twenty-three, in case you were wondering."

"I wasn't." Lie. Ever since I saw him chopping wood, I've wondered about him. Dreamt about him. What's his story? Has he ever been in love? Is he a hermit living in the woods? Is he running from something, or living his dream? "There is something I was wondering about, though. Why do you live in a cabin all the way out here when there are so many other places to live on the main part of the ranch?"

"For someone copping a squat in the attic, you seem to know a lot about Devil's Horn Ranch."

"I grew up not too far from here. When I was a kid, we used to sneak onto the ranch. Some of my friends drag raced on the old airstrip. Sometimes we'd sit in those rusted out cars, back when this place was abandoned. I even came inside one time and put my foot clean through one of the steps on the front porch. Some big dude named Matteo caught us when I was sixteen. Said he'd call the police and our parents if he ever saw any of us again."

There's a huge smile on Aaron's face.

"What?"

"I hung out on the airstrip when I was fifteen. Got in a lot of trouble back then—that's another story I'll tell you sometime if you're interested."

"You have a lot of stories," I say.

"Maybe we can swap a few one day."

"I don't have any stories to swap."

He snorts. "Somehow I think that's not true. You've pretty much been brought up to speed. Any questions?"

"Nope."

"Since you won't be needed until tomorrow, what are your plans for today? You know, now that you don't need to hide anymore."

"I thought I'd walk into town." He doesn't need to know why, but I need tampons—one thing the lodge doesn't seem to have.

He focuses on my foot. "Walk? It's five miles one way."

"I've done it plenty of times."

"Not on an injured foot. I'll drive you."

"I'm sure you have better things to do. I won't have you treating me like some charity case."

"Actually, I have to go to town for supplies." He pulls a slip of paper from his pocket and holds it out to me. "Just add what you need to the list. You can stay here and rest your foot."

I scan his list.

Toilet stopper thingy

Apples for Rueben

WD-40

Coke

Protein bars

I shake my head. "Thanks, but I'll come along."

"No time like the present. Lora will be meeting the guests shortly. We'll only be in the way."

"Let me go fix the other beds first." I walk away.

He taps my shoulder. "Don't forget this." He hands me the phone.

I stuff it into my pocket.

Ten minutes later, I'm in the kitchen, where a beautiful blonde woman with glorious spiral curls is leaning against the counter, drinking iced tea. She eyes me over the glass. I know this look. I've been on the receiving end of it many times. She doesn't like me. Why, I don't know. We've never met.

"Lora, I presume?" I say.

She sets down her glass and wipes her lower lip, appraising me as if I were a snake in the grass. "And you are?"

Aaron comes out of the office. "Oh, good. You've met."

"Not really," she says.

"Devyn, this is Lora Belmont, our events planner. Lora, this is Devyn, our new housekeeper."

Lora's eyebrows go up in surprise. "Housekeeper?"

"That's right," he says.

Her judgmental eyes travel all the way from my head to my feet. *"You're* a maid?"

"I prefer the term housekeeper," I say.

"Humph."

"Are you ready?" Aaron asks.

I hold up a finger. "Let me get my purse from my room."

"Her *room?*" Lora asks, aghast. "She's sleeping here?"

"She is," Aaron says.

I listen from the hall.

"Mrs. Garcia never did."

"Mrs. Garcia lived with her son."

"And Devyn doesn't have anyone she can live with?"

"It's no big deal, Lora. The room is empty."

"How did you find her?" She lowers her voice. "What do you know about her?"

I step back into the kitchen. "Ready. Nice to meet you, Lora. I hope I'll be seeing you around." It's a lie. I don't want to see her. She either has a thing for Aaron, or she's really protective of the lodge. Either way, she sees me as the enemy.

"You're not staying to greet the guests?" she asks.

"I think you can handle it," Aaron says. "We're running into town. Call if you need me."

I can feel her eyes burn into the back of my head as I leave. I climb into the passenger seat of his truck. "She doesn't like me much."

He chuckles. "Lora can be brusque. Give it time. She'll warm up to you."

"I think it's *you* she might want to warm up to."

"I don't think so. She's got a boyfriend."

We don't talk much on the way to town. We're not going into Fort Worth—that's the *city*, and the place I try to stay away from. People there might recognize me. Two years is a long time, but not long enough. Somehow, though, I can't bring myself to go farther away. Am I torturing myself, or trying to hold on to a piece of me I'll never get back?

I tell Aaron to stop the truck when we reach the corner where Mr. Choi's market is. "I'll meet you back here in an hour. Is that long enough for you to run your errands?"

"An hour it is."

The truck pulls away, and I bypass Mr. Choi's store and head in the other direction. This small rural town doesn't offer much, but it has what I need. I cross the street and duck into the free clinic. I step up to the front counter. "Can I please get a care package?"

No need to explain further. They know exactly what I mean. The girl gives me an inviting smile even though she knows I'm swallowing my pride to come here. She sits behind the desk at her twelve-dollar-an-hour job, dealing with indigents like me. Am I still one, now that I have a roof over my head and a sort-of job?

She hands me a nondescript box. I know exactly what's inside: tampons, pads, a stick of deodorant, small tubes of toothpaste and shampoo, a bar of soap, and two generic pairs of white granny underwear that are way too big for me. All things I can't buy with my Lone Star Card. Food products only—men must have come up with that rule.

I contemplate giving everything back except the feminine hygiene products, but then think twice about it. I don't know how long I'll be at the lodge. What if Maddox or his dad find out about me and kick me out? I should stockpile supplies just in case. I thank the girl and leave.

I'm about to go into Mr. Choi's store to ask him how much I have left on my card. I don't want to use it, but it would be nice to know. Then I remember what's in my pocket. A woman at Social Services said I could keep track of the balance online. It's been a while since I've used a phone, but they haven't changed all that much in two years. I find the website, input my card info, create an account, and *voila*! I've taken one more step toward normalcy.

I have a phone. The possibilities! I sit on the bench outside the store, open a search engine, and type *Roseanne DeMaggio*. Immediately, a picture of my stepdad pops up. Of course it does. He's a congressman. My mother, on the other hand, doesn't have much of a google-worthy history. She's a housewife—something Ed insisted on. He also insisted on adopting me, even though I didn't want him to. I had already been adopted once before, by a man who loved me. Ed didn't love me. He was doing it for show, to earn him points in the political arena. He was a district attorney running for Congress. He practically based his campaign on the fact that he had adopted a teenager.

He's still a congressman—probably won re-election by playing the pity card. I wouldn't be where I am now if it weren't for him. Bile rises in my throat. I can play the blame game all I want, but the truth is *I'm* the reason I'm where I am today.

I don't read his bio. I don't need a recap of his life. I know exactly what it will say about him *and* me.

Next, I search for Dane and Angelina, my former best friends. I see a sorority picture of Angelina. She went to Tulane, like she'd planned. She looks like she doesn't have a care in the world. Like she had no part in what happened. I often ask myself if I would have gone on with my life like nothing had happened if the tables were turned.

There's no information on Dane, but Smith is a common last name. I pull the creased picture of the three of us out of my wallet—one of my few mementos of the past. I'd never been closer to two people. Man, that seems like forever ago.

There's another picture in my wallet, and I want to look at it, but it's too painful. Instead, I look at the inscription on the back. *Kasey and me ~ August 3, 2018.* I trace the letters of her name.

When I put it away, I see the slip of paper I tucked in there months ago. It's Jill Benson's phone number. She's the only friend I've had these past few years, even if she was paid to be. I dial her number.

"Hello?"

"Hi, Jill. It's Devyn. Devyn De—"

"Goodness. Devyn, it's so nice to hear your voice. I was hoping you'd reach out to me. Is everything okay, dear?"

"Yes. That's what I was calling to tell you. I have a job on a ranch. It's nothing special, but it comes with a place to live."

"I'm delighted. I knew you'd land on your feet."

"How did you know?"

"Been doing this a long time, child."

"Well, I don't want to bother you. I just wanted you to know."

"You could never be a bother. You call me anytime, you hear?"

"Thank you. Thank you for everything."

I hang up. Then I type *Aaron Pearce* into the search field. He appears in a cap and gown. He graduated from Texas A&M just last year. He's flanked by a beautiful woman and a very attractive man with the same black hair he has. Aaron really hit the jackpot in the looks department, and I can see why. I study his chiseled jawline, his infectious smile. The tiny creases by his eyes from squinting at the sun. I get all warm and tingly inside. It's a feeling I haven't had since Billy Minton and I went to third base after graduation. I might have even gone all the way with him had his mom not come home early and busted us in the basement. Two days later, Billy, along with everyone else, dropped me like a hot potato. No one wanted to be associated with Devyn DeMaggio. Not even Devyn DeMaggio.

The article talks more about his parents than Aaron. His dad is a famous photographer, and his mom runs a restaurant in New York City. I scroll through pictures and additional articles. His uncle is a movie producer, who is married to a bestselling author. He has another uncle who was MVP for the New York Giants some years ago. He comes from serious money, but he drives an old truck and lives in a one-room log cabin. It doesn't quite add up.

A horn startles me. "You ready?" Aaron asks, leaning across the passenger seat.

I stash the phone, not wanting him to know what I was doing, and climb in. I catch my shoe on the running board and fall headfirst into the truck. The box I'm carrying pops opens, and to my horror, tampons land right in his lap.

He hands them to me without embarrassment. "I get now why you didn't want me to do your shopping, but I would have gotten them for you, Devyn. It's no big deal."

"Said no guy I've ever met." I grab the tampons and stuff everything back in the box.

"When I was a teenager, my mom punished me for disrespecting her by making me buy her a box of tampons. If she was in a really bad mood, she'd make me buy Vagisil, too."

I can't help but laugh, and it feels good. It makes me feel—I don't know—free in some way.

"True story," he says, laughing with me.

"I think I'd like your mom."

"She'd love you," he says, pulling away from the curb.

"What makes you say that? You don't even know me."

"Because she roots for the underdog."

"Is that why you're helping me? Because your mother forced you to buy tampons and likes underdogs?"

"I don't know. Maybe. Or maybe I want to do some good for once."

I study his profile. Something about the way he said it makes me think he's trying to make up for something bad. Or perhaps I'm just projecting.

"Who's Reuben?" I ask.

"What makes you ask?"

"On your list you wrote apples for Reuben."

"Reuben is a horse. He's my favorite. He's not mine, though. He's Maddox's. But Mad has a dozen horses, so he doesn't care if I ride him. I can introduce you if you want."

"To Maddox or Reuben?"

He laughs. I like his laugh. I like it even more than his smile.

"Both if you want."

"What will you tell him?"

Aaron rolls his eyes. "He's a horse, Devyn, he doesn't understand English."

I swat his arm. "I meant Maddox. What will you tell him about me? If he runs things, he'll want to know. What if he won't let me stay?"

"He doesn't have a say in the matter. He may oversee the ranch, but I run the lodge. Plus, we're not paying you. No money out of his pocket."

"He'll want to know my last name."

He glances at me briefly. "He's not the only one."

I shake my head.

"So make one up, and we'll go over to the main ranch on your next day off. You can meet Reuben, Maddox, and Owen, and anyone else who happens to be there. You'll fit right in."

"How do you know?"

"Because we're all a bunch of misfits."

"Now I'm a misfit?"

"Better than me calling you a thief."

"I think I preferred ghost."

He laughs again and butterflies take up residence in my stomach. We glance at each other, then back at the road. I get the idea working for Aaron Pearce might be very interesting.

CHAPTER NINE

Aaron

I can't sleep, which makes no sense, as I'm back in my bed after the better part of a week on a couch. I can't stop thinking about her. I couldn't care less about her stealing food and shit. I'm more worried about her leaving.

She's fully capable of working. Anyone would hire her on her appearance alone—she's gorgeous if you can get past the sad, lost look in her eyes. She also seems smart, but she's definitely hiding something. Is she running from someone and scared I might blow her cover? How long will it be before she gets spooked and runs off?

At three in the morning, I get up and pee. On my way back to bed, I stop at the window that offers me a view of the lodge in the moonlight. I look at it for a while, wondering if Devyn is finally getting a good night's sleep.

Movement on the roof makes me catch my breath. I swear I'm seeing a ghost and laugh quietly at the thought. I squint, wishing I had a pair of binoculars, but it's got to be her, and it appears she's climbing back inside the attic through a window. What was she doing? It must be more than thirty feet high. Jesus, was she going to jump and then changed her mind?

I have to keep myself from going over there. She's a grown woman. She's not my responsibility. Still, the urge to save her—from her demons, from herself—is overwhelming, and I don't get a lick of sleep the rest of the night.

I'm walking through the back door of the lodge before seven. Joe is already there, fixing breakfast. He's a retired Army cook and perfect for the job. Lives in a trailer off the main road halfway to town. Comes when we need him and watches old war movies from his BarcaLounger when we don't. A patch covers one eye. He tends to keep to himself, so I never have found out if his eye is damaged or fully missing.

"Joe." I nod.

"Morning, Aaron. You're here early. You doing the tour today?"

"Luca is. I'm just checking on our new housekeeper."

"Devyn? Already come and gone. Cute as a button, that one. If only I were fifty years younger." He chuckles and cracks eggs into a mixing bowl.

I can practically feel my blood pressure spike. "She's gone?"

"Took a muffin and a Coke. I told her I'd be happy to make her a frittata, but she simply wrote something in her journal and went on her way."

I cross the kitchen, walk down the back hallway, go past the mudroom, and push open the bedroom door. Relief sets in when I see her pack in the corner and three shirts hanging in the closet. I touch one of them. She needs more clothes, but she won't take charity. I'm determined not to make her feel like less of a person.

Whatever she's going through, she doesn't need me adding to her problems.

"Which way did she go?" I ask Joe on my way out.

He nods to the east. "Thataway. Seems to me, though, she's not the type of gal who wants to be followed."

"No, I suppose not." I glance at the basket of muffins. "Do you mind if I take one?"

"Help yourself."

I thank him and leave. After crossing the yard, I examine the roof. It looks even more dangerous from down here than it did from my cabin. The pitch is steep but not so much you couldn't walk on it. It makes me shudder, thinking of her up there. Every ounce of me feels the need to protect her. Yet somehow I know if I push too far, she'll leave.

I finish my morning chores, which mainly consist of riding the ATV along the fences to check for breaks or weaknesses and then putting more hay out for the pastured horses. Any barn worker or ranch hand could do it, but that's what I am, without a formal label. Maddox does the same things from time to time. Like me, he never complains about mundane tasks. The only difference between us, other than our nine-year age gap, is that I have a formal education. I earned my degree in petroleum engineering. If I plan to help expand this ranch and its capabilities, I need to know how to do it without fucking up the environment more than it already has been.

Maddox conveniently emerges from one of the stables the moment I pull up. He smiles. "What does the other guy look like?"

"Fuck off," I say without heat and park the ATV.

"Seriously, Aaron, what happened? Andie told me you had a shiner. You and Quinn get into some trouble in Fort Worth? Aw, hell, you didn't take up bronc riding, did you?"

"It's nothing."

He follows me all the way to Reuben's stall. "If it's nothing, why not tell me how it happened?"

"Don't you have better things to do?"

"Fine, you don't want to talk about it. Changing the subject now. Can you and Quinn wrangle up some day laborers? I want to get the entire south wall sanded and painted by next week when phase two of the project starts."

I laugh. "I know the same people you know, cousin. I'm not sure who you think I can bring to the table, but I'll ask him. You talked to the Diamond Duce or Thousand Acre Ranch yet?"

"Called them yesterday. Told them I'll pay top dollar. They said they'll send anyone they can spare. At this point, I'm willing to accept anyone who can climb a ladder. If I could get Reuben to hold a paintbrush, I'd use him, too."

I run a hand down the horse's mane, deep in thought. "How much are you paying?"

"Twenty dollars an hour."

"Do they have to fill out any paperwork?"

He shakes his head. "The way it works is each day laborer is treated as an independent contractor. Technically, I have to fill out an I-9 for each one, and I do keep up with that, but mostly for my accounting purposes. The IRS doesn't require me to submit those forms, just a good faith number and an affidavit swearing that's what we paid. If the worker makes over a certain amount, they have to claim it on their taxes."

"So if someone worked for you for, say, a few days and earned a few hundred bucks, they could do it without having to file anything or pay taxes?"

He holds up his hands. "Hey, I'm not giving tax advice. What the people do with the cash I give them is their responsibility. As long as I cover my own ass, what they do is up to them." He narrows his eyes. "Why the third degree?"

"Just trying to learn everything I can about the business side of things."

He pats me on the back. "I'm glad you're getting into it as much as you have been. Owen says you've been shadowing him at least once a week, learning all the ropes."

"Maddox, I worked here seven summers in a row. I think I know the ropes. I'm only helping out where I can."

"Earning your one percent, are you?"

"Are you ever going to ease up on me about owning seven percent more than I do?"

He chuckles. "I have to have something to hold over your head. You're damn near perfect. You have a degree and graduated with honors. You work as hard as anyone I've ever seen, and you've got the lodge starting to turn a profit in less than a year. When you're my age, you'll own a hell of a bigger percentage than I do right now."

I kick dirt. "Yeah, my life is so fucking perfect."

He looks concerned. He's one of the few people who knows about Cameron. He pats my shoulder. "Damn. Sorry."

I lead Reuben away. "Gotta get to work."

He means well, and he treats me like I'm normal, but he has no idea that I wake up every day feeling like shit when I watch the sun rise. Or that I go to sleep at night wondering why I have the right to enjoy sunsets.

I can never make up for what happened. But I sure as hell plan to do everything in my power to try.

CHAPTER TEN

Devyn

I transfer the load of plain white towels from the washer to the dryer. I get they are easier to clean, but they're boring. A place like this should have towels with more character.

I strip the sheets from the bed in guest suite eight. I can't imagine what they must have done to make them look like that. I'm careful not to touch any of the stained areas. After I finish making up the room, I spray air freshener to cover the smell of sex. At least I think that's what the smell is.

I'm a twenty-two-year-old virgin. Based on the books I've read on the e-reader, that's almost unheard of. Two horrible men tried to change that simple fact. No, not men. Monsters. Since my failed attempt to lose my virginity with Billy Minton, not having a boyfriend hasn't been by choice, only circumstance.

I've thought a lot about it over the past few days. Aaron is a nice guy. Single (I think), attractive, funny, my age. And he doesn't ask too many questions, but would he if I slept with him? Would he get all curious or clingy? That's the last thing I want. But I have needs. The way my body responds when he's near, it's like some visceral reaction I don't seem to have any control over.

I clean the next four rooms, wondering what he would do if I propositioned him.

"Devyn, right?" a man says from the doorway.

"Yes. Sorry, I'm finishing up now." I go for his trash can. "I'll be out of your hair in just a sec."

He crosses the room and removes the overflowing bag from his can. Beer bottles clink together. "Here, let me help."

"You don't have to."

"It's heavy," he says, placing the bag into my larger trash roller. "And it's my pleasure."

"Thank you."

His gaze travels the length of my body. He's attractive, in a straight-laced-banker kind of way. I wonder if there are any rules about me mingling with the guests. "Anytime," he says, touching my lower back as I exit his room.

I expect my body to react. I wait for the somersaults in my stomach, the tingles down my spine, the spontaneous exhale of a slow breath. But nothing.

"All this team-building stuff is crap," he says, following me to the doorway. "How about I skip the afternoon session and you give me a tour of the ranch?" His hand juts out. "I'm Jake."

I shake. "Devyn."

"I thought we'd already established that."

I'm terrible at flirting. Haven't had the opportunity to do it in a while.

A noise down the hall gets my attention, and I stick my head out. Aaron is on his knees, fixing a spindle along the upper balcony that broke when one of the drunken bankers fell against it last night. He looks up and lifts his chin. He briefly glances at Jake and then goes back to his task.

"I, uh… better get back to work."

"So, after lunch then?" Jake asks.

I peek at Aaron. He's listening. "Against the rules. Let me know if you need anything else."

Jake retreats into his room. I hurry past Aaron to the back stairway, not wanting to be upstairs when the other guests return. Halfway down, Aaron joins me and helps me carry the heavy trash bin the rest of the way. "It's not, you know."

"Huh?"

"Against the rules. There aren't any rules. If you wanted to do… whatever he was asking."

At the bottom of the stairs, I take the bin from him and gaze into his eyes. They are pale green; such a contrast to his dark hair. "I didn't. I don't." I gawk at him like a smitten schoolgirl and then open the back door and go out.

"Good," he says before the door shuts behind me.

I lean against it, putting a hand on my stomach as I exhale. I smile as I haul the trash across the yard to the dumpster shed. Something falls from a bag as I'm tossing it. A magazine. Congressman Ed DeMaggio's face is on the cover. He stares at me, letting me know I have no right to happiness. I toss it into the dumpster and then hide behind it and cry.

Upon my return, I don't expect Joe, the cook, to be in the kitchen. There's no avoiding him; I have to walk past him to get to my room. One look at me, and he guides me to the table. "Sit. I'm gonna make you some tea."

"I'm fine."

"Nonsense. Just wait 'til you taste it. My tea could charm the feathers off a bird."

I wipe away one remaining tear. "That good, huh?"

He makes small talk while the water boils and he fixes lunch for the guests, then he sets two mugs on the table and takes the seat next to me. "We're a lot alike, you and me."

I try not to laugh. He's at least seventy years old, African American, and Aaron tells me he's an Army vet. His left eye is covered with a patch. We couldn't be more different.

I blow on my tea. "How so?"

"We both got secrets. War wounds. Things we ain't never told nobody. Difference is, your wounds are still fresh."

I sip. "Wow, this is good."

"Lots of folks around here got 'em—secrets, that is. We all got that same look about us. A guilt that burns deep in our gut. Take it from an old man whose secrets got buried long ago. They'll eat you up from the inside."

I quietly drink my tea. I'm sure Joe has good intentions. He's undoubtedly been through a lot. But that doesn't mean he would understand. It doesn't mean he would accept me for who I am and what I've done.

"Thank you for the tea." I wash my mug and put it back in the cabinet. When I turn to leave, Joe hands me a cup of yogurt and a spoon.

"I know it's your favorite. I made sure to order extra these past few weeks." He winks at me.

My cheeks heat. "You knew?"

"Been fixin' food here for the better part of a year, Missy. A good cook knows exactly how much food is in his kitchen. Well, that, and I saw you casing the place last month. Figured if all you wanted was food, you couldn't exactly be a hardened criminal."

I swallow. "Thank you for not saying anything."

"Like I said, we all got our secrets. Ain't my place to go tellin' any of yours." He winks and I take the yogurt and leave the room. He calls out after me. "My eyes may not be what they used to be, but I got me a perfectly fine set of ears. And they're real good for listening. Got me?"

I nod and hold up the yogurt. "Thanks, Joe."

That night in bed, I can't sleep. I look at the clock. It's after one in the morning. For a month, I slept during the day. Nighttime is when I came out of the attic. It's been hard getting my body back on a regular sleep schedule. At two, I give up and make my way to the attic. Out of habit, I'm quiet and careful to avoid the creaky steps.

I go to the window, as I've done so many times. I still oil it daily with cooking spray I borrowed from the kitchen. The stick I use to prop it open lies at my feet. I jam it in the window and climb through, bringing an old blanket with me.

I love it out here. It reminds me of when I was a kid. I try to remember the names of the constellations and the gods and goddesses they were named after.

I startle when I hear a noise behind me.

"Don't get up," Aaron says. "I didn't mean to scare you."

"What are you doing here?"

"Couldn't sleep."

"Me neither."

"I saw you up here the other night. Do you come up here a lot?"

"Sometimes I would lie for hours, waiting for the guests to go to sleep."

"Seems risky."

"I don't think anyone ever heard me."

He peers over the edge. "That's not what I meant."

I make room for him on the blanket, and he sits.

"My friends and I used to get in the convertible or the car with the rusted-out roof and look at the stars. I've been meaning to ask why you haven't had them removed. Seems kind of strange to keep a pile of junk cars on the property."

"I don't think it's strange at all. It adds to the ambiance. Besides, there's probably a story there. Maybe some of them were used to drag race on the airstrip back in the fifties."

"Maybe some guy took his girlfriend in the convertible to a drive-in movie."

"What if one of them was used by Bonnie and Clyde?"

We laugh as we come up with even more outrageous scenarios.

Eventually we stop talking, lie back, and gaze quietly at the stars. He's so close, I can feel the hair on his arm. Part of me wants him to climb on top of me. Make love to me right here. Would it be like in the books I've been reading?

I turn and catch him staring. Not at the stars. At me.

"You don't have to keep track of the food you eat anymore. I told you, it's part of the deal." When I'm silent, he continues. "Joe said you wrote something on your notepad after you took a muffin and drink."

"Are you keeping tabs on me?"

"I simply want to be clear that you don't owe me or the lodge anything. You're doing a great job."

"Thanks."

"I wish I could pay you, but I can't risk getting my uncle's business in trouble. Are you sure we can't make you an official employee?"

I sit up. "I like things the way they are."

"But everyone needs money. For clothes if nothing else."

"I've learned to make do with what I have."

"You shouldn't have to." He sits up, too. "There's a way for you to make a little money if you're game."

My jaw drops. I flashback to the first time someone said those words to me and start to rise. He pulls me back down, and I lose my balance and almost topple off the roof. He grabs me tightly, and we hunker down.

"Jesus, Devyn. You almost fell. You could have died." He rolls off me and blows out a few breaths. "I swear, what I said came out the wrong way. What I meant is that ranches sometimes need more help than they can get from their employees, so they hire day laborers. They're paid in cash. We keep a file for everyone who works, but you can fill out the form as Jane Doe for all we care. It's up to you if you want to pay taxes on the money."

"I don't know. I'm a woman, and not a very strong one."

"I'd beg to differ." He points to the bruise under his eye. "Can you climb a ladder? Use a paintbrush?"

"Probably not very well."

"We're not painting the Sistine Chapel, Devyn. It's a stable, and it pays twenty bucks an hour. Maddox needs everyone he can get to complete the job on time. We don't have any guests booked at the lodge Monday through Wednesday. You could bank a lot of cash in that time."

"You promise me this isn't charity?"

I cross my heart. "I swear. Ask Maddox."

I do the math in my head. Twenty dollars an hour over three days. That's more money than I've seen since I worked at the supermarket. "I'll do it, but I was sort of looking forward to meeting Reuben."

"You want to learn how to ride?"

I nod and he smiles in the moonlight. I smile back. Fleeting glimpses of happiness. That's what I get now, though I don't deserve even that much.

CHAPTER ELEVEN

Aaron

The waitress brings drinks to our table. Quinn immediately throws back his shot and orders another. As always, I slowly sip my beer.

Twenty minutes later, my wingman is feeling pretty lively. "Want to see me rodeo tomorrow?"

"Watching you get your ass kicked by bucking broncs is not my idea of a good time."

"I'm getting better. They don't always kick my ass."

"Yet you always seem to be battered and bruised."

"The ladies love that shit. Seriously though, I stayed on the whole eight seconds last time."

"And then you almost busted your ribs trying to get off him."

He shrugs. "Nature of the beast, brother. Badges of honor."

"You're going to get yourself killed one of these days. I'd rather not lose another friend."

He looks guilty for half a second, then shakes it off and takes another shot. "Dude—won't happen." He looks over my shoulder. "Those two," he shouts over the band, pointing to a couple of petite blondes.

"Whatever you want, man."

"What the hell is with you tonight?"

"Nothing, why?"

"Nothing, my right nut. You've usually propositioned half a dozen women by now. What gives?"

"*You've* usually propositioned that many," I say. "I never need to ask more than one."

He punches my right arm, and I laugh. Quinn and I never end the night alone. Even if we don't go home with the women we pick up, we always end up doing something with them, whether it's in someone's car, in a back hallway of a club—hell, even the bathroom of an all-night diner.

The Dallas/Fort Worth area is pretty large, but it's getting harder to find places populated by women Quinn hasn't slept with. Me, not so much, because I was away at college most of the time. But Quinn—he's been slapped, punched, and spit on. One girl even keyed the Ford F-150 his mom gave him for his twenty-fifth birthday. It's not that he's a dick; he just doesn't like second dates. Some people would say that makes him a dick. I say it's fair game as long as he's clear about it up front, which he is.

I call them the next day. Even had a few second dates. None of them were anything to write home about. Most are too into drinking. That's what I get for picking up women in a bar.

The blonde women see his inviting gesture and come over. The one with the plunging neckline holds out her hand to Quinn. "I'm Ashlyn." The other one sidles up next to me. "I'm Raven."

I peer sideways. "Devyn?"

"No, Raven," she yells in my ear.

I introduce myself, wishing she *was* Devyn. It hits me like a ton of bricks. I don't want some blonde I pick up in a club. Some perky sorority girl looking for an ego boost and a good time. I want the mysterious brown-haired, hazel-eyed woman who lies on the roof and stares at the stars. The one who has nothing but won't accept a handout from anyone. The one who's hiding—running even—from her past.

"Aaron?"

I stare blankly at Quinn and the others, who are waiting for me to say something. "Uh, what?"

"I was telling Raven what an entrepreneur you are," he says with a wink.

It's something we do. We talk each other up. Sometimes we make shit up, sometimes we don't. Occasionally, I tell them he comes from a family of mobsters, which isn't far from the truth. Makes him seem dangerous. Surprisingly, girls love that stuff.

Raven touches my thigh, then runs her hand up to my crotch. "Oil wells. Impressive."

I roll my eyes. "Oil well, as in *one*. And it's not what you think."

"What do I think?"

I almost go into my spiel, the one about me not getting into it for the money, but with the way she's gawking at me, I doubt she cares about anything except how long I can bone her.

A waitress comes by and saves me from having to answer. "Can I get you anything?"

Raven looks at my half-full beer. "Are you the designated driver or something?"

"Or something."

She giggles far too boisterously, then leans in. "I guarantee by the time you leave, I'll have fucked you sober." She turns to the waitress. "Another round, and an extra shot of Jägermeister for him." She pats my arm possessively.

I get the attention of the waitress behind Raven's back and give her the cutthroat sign. When she brings our drinks a few minutes later, the extra shot is missing from the tray. I smile my thanks at her even though Raven barks her displeasure.

"What's the matter?" Ashlyn asks. "You don't like to have a good time?"

"I like to have fun. I just don't like the taste of hard liquor." That's a lie. I do, especially whiskey, but I'll never drink it again.

"There must be something you like." Raven claps her hands excitedly. "I know, let's get the waitress back here and order one of every drink." She pulls a wad of cash from her back pocket. "It'll be fun."

"Put away your money. We're not doing that."

"Buzzkill." She pushes a fresh beer over to me, even though I'm still working on my original. "Come on, drink with me." She tosses back another shot. I take a small sip of the beer but leave the mug tipped against my lips to make it appear I'm drinking more than I am.

"That's more like it. Hey, do you guys want to dance?"

Ashlyn pulls Quinn onto the dance floor. I resist. "I have to hit the bathroom."

Raven stands. "I'll go with them. Meet me out there."

In the hallway to the bathroom, I pull out my phone and check the time. It's not even ten o'clock. I look at my recent calls and see Devyn's name. She called me earlier today about a clogged sink. Stupid me, I thought she was calling to talk. As far as I know, it was the first time she'd ever made a call on her new phone. I get the idea she doesn't know anyone. If she did, she would have been living with them and not under a goddamn bridge somewhere.

It still saddens me to know she was on the streets. *Her.* Beautiful, interesting, capable. How does someone like her end up with nothing? It makes no sense. Maybe she was in an abusive relationship, and he swore to hunt her down and kill her if she ever left him. Maybe she doesn't have family to go to, or she does and he threatened them too, and she's protecting them by staying away.

Whatever happened was just over two months ago. She said she'd gotten three months' worth of assistance, and it was running out.

"Dude!" the guy behind me says. "Do you mind? Some of us have to take a piss."

I step out of line and lean against the wall. What is she doing now? Is she up on the roof again? I have an overwhelming urge to know. I forget about having to pee and head out to find Quinn.

"There you are!" Raven yells exuberantly. She pulls me close and grinds into me.

I lean toward Quinn. "I'm gonna bail. There's something I have to do back home."

Raven's bottom lip juts out. "You're leaving me?"

"Duty calls. Life on a ranch never stops."

"I could go with you. Quinn says you have a lovely little cabin in the woods."

"Some other time." I turn back to Quinn. "I'll see ya."

"But we came in my truck."

"I'll Uber."

"All the way to the ranch? It'll cost you a hundred bucks."

"Yeah, maybe." I glance at our table with all the empty shot glasses. "You should Uber too, if you keep this up."

"Sure thing," he says. I give him the stink eye. "No, I will. I promise."

"Well then," Raven says. "I guess it's your loss." Without skipping a beat, she moves her arms from me to Quinn. Ashlyn doesn't seem to mind sharing. I get the idea this isn't their first rodeo. Judging by the smile on his face, Quinn is one hundred percent on board. I'm pretty sure he'll be thanking me tomorrow.

It doesn't take me long to get a ride, but when the driver finds out where I'm going, he's less than pleased. There's not much chance of him getting another fare back to town. I lean forward. "I live in the boonies, but there's a good tip in it for you."

"Then it looks like I might be done for the night."

After he drives into the back entrance of the ranch and down the dirt road leading to my cabin, I have him stop. "You can drop me here."

He glances around. "We're in the middle of nowhere."

I point. "My place is just up there."

"Sneaking up on someone?"

"I suppose you could say that." I can tip on the app, but I pull two twenties from my wallet and hand them to him.

"Thanks, man."

"Just be sure to back out."

He salutes me. "Gotcha."

His car disappears, and I use the flashlight on my phone to navigate the rest of the way. I shut it off as I approach my cabin. It's dark with the exception of the porch light. But it's not the cabin I'm interested in. I look over at the lodge and see movement downstairs. People are in the rec room, probably playing pool. But I'm not interested in that either. I look at the roof and there's a lump on it. Devyn is lying down. I picture her on the blanket we sat on the other night.

The urge to join her is strong. I've known her less than a week, but I've never felt this way about anyone. If I asked her out, would I scare her away?

I reluctantly go inside my cabin. I don't turn on any lights. I stare out the window, hoping to see any semblance of movement on the roof. Wanting her to stand up just so I can admire her silhouette in the dim light of the half-moon. Needing her to glance over; give me some indication that she might be interested in me, even if she never does anything about it. But she's completely still. Maybe she's fallen asleep.

My legs grow tired from standing. I lean against the table and unbuckle my pants, wishing she were the one doing it. I fist myself as I gaze out the window, fantasizing about the woman who makes nightly appearances in my dreams.

I come hard and wonder if it's the closest I'll ever get to being with Devyn Just Devyn.

CHAPTER TWELVE

Deryn

Aaron let me borrow his truck to drive into town. Though I'm a licensed driver, I have no idea where my license is. Not that he seemed to care. He told me fourteen-year-old kids drive trucks out here in the rural areas.

I peek in my wallet for the tenth time when I stop at the one and only traffic light. Three hundred eighty dollars. I feel rich. I tried to give Aaron a hundred dollars to pay him back for the food I took, but he wouldn't take the money. I left it sitting on the kitchen counter. A promise is a promise.

I bypass the small strip mall clothing stores, knowing I can get way more for my money at the thrift shop on the other side of town. People don't realize there are actually good clothes in thrift shops. You just have to know how to find them.

When I get out of the truck, I don't bother looking around. Nobody I know would be caught dead coming to a place like this. I go inside. I may be in a secondhand shop, but the feeling I get perusing the rows and rows of clothing is hard to describe. Or maybe it isn't. It feels like freedom. Freedom to pick out what I want and wear it when I choose without anyone telling me what or when to do it. I take my time and enjoy every second.

An hour later, I hand the middle-aged cashier sixty-nine dollars and fifty cents, and he stuffs twelve shirts, three pairs of pants, a skirt, and two pairs of shoes into a bag. Some of them still have the tags on them—never worn! I even found a hair straightener for a buck. The lodge has plenty of hair dryers, but no straighteners. Oh, how I've missed mine.

One thing I don't have to buy is a cowboy hat. Good thing, because even here, they're expensive. The first thing Maddox McBride did after greeting me was take me to a room in the stable with riding gear and hats. He made me pick one out. Said his grandmother, who used to own this ranch, had a rule that everyone wore a cowboy hat. I pretty much grew up in Texas and never had occasion to wear one. His wife, Andie, said the one I picked fit me so well, she insisted I keep it.

On my way out the door, I see a table-top sewing machine on a table of random things. The man behind the counter sees me admiring it. "You know what that is?" he asks.

It's hard not to remember the days I spent using one like this. I remove the cover. Well, not just like this. The ones I used were pieces of crap. This one, while old, has some bells and whistles. "Sure do."

He comes out from behind the counter. "Not many people your age have even seen one of these, not to mention used one. I'll sell it to you for ten dollars."

The price marked is twenty-five. "Really? Does it work?"

"Sure does. Try it if you like. Can't seem to get rid of it. It's just taking up space. My wife insisted someone would buy it, but it's been here for damn near a month." He picks up a bag full of thread and other sewing accessories. "I'll even throw these in." He looks over his shoulder. "Don't tell June if you see her, deal?"

I think of how Aaron wouldn't take the money. It'll still be on the table when I return. Maybe there's another way to repay him.

"Ten dollars, you say?"

"Yes, ma'am."

"I'll take it." I pull a ten from my wallet and hand it over.

"You want to try it out first?"

I shake my head. "If you say it works, I believe you." At the last second, I notice something else on the table. "I'll take this as well." I pick up the book and hand the man two quarters.

He carries the sewing machine to the truck for me. "You get home and have any problems with it, you come see me, not the wife, capisce?"

"I'm sure it will work just fine. Thank you."

In the truck, I open the bag full of thread, happy to see it contains everything I need. More guests are arriving tomorrow afternoon. That should give me plenty of time to accomplish my task.

I still have three hundred dollars. More, if you count the money Aaron wouldn't take. I'm saving it. That money, along with what's left on my Lone Star Card, could come in real handy if I have to leave. I'm not foolish enough to believe this gig will last forever. Someone will recognize me. The other shoe will inevitably drop. The only question is when.

Back at the lodge, I carry the sewing machine into my room. It barely fits on the small desk in the corner. I spill the contents of the sewing bag on my bed and sift through it for the right color thread. Then I go to the supply closet and gather what I need.

It takes me a while to figure out the machine. It has a button in place of a foot pedal. I've never used one like this. I do, however, like the bobbin being visible versus inside the machine. It allows me to see how much thread remains. I'm excited about doing a job I once came to dread.

I practice on one of my old shirts and mess up a few times, but it all comes back to me.

Three hours later, I'm staring at my hard work when my stomach tenses. I did all of them. What if he hates it? What if I just cost the lodge hundreds of dollars if he insists on replacing them? I pick up a towel and run my hand over the stitching. Maybe I should have only done one and run it past him.

It's too late to second-guess myself now. I take the towels to each guest suite. I'm finishing up in the last room when Aaron says, "There you are."

I straighten the towel and hold my breath. "What do you think?"

He removes it and traces the blue DHR I stitched into it. "Where in the hell did you find these?"

"I made them. I mean, I embroidered them."

He picks up the hand towel next to the sink with matching embroidery and compares the two. "Jesus, Devyn, you got the logo dead on. These are incredible."

"You have no idea how happy I am to hear you say that, because I did them all."

"I love them, but how did you have the time?"

"I picked up a used sewing machine at the secondhand store."

"To make your own clothes?"

"No, to do this. I saw the machine, thought of the plain white towels, and figured it would give them some character."

"How much did you pay for it?"

"Hardly anything," I say. "The guy practically gave it to me."

He pulls money from his back pocket. "You left this in the kitchen, and I wanted to give it back to you. Now I feel it's not enough."

I try and control my excitement as I tuck the bills into my pocket. "How about we call it even?"

"No way, because now that I've seen what you can do, I want more." He crosses to the bed and picks up a pillow covered in a white pillow sham. "Can you do the same with this?"

"Of course. In fact, why don't I replicate the entire Devil's Horn Ranch brand on these?"

"You mean the horns and everything? You can do that?"

I nod. "It would look really classy."

He stares me down. "I think *you're* really classy."

I laugh. "Nobody has ever called me that."

"I'm serious, Devyn. I have no idea what happened to you before you came here, but you're a real class act, and I don't say that lightly. You have a fantastic work ethic. Everyone at the ranch loves you. You're pretty much the whole package."

My cheeks flush. I'm not used to getting compliments. In fact, quite the opposite. Put-downs and denigrations are all I've gotten. "You don't know what you're talking about." I start for the door.

His hand on my arm stops me. "I think I do."

He gazes at me longer than anyone has ever gazed at me. It's like he's talking with his eyes, telling me all the things I've never heard a man say outside of my dreams. I try to push down these feelings I have for him. They're too intense. Also exciting and confusing. Maybe it's because he's the first man who's been nice to me, not counting Mr. Choi or Joe, who are both decades older than I am.

My heartbeat races when he strokes my arm and then laces his fingers with mine. He's going to kiss me. I lick my lips in anticipation.

"Hello?" someone calls from downstairs.

When Aaron walks to the door, I miss him. He turns back, and I almost think he's as upset as I am about the interruption. "Sorry. Lora is here for a meeting. Can we continue this later?"

What is it he wants to continue exactly? Our discussion about the pillows or the kiss that almost happened? I can't speak so all I do is nod.

His smile before he leaves the room is brilliant. "And the towels? Really nice. Thanks."

CHAPTER THIRTEEN

Aaron

Maddox rides up on Doc, his favorite horse. "Aaron?"

"Whoa, boy." I pull Reuben to a stop.

"I called to you ten times."

"Didn't hear you." I'd been lost in thoughts of Devyn. I've never spent as much time in the shower as I have over the past week. I can't even think about her without getting hard. And the other day when we almost kissed—

He chuckles. "I remember a time when I was oblivious to the world, too."

"What are you talking about?"

"It's Devyn, isn't it? She's all up in your head."

"She works for me, Maddox. Or the ranch, anyway. I'm pretty much her boss. It wouldn't be right."

He shrugs. "I've never signed a paycheck, so technically—"

"Semantics. She works for me, and we both know it."

"Who cares? Look at Andie and me. She worked at the ranch long before we got together."

"That's different."

"How so?"

"If Devyn and I hook up and things go south, she'd have nowhere to go."

"What's her story?"

"I have no idea. She's super private. Never talks about herself. I get the idea she doesn't want someone to find her."

"Bad breakup?"

"Maybe. Or worse."

"You think someone hurt her?"

"Like I said, I have no idea. A relationship is probably the last thing she wants."

"Relationship?" He cocks his head in surprise. "This is a whole new you, Aaron. I wasn't sure that word was even in your vocabulary. What if you get with her and then decide she's like every other girl? What then?"

"Two seconds ago, you were encouraging this."

"That was when I thought you were talking something casual."

I shake my head. "She's different. Not like the others."

"But you barely know her."

"She's not easy to get to know."

"Bring her by the house for supper. We'll invite Christina and Tara. With those two and Andie, they're bound to get some details."

"I'm not tricking her into getting grilled by your wife and her friends."

"It won't be like that. I promise to tell Andie to go easy."

"She might not come. She doesn't seem the social type."

"You'll never know until you ask."

"I don't know. I'll see how things go."

"Andie showed me a picture of the pillows and towels. She's great with a sewing machine. An unusual talent for someone her age."

"I told you, she's not like the others."

He laughs.

"What?"

"Cousin, you've got it bad."

"Fuck off." I click my tongue and squeeze Reuben with my legs, and we take off.

"Friday night?" he calls after me.

I flip him off without turning.

Back at the lodge, I water Reuben, tie him up, and go inside.

Yesterday, when I asked Devyn about learning to ride again, she seemed unsure. She's reading a book in the living room. Not her electronic book thing, but an actual paperback. I step closer. It's a book about constellations. "Studying up on the stars?"

"Thought I could use a hobby."

"You mean besides sewing?"

"Sewing isn't a hobby."

"Then how did you learn—"

"Did you know there are eighty-eight official constellations, and the word constellation means 'set with stars'?"

"I didn't know that."

"Living on a ranch, you might be interested in this fact: farmers were the first to use constellations. In some areas of the world, the changing of the seasons is so subtle that they depended on the stars to know when it was time to plant and harvest."

"Is that so? I guess you're becoming an astronomy expert."

"Ha! Hardly." She puts the book on the table.

"Can you come outside?"

"Why?"

"I was hoping we could go for a ride."

"In your truck?"

"No."

She sighs. "I'm a little nervous about getting on a horse."

"We'll ride together. Reuben is strong, and we should both fit in the saddle I put on him."

She's still hesitating.

"You live on a ranch now, Devyn. Horses come with the territory. Besides, you said you needed a hobby. Maybe now you can have two: stars *and* horses."

"What if they hate me?"

"Horses don't hate anyone."

After a moment, she says, "I'll get my hat."

Out front, I untie Reuben and mount up. When she appears, I hold my hand out and pull her up in front of me. We fit in the saddle, but it's snug. I slip my arms around her and pick up the reins. It's as close as we've ever been. My chest is pressed against her back, and when Reuben starts walking, the friction between us causes an unintentional reaction.

"Keep your legs slack, otherwise it will confuse Reuben."

"Where are we going?"

"You'll see."

We go slow. I don't want to put undue stress on the horse. We head away from the ridge and onto the airstrip.

"Wow," she says. "It's even more overgrown than I remember. I walked past here last month on my way to the lodge, but it didn't really hit me how dilapidated it was. Do you think anyone will ever make use of it again?"

"We don't have much use for it. The airport is only forty minutes away. This was built way back."

"But wouldn't it be cool if your guests could fly directly here? Like have VIP plane service from the airport and then get on horses to the lodge? It would add to the overall experience. And as long as we're dreaming, you know what else would be great? Helicopter tours. Think about it. You do horseback rides, but the ranch is so big, there's no way for them to see it all. I'll bet it looks amazing from the air."

"It does. I've seen it. The ridges to the east of the lodge are what this place is named after."

"The devil's horns. I'd love to see them."

"I'd love to show you. You got a few extra million lying around to fix the runway and add a helipad? Not to mention we'd need a pilot, or do you want to add that to your list of hobbies?"

She leans back into me with a sharp nudge. My arms tighten below her breasts, and I hold her against me. Her heart is racing, and she stops breathing for a moment. I think I do, too.

We reach the clearing at the end of the runway.

"What's that?" she asks.

"It's my oil well."

She turns so I can see her surprised expression. "Yours, Aaron Pearce's, or yours, DHR's?"

"It's mine."

Her eyebrows shoot up. "Do you bring *all* the girls out here to impress them?"

I lift her hat and put my lips to her ear. "You're the only one." I circle Reuben around it.

"So you're rich?"

I chuckle. "One oil well won't make you rich."

"But you must make something off it, otherwise why have it?"

"I don't keep the profits."

"Why not?"

"That's not why it's here. I have it for research."

"What are you researching?"

"Better, cleaner ways to drill for oil."

"You mean because of the impact on climate change? Isn't that why people want renewable energy, like solar and wind? Won't oil drilling be obsolete someday?"

"Oil isn't only used for energy. It's a natural resource critical in the production of lots of things, like rubber, detergents, clothing—even pharmaceuticals. It's not going away anytime soon. Until then, it's my mission to make it more eco-friendly. This is called a wildcat well. That means it's away from any established oil fields. I specifically chose this location on the ranch so it wouldn't impact any of the wildlife or forestry."

She tilts her head. "Who knew you were a save-the-world kind of guy?"

"Just trying to do my part. We should head back before Reuben gets too worn out." I turn the horse in the direction of the lodge. "I'm going to the main ranch for supper tomorrow, and my cousin wanted me to invite you along. What do you say?"

She tenses. "That depends. What have you told him about me?"

"Devyn, I don't know anything about you, so there's nothing to tell."

"You didn't mention me stealing food or living in the attic?"

"Of course not."

She turns slightly. "Why didn't you?"

"I figured it was nobody's business. So, supper?"

"It would be a nice change."

"You won't be sorry. Andie is a spectacular cook. Want to take the reins?"

"No, thanks."

"Come on, it's easy," I say. She reluctantly takes the reins from me. To reassure her, I rest my hands lightly on the back of hers. "You barely have to pull; a little tug will let him know which direction you want him to go. Use the pressure of your legs and thighs to tell him how fast. Squeezing your legs will speed him up, releasing them will slow him down. Try it."

As we pass the airstrip, I remember what she said. It's kind of an outrageous idea but one I plan to keep in the back of my mind.

With her guiding the horse, I sit back and enjoy the feel of her in my arms. I could do this every day, and it would never get old. She's everything I want in a woman, which is laughable because I know precisely nothing about her. My thumb is grazing circles along her forearm, and I can feel goose bumps arise. Reuben starts to trot. She must be squeezing him. "Relax," I whisper. Reuben slows and she leans into me. Fuck. I've never wanted anyone more than I want her.

When we ride up to the lodge, Joe is sitting on the front porch with lemonade. I like the man, but I'm disappointed to see him. Guests don't arrive until tomorrow. I was hoping Devyn and I might continue what we started.

"Joe!" Devyn shouts gleefully.

He raises his glass. "Thought I'd try out a new recipe on the two of you before I poison any of the payin' customers. You game?"

"Yes," she says. "I'm sure it will be incredible, like all your creations."

"How 'bout you, son?"

I help Devyn down off the horse. "Sure. Just let me get Reuben back to the stable."

Joe and Devyn start a conversation before I have Reuben turned around. She's really taken to him. Maybe he's like a father figure to her.

Will I ruin everything if I try to be with her?

CHAPTER FOURTEEN

Deryn

My belly hurts from laughing. Joe may have deep dark secrets, but he sure is a funny guy. I get up to clear the table, but he won't let me. Aaron and I enjoy a decadent dessert as Joe does the dishes. When he sits back down, he pulls a flask from his breast pocket.

I raise a brow.

"You don't think an old man can relax with a shot of gin after supper?" He pulls two glasses from the cabinet. "Care to join me?"

"I… I guess. But go easy on me. I haven't had a drink in forever. I've forgotten what alcohol tastes like."

Aaron studies me as Joe puts ice in my glass and pours a small amount of gin over it. There are only two glasses on the table. I stand and open the cabinet for a third.

"Don't bother." Joe thumbs at Aaron. "This one don't drink much."

"Oh." I push my glass away. "Then maybe I shouldn't."

"It's fine," Aaron says. "I'm not an alcoholic, if that's what you're thinking. I simply prefer soda." He moves my glass closer. "Go ahead. Just be careful."

Careful? It's not like I'll be driving anywhere. I wonder why he seems a bit uneasy, but the glass looks inviting, so I sip the gin. It warms my throat all the way down to my stomach.

"You wouldn't happen to play gin as well as drink it, would you, Joe?"

He seems pleased. "I think I've died and gone to heaven. I haven't run into a young'un who likes to play gin in thirty years."

"I'll get my cards." I race to my room. In the past, playing gin may have simply been a way to pass the time, but I got really good at it. I deal three hands.

Aaron laughs. "I have no idea how to play."

"We'll teach you."

I spend the next two hours playing, laughing, and flirting with both of them. It's been the best night I can remember.

Joe notices the time. "I may just turn into a pumpkin if I don't leave now." He puts away his flask and leans over to plant a kiss on my cheek. "Thank you for a lovely evening, Missy."

"No, thank *you*. The food was to die for."

"I'm glad you approve. I'll add it into the rotation."

Joe leaves. I put the cards away and hear his old truck rumble to life, then loudly sputter down the drive. I giggle. "Talk about being bad for the environment."

I wash the two glasses, then dry them, realizing I'm being watched the entire time. I turn and lean against the counter.

"I guess I should go, too," Aaron says. "It's late and we have guests coming tomorrow."

"Okay."

"You didn't want to play more cards or anything, did you?"

"No." I want to kick myself when the word leaves my mouth. Of course I don't want him to go, but I don't know what to say to get him to stay either.

He crosses to the door. "I'll see you tomorrow, then."

"Yes."

He hesitates, then walks through. I sit heavily on a chair and bang my forehead on the table. I should have asked him to stay.

The entire time we played cards, my shoe was resting against his. My leg went numb a few times because I refused to move it. We weren't touching, not really, but I swear I could feel him. And I couldn't help but think of the hour I spent on the horse with his strong arms around me. And when he whispered in my ear, I almost detonated on the spot.

I'd never played cards so poorly.

I watch the door, almost expecting him to come back and tell me he's changed his mind. I fantasize about him carrying me up the stairs to one of the guest rooms. We'd make love on the bed, the chair, even in the large tub, and he'd tell me I'm a good person. For a second, I'd believe him.

After I change into the T-shirt I've been sleeping in, I go out on the roof. I love being here when there are no guests. I can turn off all the outside lights and enjoy an amazing view. I glance at Aaron's cabin and see movement in one dimly lit window. Is he getting ready for bed? Does he sleep naked?

I lie down and look for the Big Dipper. It's technically not a constellation, because it's part of a larger one. But it's the most recognizable and a good place to start for a novice like me.

I'm tracing it with my finger when I hear noise inside. Someone takes a tumble.

"Shit," Aaron curses. "Shit, shit, shit."

I rise on my elbows. "You okay?"

"Hit my knee on the corner of something."

"You could have used a light."

"I was going for the element of surprise."

"You wanted to scare me into falling off the roof?"

He sighs. "Maybe I didn't think it through." He climbs through the window. "Couldn't sleep either?"

"Didn't even try."

"Me neither. Mind if I join you?"

I scoot over, and he lies next to me. I pick up his hand and put it underneath mine, then retrace the stars. "Do you see it?"

"The Big Dipper. It's one of the two I know."

"Let me guess, the other is the Little Dipper."

"I'm lame, I know."

"You're not lame." I put his hand down.

He takes my hand in his. "Tell me about the stars."

"I don't know much. The Big Dipper is part of a larger constellation called Ursa Major, which is the third largest constellation. It covers over three percent of the sky."

"That's huge."

"It borders eight other constellations. Draco, Leo, Leo Minor, and some others I can't remember. It's a twenty-eight-sided irregular polygon. Ursa Major was the inspiration for Vincent van Gogh's Starry Night painting."

"You remembered that stuff from your book? That's pretty good. If your memory's that good, maybe you should consider counting cards in Vegas."

I laugh and pull my hand away.

He captures it again. "What happened to you, Devyn?"

My smile fades. "What happened to *you?*"

"What do you mean?"

"Joe said we all have secrets. I got the feeling he was talking about himself *and* you."

"I could tell you, but I get the feeling you kind of like me. I'd rather not change that."

I stare at the side of his head. I could have said the exact same thing. Is he reading my mind? "I get the feeling you kind of like me, too."

He scoots closer. Our faces are inches apart. "So we can agree that we like each other and everyone has secrets?"

"I suppose we can."

"Can we agree that I want to kiss you, and you're going to let me?"

The smile returns. Without thinking much about it, I straddle him. We stare at each other. Then at the exact same time, he stretches up, I lean down, and our lips meet.

Days, weeks of sexual tension and pure animal attraction culminate in a kiss like I've never experienced. The heat of his lips. The pressure of his hands on the back of my head. The intense feeling of our bodies finally mashing together the way we might have both dreamed. It's explosive.

It lasts minutes, maybe hours. I have no idea. I've lost track of time. He flips me over so I'm beneath him, and he murmurs something into my mouth. I think he says, "Oh my god," but I probably only think it because those exact words are on repeat in my head.

I gaze at the stars as his lips work on my neck. The feel of his tongue on my skin mesmerizes me as much as the view above. It's the most perfect moment of my life.

He balances himself on his elbows. "Jesus, Devyn."

"You too?"

"What the hell is happening?"

"I don't know. All I know is I don't want it to stop."

He sits up and grasps the hem of my T-shirt. He waits for permission. I guide his hands up and over my head, and my shirt comes off, leaving me naked except for panties.

He looks at my breasts. I don't wait for him to make a move. I place his hands on me.

I tuck my hands into the back of his pants, needing to feel skin. I can't get leverage, so I unbutton his jeans and push them down, then reach around and grab his ass. He tears his shirt off.

Seeing him shirtless in the moonlight is something out of my dreams. My deepest fantasies. I tug at his pants. "Off. Now."

He removes his pants but keeps on his skivvies. That's fair; I'm still wearing mine.

I run my finger under the waistband. "More."

"Are you sure?"

"More."

He strips off his boxer briefs, and his erection springs free, its silhouette standing proud and tall against the starlit night sky. I don't deserve this. I've done nothing to earn this. But I'm going to take as much as he wants to give me.

"Now me," I say, guiding his hands to my underwear.

I've had men try to rip them off and take what wasn't theirs, but not him. He slowly slides my panties down my legs and then appraises me as if he's never seen a naked woman before. I heard the guys talking when I was painting the stable. He's seen plenty, probably more than he can remember. What he doesn't know is this is the first time I've seen a naked man. In the flesh anyway.

He's breathing so hard I can feel the puffs of breath across my chest. He looks into my eyes, and for a moment, I think he's going to stop. It almost seems like he's in pain.

He says, "I've never seen anything so fucking gorgeous in my life."

That's it. I'm done. My heart melts. "Aaron, will you make love to me?"

He lowers himself to me, and his erection presses against my thigh. "Hell yes, I will. But not yet."

He takes my nipple into his mouth, and my head goes back at the exquisite feeling. He teases me, tastes me, tempts me. His tongue blazes a path lower, down my abdomen and across my belly. I tense. No man has ever put his mouth on me there, but this is Aaron. He's the one I want there. He's the one I want everywhere.

When he puts his tongue on me, I shudder. I've read about it. Dreamt about it. But words can't possibly describe the way this feels. I'm in heaven, surrounded by stars, with this man touching me like I'm the most precious thing in the world.

He inserts a finger, then another. He moves them around as if he's a musician and I'm his instrument. I'm building like a crescendo. My hands ball into fists. My teeth dig into my lower lip. A sound I've never heard escapes my throat, and I shout.

When I stop pulsating, he climbs up my body. "Holy shit, Dev. Now I've seen *and* heard the most gorgeous things."

He called me Dev. Only one other person has ever used that nickname for me. The only person who ever loved me.

Tears spill down my face. I hope he doesn't notice.

Fat chance. He leans over and kisses one. I'm embarrassed, but he doesn't seem to mind. In fact, the way he's looking at me tells me just the opposite. He wants more. *I* want more.

He hovers over me like he's asking for permission again.

My body is humming. I don't have a choice. The answer is yes. Hell yes. Holy fucking god, yes.

I pull him toward me and touch his stiff, velvety penis. He pulls back, and I think maybe I'm being too aggressive. But he grabs his pants, retrieves his wallet, and removes a condom.

Of course. What was I thinking? I'm glad one of us has their wits about them.

He holds the condom up. "If you touch me, I'll explode, so which is it?"

"Put it on."

He smiles. I thought I knew every one of his smiles, but this one is different. It transports me to places I've never been. To feelings I've never had. To wants I've never experienced.

He rolls it on and gets into position. He locks eyes with me as he guides himself inside me. I wait for pain, the pinch, a sting I've read about. It never comes. He glides in and out with ease, setting a slow pace that I match with my hips.

As he gazes down on me, all I can think of is I've found it. The holy grail, the fountain of youth, the key to humanity—all of it. Tears threaten a second time. Is it like this for everyone?

"Aaron?"

He stills. "Are you okay?"

How do I tell him I'm not okay? I'm the farthest from okay I've ever been. I'm floating, I'm flying, I'm soaring among the stars. "I'm… I'm…"

He tucks a piece of hair behind my ear. "Me, too."

I run my fingernails down his back. Across his ass. Up his ribs. He pumps faster. He must be close; I can feel his desperation.

"Dev… oh god." He tenses.

I watch his face as he comes. It looks like it hurts, but that's followed by complete and total elation. That's exactly what he did to me. My life as I know it is forever changed. I'm not the same person I was twenty minutes ago. Is he?

He collapses on me, breathing heavily.

When he rolls off me, we both look at the sky. Clouds are rolling in and covering the stars.

"Jesus, Devyn."

I get up on an elbow. "You're welcome?"

We fall into a fit of laughter, and I realize this might just be the very best moment of my entire life.

We dress and go downstairs. Neither of us seems sure what should happen next.

He kisses my forehead. "I'll see you tomorrow?"

I nod.

He leaves, and my stomach heaves. I run to the bathroom and vomit, knowing I'm the last person in the world who deserves to feel what I just felt—deliriously happy.

CHAPTER FIFTEEN

Aaron

I walk blindly around the store. I don't know how to do this. I've never bought flowers for a woman. Hell, I've never bought anything for a woman.

"Can't go wrong with roses," the lady behind the counter says. "Everyone loves roses."

I shake my head. "She's definitely not everyone."

"Ah, one of those." She closes her eyes and sighs. "Had me one of those once, God rest his soul."

Something catches my eye. I pick up an arrangement of white lilies.

The lady rushes over. "It ain't Easter, and I'm pretty darn sure you're not off to a funeral." She takes them from me.

I want to tell her that some people like them anyway. People like my mom. And my guardian angel.

She must sense what I'm feeling. She picks up another. "If you're dead set on lilies, go for the colorful ones. Shall I have them delivered?"

"No, I'll deliver them myself."

"Good for you," she says. "Chivalry is all but dead these days. Best to own up to your feelin's rather than sit by the phone and hope she calls, eh?"

"I suppose."

She rings me up. "You look her right in the eye when you give these to her. If she's special, you need to let her know right away. Never stop lettin' her know."

"Yes, ma'am."

She puts the arrangement in a box that will keep it from falling over on the way home.

I haven't stopped thinking about Devyn since I left last night. I got up far before my alarm and raced through my morning chores so I could go into town and get these to her before the guests arrive.

Last night was unbelievable. We connected on some level I didn't know existed. It wasn't just sex. It was... Well, whatever's better than sex.

I pull up to the lodge and remove the vase from the box. I pass Lora's car on my way to the door. She's early. I contemplate waiting until later to do this. But what if Devyn and I run into each other, I don't have the flowers, and it's awkward because she doesn't know how I feel about last night, and I can't say anything until I give her the flowers? It's best to take them in now.

Get a grip, I chastise myself. *You're not thirteen.*

I enter through the back. Lora is leaning against the counter, sipping coffee. She eyes the flowers. "Table decoration?"

"No." I glance at Devyn's room. The door is open, but the lights aren't on. "Have you seen Devyn?"

Her nose turns up so slightly that it's almost imperceptible. I wonder if Devyn was right about her. "She's probably doing whatever maids do."

"She's not a maid, Lora."

"Housekeeper. Cleaner. Servant. Which word do you prefer?"

The claws are definitely out.

I cross the kitchen to the rec room. Lora follows.

"I can find her myself," I say. "Why don't you hang out in the kitchen and finish your drink?"

She seems upset as she spins on her heels and leaves.

After searching every room and guest suite, I try the attic. "Devyn? You up there?"

"One sec!"

I put the vase on the floor beside the door. She appears at the top of the stairs, and I wonder how she's gotten more beautiful since last night. She smiles. I almost sigh in relief. I wondered if she would think it was a mistake. We did kind of go from zero to sixty in two-point-five seconds.

"What are you doing up there?"

"Just thinking."

"In the attic?"

"Nobody ever bothers me here."

"Do you want me to leave you alone?"

She descends the stairs. "No. I want to check the suites one last time before the guests arrive. Did you see the pillowcases?"

"You did them?"

"Did a few this morning. I'll need more thread for the rest." She hops off the bottom step and sees the flowers. "What are those?"

I pick them up and hand them to her. "They're for you." I kiss her cheek.

"They're beautiful. Thank you." She smells them. "I've never gotten flowers before. What kind are they?"

"Lilies." My eyes narrow in surprise. "Never? That's not possible."

Voices echo in the grand hall below. The guests have arrived. She shoves the flowers at me. "Please put these in my room. I really want to double-check everything before they come up."

"Are we still on for supper at the main house?"

"Yeah, fine." She races away and says over her shoulder, "Come find me later."

I go down the back stairs and into Devyn's bedroom. I haven't been in here since it became hers. I'm not sure what I expected, but there are no personal touches. She really did come with nothing. There's not much choice about where to put the flowers. The sewing machine takes up the desk in the corner. When I move her notepad on the nightstand so I can place the vase next to it, I see her writing and can't help reading it.

Last night is the first night I can remember not having a nightmare.

I want to read on but know I shouldn't. These are her private thoughts. I shut the notebook, not wanting her to know she left it open.

She has nightmares? About him? The ex-husband or boyfriend who is after her? The one who never got her flowers? More than ever, I want to know what she's running from. I need her to know she can tell me. That I won't think any less of her. I lean against the wall. Would she think less of me if she knew what

I've done? Did last night change anything? Are we dating now? Do I want to be? Does she?

These questions plague me all afternoon as I work around the ranch.

Later, Devyn and I are in my truck, pulling up to Maddox's place. She sees other cars in the driveway. "We aren't the only guests?"

"Maddox said Andie's best friends are coming. And Owen—you remember him?"

"What if someone asks my last name?"

"Tell them whatever you want. Make one up if you want to."

"Dunlop," she says without hesitation.

My eyebrows shoot up. "Sure didn't take you long to come up with one. Old boyfriend?"

I want to kick myself as soon as the words are out of my mouth. If she's hiding from an old flame, she sure as shit wouldn't use his last name, and it makes me seem like a jealous asshole to even ask. But jealous is exactly what I am.

"Not an old boyfriend."

I get out of the truck, then turn to her. "In light of what we did last night, I'm wondering if I have the right to ask if there's been a lot of them. Old boyfriends."

"There haven't. Can we go in now?"

She doesn't want to talk about it. I understand. She needs time—time to trust me.

I grab the bottle of wine and we go up on the porch. Maddox's old dog, Beau, lifts his head in greeting. I lean down and give him a pat.

She looks at the pooch. "Why don't you have a dog? Don't all cowboys have them?"

I laugh. "The poor thing would probably starve to death if I was responsible for it."

Andie opens the front door before we can knock and pulls me in for a hug. Then she hugs Devyn, who appears uncomfortable, but Andie doesn't seem to notice.

"I'm so glad you could come." Andie pulls Devyn inside. "I'd like you to meet my two best friends, Christina and Tara."

They put down their wine glasses and greet Devyn with more hugs. Devyn doesn't seem to know what to do with her arms. She lifts them and then drops them, then she gives one of them a quick pat on the back, like how you'd pat a dog on the head. I get the feeling she hasn't been hugged much.

"You already know Owen," I say. "He and Tara are—" I turn to her. "What exactly are you again?"

Owen steps forward. "Yeah, I'd like to hear the answer to that."

"Gee, thanks for putting me on the spot, Aaron," Tara says. "We're… dating."

"For over seven years," Owen adds, putting emphasis on *seven* as if it's been an eternity.

"Seven years of pure bliss," Tara adds.

Owen rolls his eyes. "Yeah. Whatever." He kisses her dramatically, and we all laugh.

"I don't get it," Devyn says. "What's so funny?"

"It's a long-standing joke around here that Tara won't let Owen put a ring on her finger."

"Got a big sparkly diamond on my nightstand," he says. "Ask her every chance I get. She always says no."

"I like the way things are," she says.

"I know, babe." He pulls her close. "Don't mean I'm gonna stop tryin'."

Matt appears with a tray of hors d'oeuvres. I guide Devyn over. "And this is Christina's husband, Matt."

"Nice to meet you," she says.

After we settle on the couch, Devyn goes completely rigid.

"What is it?" I ask.

She doesn't answer right away. She's staring at the corner of the room where they keep Vivian's playpen and toys. "You didn't tell me Andie and Maddox have a kid."

"I didn't? Guess it never came up. Vivian is almost seven months old. She's amazing. I'd never been around babies before her. Do you like kids?"

She swallows, looking almost ashen. Before I can ask what's wrong, Andie comes over with a bottle of wine and some glasses. "Who wants wine?"

"I'll pass. Devyn?"

Andie starts to hand her a glass and then pulls back playfully. "You're old enough, right?"

Devyn doesn't laugh. She's still focused on the playpen.

"Devyn?" I touch her arm, and the trance is broken. "Wine?"

"Oh, sure, I'll have a glass."

"She's twenty-two," I say, as if Andie cared. "Where's the rug rat?"

"Sleeping. Thank God I got her down for a nap. She might even sleep through dinner." She turns to Tara. "You could have brought Trey, you know. Vivian loves him."

Devyn stills. "There's another one?"

"Tara has a ten-year-old," I say. "He loves Owen like a dad. He's a real cowboy in the making."

She swallows a large mouthful of wine. Guess she isn't a fan of kids.

Devyn is quiet. Observant. Hesitant. Andie and her friends joke and laugh and drink for an hour, including Devyn as much as she'll allow. I'm grateful because I get the idea Devyn can use all the friends she can get. With every passing minute, she becomes more comfortable. The tension leaves her body, and when I see her smile at me from across the room, I swear part of my heart melts. This is the first time I've ever brought a woman here.

I've only known her for a few weeks; only been with her for one brief encounter. So how can I be so damn sure? But I am. I want this. The couple thing. The Devyn thing. The *whole* thing. And the realization about knocks me on my ass.

"You sure you don't want a drink?" Owen asks. "Seems like you might be needin' one."

"I'm good."

He looks at Devyn and back at me, raising a brow as if he knows exactly how it feels to be hit by a ton of bricks. He slaps me on the shoulder and walks away.

During dinner, Andie makes a joke about Matt, calling him Victor. Christina snorts wine through her nose. Everyone is laughing except Devyn.

"I apologize, Devyn," Andie says. "Seems we have a lot of inside jokes around here. Matt and I used to date. Well, sort of. He was being investigated by the FBI, and they asked me to help. Turns out it was all a big mistake, but by the time I knew it, I'd fallen for this one." She puts her hand on Maddox's arm.

"He was my landscaper at the time," Christina says. "He became a suspect in a missing persons case. But the woman, a single mother, was eventually found in Costa Rica with some guy forty years older than she was. Turns out money was more important to her than her kid that she abandoned at daycare and who ended up living with her grandparents, not knowing for years if her mother was dead or alive."

"That's—" Devyn glances at everyone at the table. "You guys have some stories, don't you?"

"Oh, you don't know the half of it," I say. "Christina's ex-husband kidnapped Andie and held her at gunpoint."

"Oh my god," Devyn says. "Where is he now?"

"Prison," Andie says.

"When does he come up for parole again?" Owen asks.

"In a few months. You can bet I'll be there with bells on, doing everything I can to keep him behind bars, where murderers belong."

Devyn chokes on her wine. She looks sick.

"You okay?"

"I thought you said he was a kidnapper," she says softly.

"He was a lot of things," I tell her. "We're pretty sure he was at least partly responsible for the death of Maddox's grandmother, the woman who used to run this ranch, but the prosecutor could never prove it, so he only got put away for what he did to Andie, plus some drug charges."

Devyn's breathing quickens and sweat dots her forehead. It looks like she's on the verge of a panic attack.

"Excuse us for a second." I guide Devyn to the living room and sit her on the couch. "I promise you'll be safe here. I know it seems like there's a lot of weird shit going on, but it's in the past."

She breathes in and out. "This is overwhelming."

I chuckle. "Maybe we should have just started with the four of us and worked our way up from there."

Screams come through the baby monitor. "There's the little princess," Maddox says, rising from the table. "You stay, darlin'. I'll get her."

Andie smiles sweetly, and they share a look of mutual admiration. "Thanks, babe."

Suddenly I can see myself in five years. Ten. Saying the same thing, sharing the same smile. With Devyn. What's happening to me?

A timer goes off in the kitchen. Andie rises to get dessert from the oven. A second timer sounds from Maddox's pocket as he enters the room with Vivian. "I have to turn off the grill." He turns to Devyn. "Can you hold her for a second?"

Devyn turns as white as a ghost. "Me? No."

Andie walks past the opening to the kitchen, holding a steaming dish with potholders. "It's okay, Devyn. Kids aren't as fragile as you think. You won't break her."

"I'm sorry. I have to go." Devyn gets up, walks right past Maddox and Vivian and out the front door.

"What the hell just happened?" Maddox asks.

"I have no idea." I run out after her. She's halfway down the driveway. "Devyn!"

She doesn't stop. I have no idea where she thinks she's going. It's a few miles back to the lodge, and the shoes she's wearing are not for walking. I run to my truck, back out, and pull down the driveway. She's in the road when I catch up to her. I pull alongside, stop, and lean over to open the passenger door. "Get in."

"I can't do this," she says, standing on the blacktop.

My heart falls. Can't do what? Us? "Devyn, get in and I'll drive you home. You don't have to do anything right now."

She slides in next to me, the tears in her eyes glistening from the lights on my dashboard. "Whatever it is, it'll be okay."

She looks out the window. "It'll never be okay."

I desperately want to know why. My need to protect her is fierce. But I remain silent because she's fragile, and unlike Vivian, I'm afraid one wrong move might break her.

CHAPTER SIXTEEN

Devyn

I'm taken to a small room with concrete walls. There are no sheets on the thin stained mattress. Behind me, the doors clank shut. I sink to the floor, barely remembering the last hour of my life. Cameras flashed, fingerprints were taken, then I was stripped out of my clothes and given an orange jumpsuit. I was moved from room to room. My hair is wet and full of tangles. There aren't any windows, but I know it must be late—the middle of the night probably.

I relive what happened earlier over and over, my heart pounding and my stomach churning. This must all be a sick, twisted dream. I bang my head on the wall, hoping to wake up. Then I cry myself to sleep.

"DeMaggio!" a woman yells. I wake, sore from sleeping on a mattress that smells like a dumpster.

She leads me down a hallway, past other cells, to a door. On the other side of the door is an officer with a gun strapped to his side. He's standing tall, eyeing me, his hand on the gun still in the holster. I want to tell him he's got this all wrong. I'm not who he thinks I am. I'm not a criminal. Not a murderer. But I don't tell him that.

Because I am.

There are four other people in the van. We're shackled to the floor. The drive isn't long. We could have walked to wherever they're taking us.

"Out!" the lady guard says.

We file into a tunnel attached to the back of a huge building. We're escorted down a long hallway and taken to a place they call a holding room.

One by one, the five of us are called to go into a different room. When it's my turn, I realize where we are. I've only ever seen a courtroom on TV. A new guard takes me by the upper arm and moves me to a table.

The man sitting at the front of the room, the judge I presume, looks upset when he sees me. "Do you not have any representation, young lady?"

I clear my throat. It's sore from crying. "Uh… I don't understand. Everything just happened last night." As soon as the words leave my mouth, my eyes flood with tears.

A man enters the room behind me and runs up to my side. "My apologies, Your Honor. I was just assigned to Ms. DeMaggio's case twenty minutes ago."

"We've got a lot to get through this morning," the judge says. "Let's move this along. Young lady, are you aware of the charges against you? Do you understand you're here for arraignment? That means you get to make a plea."

"Give me one minute, Your Honor," the man says.

The judge waves a hand, agreeing, but clearly not happy about it.

The man to my right quickly whispers a bunch of legal stuff I don't understand. I'm still trying to wrap my mind around what happened. "You'll plead not guilty," he says. They're the only words I comprehend.

I shake my head. "But I can't. I'm guilty."

"I've read your file. Well, I've skimmed it. You want to plead not guilty. Trust me, I'm your lawyer now."

"I can't afford you. Did my mom hire you?"

"I'm a public defender. I represent people who can't pay for an attorney."

"Mr. Craddick?" the judge says impatiently.

My lawyer leans close. "Tell him you understand the charges and plead not guilty. Do it now. He's not going to wait forever."

"I understand the charges," I say.

"How do you plead?" the judge asks.

I glance at Mr. Craddick. He nods. "N-not g-guilty."

I close my eyes. Now I'm not only a criminal but a liar, too.

The judge, Mr. Craddick, and the lady at the next table have a discussion about bail—more legal jargon I tune out. The judge says stuff to me, and I nod like I'm listening. I should tell him I've changed my mind. That I'm guilty. That I deserve whatever they want to do to me. Does Texas have an electric chair?

Mr. Craddick leaves, and I'm taken back to the holding room. An hour later, after being shackled to the floor of the van and driven back to jail, I'm in yet another room, being handed the clothes I wore last night when I came in. They're damp.

"You can change in there," the lady says, motioning to a door.

Why do they want me to put my clothes back on? I stare at her blankly.

"Honey, you're being released on bail. You know this, right?"

"I'm being released?"

"They didn't explain it to you?"

I shake my head. They might have, but I can't remember.

She rolls her eyes. "I sure am gettin' sick and tired of doing everyone else's job. You get to go home until your trial. My advice is to get yourself a good lawyer."

"They gave me one."

She laughs. "Honey, if you think some public defender fresh out of law school gives a shit about what happens to you, you can call me the Queen of England, 'cause you livin' in fantasy land."

I enter a dirty bathroom. I'm happy to get out of the jumpsuit, but putting on my clothes is a reminder of what I've done.

The guard takes me out of the cell area and through the front of the building. "Now go, and try not to ever come back. You're too young to throw your life away."

She retreats into the building, leaving me on the sidewalk. I look left and right. Nobody is here for me. She told me I could go home, but I know I can't. I don't even have my phone. It must have fallen out of my pocket last night.

There's a convenience store on the corner, and I tell the guy behind the counter that my phone is dead and ask if I can use his. He pulls a landline from behind the counter, and I dial Angelina's number.

"Hello?"

"It's me."

"Where are you?"

"They let me go. I'm at a store by the jail. Can you pick me up?"

"I can't." She pauses. "They told me not to talk to you."

"Who told you?"

"My parents. Their lawyer. The police."

"Why not?"

Someone talks to her in the background. "I'm really sorry, Devyn. I have to go. You'd better not call back."

The line goes dead. I call Dane, and he tells me the same thing. When I call Billy, he hangs up on me. What is happening? I hand the phone back to the cashier and go to the door. "You aren't even going to buy anything?" he shouts after me.

I don't answer him. I sit on a nearby bench. I have no money. No phone. And, apparently no friends.

I have nothing. And it's still more than I deserve.

I wake in a sweat. I have nightmares all the time, but they usually aren't so detailed. I change my shirt and try to go back to sleep, knowing I won't. I reach for my phone, turn on the flashlight, and point it to the ceiling. I used to count dirty ceiling tiles when I couldn't sleep, but this ceiling is smooth, nothing like the one I stared at for 730 days. I put down the phone and get out of bed. I'll count stars instead.

I've counted hundreds, maybe thousands, when Aaron climbs out the window.

"Don't you ever sleep?" I ask.

"Don't you?" He sits on the blanket next to me. "Want to talk about it?"

"Talk about what?"

"Why you don't sleep."

"No."

"Then how about you tell me what happened earlier. Why'd you freak out at Maddox's?"

"I'd rather not talk about that either."

"What *do* you want to talk about?"

I take his hand. "I don't want to talk at all." I put it on my breast.

"Devyn," he says like he's my third-grade teacher scolding me. "This won't make it go away."

I push him down and straddle him. "You're wrong. It will."

"For a few minutes maybe."

"Maybe that's all I need." I lean down and kiss him. He stiff lips me. "Don't you want this?"

"Jesus, Dev, of course I want this. Last night was incredible. It was perfect. *You're* perfect."

I roll off him. "Don't say that."

"Okay, you're not perfect. Neither am I. No one is. But it's damn clear to me that we're perfect together." He pulls me against him. "What happened to you is in the past. Believe me when I say I know what I'm talking about."

I shake my head. "You couldn't possibly know."

"Do you deny that we're perfect together?"

"We've only known each other a few weeks."

"Doesn't matter. I asked you a question. Do you want to be with me, Devyn?"

I put a hand on his chest. "I was trying to. You pushed me away."

"I wasn't talking about sex. I mean, yeah, I want to have sex. Lots and lots of it. But I want to be with you and only you."

"As in you want to be my boyfriend?"

"If you'll let me."

"I've never had one before."

He seems stunned. "How is that even possible?"

"Back in high school, there was a guy, but it wasn't anything really. Since then, well, there just haven't been many opportunities."

"Then what—" He stops talking suddenly. "You know what, it doesn't matter. What's your answer?"

"You said something about sex?"

He laughs. "Lots and lots of it."

I climb on top of him again.

"Is that a yes?"

I kiss my answer, then he makes everything go away. He makes it go away two times over.

CHAPTER SEVENTEEN

Aaron

"You ready?" Quinn asks, riding up behind me on a horse.

I can't stop staring at Devyn, who's shaking out a rug on the porch.

Devyn sees us and waves.

Quinn sits up straighter. "Damn, she's hot."

Before I can get a word in, he's trotting over to her. I pull up alongside him as we reach the porch.

"I don't believe we've met," he says. "But I'm not sure why the hell not." He reaches over the railing and holds out a hand. "Quinn Thompson."

She puts the rug down, steps over, and shakes. "Devyn."

"Devyn…?"

"Just Devyn."

"I can see why Aaron has kept you a secret. Where are you from?"

"Around."

"Well, if you're new to town, I'm happy to volunteer my services as tour guide." Devyn glances at me. Quinn does, too. "Oh, are you two—"

"Yes," I say. "Can we get to work now?"

He holds up his hands in surrender. "No harm, no foul. Nice to meet you, Devyn."

"And you." She locks eyes with me. "See you later?"

"Count on it."

Quinn chuckles as we knee our horses into a walk. "Is that the reason you took off on me last week?"

"Do you think it's possible to fall for someone after only a few weeks?"

He grimaces. "Like love and shit?"

"I don't know. Maybe."

He brings Tucker to a stop. "Are you fucking kidding me?"

I shake my head.

"Well, damn. I'm the wrong person to ask. Like the way wrong person."

"Three weeks ago, I was just like you. I would have laughed if you'd told me I'd spend every waking minute thinking about a woman."

"Who'd have thought one of us would get a girlfriend before we turned thirty?"

"She's not *just* a girlfriend. I can't get her out of my head. I'm thinking crazy shit, brother. Like tuxedos, vacations on a secluded beach, matching headstones—all of it."

"Shit."

"Yeah."

He narrows his eyes at me. "Maybe it's because she's so hot. I bet in a few weeks you'll be your old self again."

"I don't think so. Have you ever stopped to think why we are the way we are? We go from woman to woman. What are we looking for? Could be we just hadn't found it yet."

"And you think she's *it?*"

"She's smart, mysterious, and sexy as hell. She even has ideas about the ranch."

"Like what?"

"We were out at my oil well the other day. When we rode on the airstrip, she said how great it would be to offer guests helicopter tours of the ranch or fly VIPs right to the property from the airport. It's genius. I wish I could make it happen."

"Why can't you?"

"One, the airstrip is a piece of crumbled crap. Two, I'm not a pilot, nor do I know any."

"Let's think about this for a minute. What if you could fix the airstrip?"

"Not a chance. It would cost millions. Maddox and Gavin would never go for it."

"What if someone donated the money?"

We reach the edge of the property, and I dismount. "Dude, I'm not letting you spend your trust fund on a crazy idea."

"What's crazy about it? She's right. Can you imagine the business you'd get if you advertised private plane service or helicopter tours? Rich people eat that shit up, trust me."

"It's not happening. Besides, you never dip into your inheritance."

"Because it's blood money. But this would be for a good cause. Think about it. You could expand more than just the lodge business. Having a working airstrip might give you opportunities for the rest of the ranch."

"Even if we fixed the airstrip, I'd never be able to afford to pay a pilot."

"So I'll do it."

"I'm not letting you pay a pilot for us."

"No, I mean I'll be your pilot."

"You're out of your mind."

He laughs. "No, I'm not. It's perfect. I'd love to learn how to fly. I feel fucking useless around here. Nobody will hire me because I'm a Thompson. College is for pussies—no offense. But what the hell else am I going to do with my life?" He pulls out his phone.

"What are you doing?"

"Finding out how to become a pilot."

I laugh. "I suppose you're going to buy a plane, too. And a helicopter?"

"How about we cross that bridge when we get to it? Besides, anything can be rented. Hot damn, I don't think I've been this excited about anything in a long time. Do you know how much chicks dig pilots? I'm going to get so much tail."

I shake my head. "As if you don't already. Mind if we get to work and pull our heads out of the clouds? I told Maddox we'd test all the water sources by the end of the day."

"Oh, I'm the one with my head in the clouds? You and the future Mrs. Pearce back there… Where's she from anyway? I've never seen her around."

"I'm not really sure."

"What did she do before she worked here?"

"I don't know."

"But you're in love with the girl? You don't know anything about her. It's the sex, isn't it? She looks like she'd be unbelievable in bed."

"She is, but that's beside the point."

He laughs and pats me on the back. "Man, that *is* the point. That's the *whole* point."

I hit him.

"What's her last name?"

"I don't know that either."

"You have got to be kidding. But she works for you."

"For room and board. I don't pay her a wage."

"Still, she hasn't told you her name? She could be a psycho. A gold digger. An underage runaway. She does look young. Oh, shit, you could be screwing jailbait."

"She's twenty-two."

"And you believe her? When she won't tell you anything else?"

"I do."

"You should hire a PI before you get in too deep."

"What don't you understand about everything I've said? I'm already in deep. I don't care who she was before she came here. I'm the last person to judge anyone."

"Does she know about Cameron?"

"No."

"Why not? Seems like maybe the two of you do nothing but fuck."

I zip up my test kit, put it in the saddlebag, and mount up. "Go home. I don't need your help today."

He catches up to me. "Hey, I'm sorry. I'm just looking out for you. If you say she's the real deal, I'll back off."

"She's the real deal."

"Fine. I won't say another word."

We ride in silence to the next watering hole. Quinn may be from a crappy crime-ridden family, but he's the closest thing to a brother I've ever had. "I haven't told her about Cam because if she knew my secrets, she'd feel pressured to tell me hers. I think she may be running from an abusive ex. Then again, she told me last night that she's never had a boyfriend. She's been through the wringer, for sure. Someone like her doesn't just end up on the streets."

"She was homeless?"

I instantly regret saying anything. Though I trust him like a brother, I don't want him viewing her differently. "You have to promise you'll never repeat that or make her feel like any less of a person. If you do, I'll kick your ass into next week, and you'll look far worse than any bucking bronc would leave you."

He grins. "Oh, you think you can kick my ass?"

"I've done it once. I'll do it again."

"I was seventeen. I'm older and bigger now."

"Yeah, but I was fifteen at the time. Pretty embarrassing for you, if I recall."

"You're goddamn right it was. But somehow I ended up supplying you with weed and buying you a phone."

"It's my charm. Nobody can resist it."

We reminisce about our sordid past on the way to our next stop.

After we drop off the samples and the horses at the main ranch, I thank him. "You don't have to keep helping me around here. I'm sure you have better things to do."

"I *don't* have better things to do. Why do you think I'm here all the time? Hey, speaking of that, do you think Maddox would mind if I crashed in one of the empty apartments for a while?"

"Sick of living in your mom's guest house?" I narrow my eyes. "You could rent anything you want. Why live here?"

"Maybe I like being around people who don't treat me like a pariah."

"I'll talk to him. I'm sure it'll be okay."

"Thanks." He looks at his phone. "And just so you know, I may have better things to do after all."

"Like?"

"Like going to flight school, baby."

"You're serious about this?"

"As serious as a fat man at a buffet, brother."

I imagine how great it would be to offer VIP flights and helicopter tours. It would put DHR on the map of private ranch destinations. I can't wait to tell Devyn.

CHAPTER EIGHTEEN

Devyn

"You're getting good," Aaron says as I ride Jasmine around the paddock.

For weeks, he's been giving me riding lessons on my days off. Jasmine is one of the smaller, gentler mares, and she's been very patient with me. I walk her in a circle, then turn and go the opposite direction.

Andie gives me a thumbs-up from the other side of the paddock. She's been trying to be my friend. I know she means well, but I'm not sure I'm ready for friends like her. I'm not sure I'll ever be ready.

Aaron helps me down off Jasmine, and we walk her back to her stall. I glance around in thought. "Is it expensive to build a stable?"

"Depends. One like this, yes. Why?"

"You should have one at the lodge. You're always having to take an ATV over here and move horses back to the lodge for the guests. If you had a stable there, wouldn't it be more efficient? And there are plenty of ranch hands to swing by and feed them or whatever. Think of when you're booked solid—you know it's going to happen. The lodge is getting more popular. It sure would make things easier."

He smiles. "Don't lie. You just want to be able to go riding whenever you want, don't you?"

"Yes, but I also think it's good for business."

"You're right. I've been turning over similar ideas in my head. Maybe we could work on it together."

"I think I might like that."

"Devyn!" Andie sees me from the south stable and rushes over. "You should join me Sunday by the pool. It's my only day off, and I like to make Maddox feel like building it last year wasn't a wasted investment." She leans close. "I think he just likes to watch me walk around in a bikini."

"Pool? I don't, uh, swim."

"That's okay. You can lie out and get some sun while keeping me company."

"Sunday is a turnover day. I'm usually pretty busy."

"No guests are arriving until Wednesday," Aaron says. "You don't need to get everything done Sunday."

"Still—"

"Come on. It'll be fun," Andie says. "Besides, I always swim during Vivian's nap. It'll be boring without you. What do you say?"

Aaron gives me an encouraging nod. I know how much he wants me to be friends with his friends. I guess he's never had occasion to test their loyalty. He's never found out that with some friends, you'd be better off with enemies.

"What time?"

Andie squeals in pleasure. "Two o'clock. Vivian's naps are like clockwork. We should have a full two hours to ourselves. I'll even make margaritas. Sound good?"

Sounds like torture to me, but to make Aaron happy, I agree.

Andie leaves, and Aaron steps away to answer a phone call. I stand by the arena, mesmerized by how the trainers are able to make horses move exactly the way they want them to. A horse backs up, something I'm told is hard to teach, and Mickey, the head trainer, looks pleased.

He catches me observing. "Want to give it a try?"

"Me? I can hardly ride."

"I've seen you. You're a quick learner." He waves me over. "Come on. I'll show you."

I climb over the fence and go to him.

"Georgie won't bite," he says, giving the gelding a pat. "He's our newest boarding horse. Never been formally trained." He hands me a crop and the lead rope attached to his halter. "Training a horse to back up is called backing, and it's easiest to do when you're standing on the ground. Once he's got it, you move to saddle training. Stand about four feet in front of him with the rope extended and lightly tap it with the crop while moving toward him. That will make him back up."

"I'm nervous."

"Don't be. I'm right here."

I do as he asks, and Georgie doesn't move. "I'm doing it wrong."

"Tap it a little harder. The rope barely moved when you did it the first time."

I add a bit of force, and the horse obediently steps back. "He did it," I say enthusiastically. "Good boy, Georgie! Good boy."

"Well done," Mickey says. "Lighten your grip now—it's his reward for doing his job. Would you like to try another trick with him?"

"Yes!"

"I started working on this with him yesterday. It's called leg up. Romeo will be your best friend if Georgie learns this one. He's our farrier."

"Farrier?"

"The one who tortures the horses with shoes. I'm only kidding. The shoes are nailed into a part of the hoof that doesn't cause them pain. Anyway, if they learn leg up, his job is easier. Let me show you." He stands beside Georgie. "You need to be close enough that your shoulder touches the horse's shoulder, or his hindquarters, if you are picking up the back legs. Place the hand closest to the horse on him, like this, and run your other hand down his leg until you reach his fetlock or ankle. If he hasn't started to pick his foot up by the time you get to the fetlock, squeeze the back of his leg gently, and he will lift his hoof." Georgie lifts his foot. "Now you try."

I give the horse a pat. "Let's do this, Georgie." I run through all the steps in my head and then begin.

"Use your left hand," he says. I switch. "That's correct. Now run the other hand down his leg." Georgie lifts his leg before I have to squeeze his ankle. "Would you look at that? Devyn, you've found your calling."

I hear applause and turn to see Aaron clapping from the other side of the fence. "Did you see that?" I ask excitedly.

"You're a natural!"

I hand Mickey the rope. "Thanks. That was fun."

"Come back anytime."

Aaron and I walk to his truck. "He likes you."

"Which one, the man or the horse?"

"Both, I presume. Mickey is great—a patient and persistent teacher."

"Seems that way."

He holds up his phone. "The call I got was about a pick-up at Home Depot. Want to keep me company?"

"Into Fort Worth? No."

"Come on. We'll listen to country music. See who can find the most depressing song on the radio."

"I prefer to hang around here."

"Stay in the truck if you like. There and back. I promise it will be painless." He offers up his charming grin. How can I say no?

"All right."

He tucks his phone away and opens the passenger door for me. "You can pick the first station."

After a few minutes of listening to depressing country songs, I turn off the radio. "I wanted to be a teacher once."

"Really?" Aaron takes his eyes off the road and glances at me in surprise. "Tell me more."

I shrug. "Not much to tell. It was a dream I had when I was little."

"There's a great community college half an hour from the ranch. You could take classes."

"I can't be a teacher."

"Why?"

"I just can't."

"I bet you'd be great at it. Look what you did with Georgie." He stops at a light. "Hey, you like horses now, right?"

"I love them."

"So teach *them*. You don't need a degree or anything. Mickey would love to have you as an apprentice. You can do it on your days off."

"Tempting, but you get it's not the same, right?" Still, I think about it.

"What would you have taught?"

"Math. High school algebra. Maybe even calculus."

"I knew you were a brainiac. Don't ask me to solve any math problems. That's what calculators are for."

"What did you want to be when you were a kid?"

"The truth? I thought about going into teaching, too. Then I got sent down here for a summer and fell in love with the ranch."

"You, a teacher?" I consider that. He's lean, rugged, and sexy. "The girls would have clawed each other's eyes out to be in your class."

"You think I'm hot, huh?"

I swat his thigh and he captures my hand and holds it. I move as close to him as my seatbelt will allow. "I'd have taken your class. But why teaching if your dad was a photographer and your mom's in the restaurant business?"

"Because of my guardian angel."

"Your *what?*"

"I know it's crazy, but I really do have one. Erin was supposed to be my adoptive mom. She couldn't have kids of her own so her and my dad, who was her husband at the time, hired my mom, Skylar, to have a baby for them. But then Erin got cancer and knew she was going to die, so she made my parents fall in love with each other. It's kind of a crazy story. Anyway, she wrote all these letters before she died, for my parents and for me. I get them from time to time, like when I graduated high school and stuff. Oh, and I'm named after her."

"That's an amazing story."

"I know. My aunt, Maddox's mom, even made it into a book."

"I think I know what I'll be reading next."

"Don't buy it," he says. "Andie has all of Aunt Baylor's books lying around. She'll be happy to let you borrow it."

"Great. I'll pick it up on Sunday."

"Right. You're going swimming. Do you think you two are becoming friends?"

"Hard to say. I don't make friends easily these days." We're stopped at another light when I see something out the window. "What I wouldn't give for a Chick-fil-A sandwich."

Aaron steps on the gas, pulls in front of another car, gets honked at, and turns into the drive-thru line.

"Are you crazy?"

"My girl wants a chicken sandwich."

His girl. I have a hard time containing my grin. That is until I remember I don't have any money. "I… didn't bring my purse."

He gets out his wallet. "I think I can swing it. See, this is what boyfriends do for their girlfriends. Buy them lunch and stuff."

A welcome warmness flows through me. "Is that so?"

We order, get our food, and park. He shuts off the engine, then hands me my sandwich with a wonky grin. "This is sort of like our first date. Sorry it wasn't a steakhouse or something fancy."

"I don't need fancy."

"You don't, do you?"

I'm salivating before I even take a bite. I haven't had one of these in years. "Oh, god," I say when I rip into the first piece.

Aaron gives me a look.

"Yours not any good?" I ask, inching away. "Because I'm not giving up mine."

"I'm sure it is, but watching you eat is giving me a fucking woody, Dev."

My cheeks flame. "It's been a while since I had one of these. It's so good." I pop a waffle fry into my mouth. "How come you call me Dev sometimes?"

"I don't know. I guess it just slips out. Is it a problem?"

I shake my head. "I kind of like it. Too bad you don't have a name that can be shortened. What's your middle name?"

"I'll tell you mine if you tell me yours."

I look away.

"Fine, you don't have to answer," he says. "But hey, I found out one thing about you today. Your dream job was to be a math teacher."

"Is that enough for you?"

"It is."

I sigh. "For now, right? Isn't that what you want to say?"

"Do I want to know more about you? Yes. But I'd rather be with you and not know all that stuff than not be with you at all." After we finish eating, he starts the truck. "Home Depot is right around the corner." We park in the huge lot. "You sure you don't want to come in?"

"I'm fine here."

"Want me to keep the truck running?"

I roll down my window. "No need. It's a beautiful day."

"I'll be back in five minutes. Ten tops."

I pull out my phone and search for his aunt's books. I find the one that looks like it might be about his parents. Maybe I will ask Andie if I can borrow it. I pull up the free snippet and start to read.

"DeeDee?" a boisterous voice shouts from a few cars down.

I stiffen. I immediately look at the Home Depot exit for Aaron. When I don't see him, I turn in the direction of the voice. Delta Brown is already coming toward me.

"It *is* you," she says. She sticks her head inside and looks me up and down. "Girl, you clean up real nice. When you get out?"

I start stress sweating. "A few months ago."

"I told you to look me up. Got me a place on the other side of Fort Worth. Willy got me a job cleaning the movie theater. Don't pay shit, but I get by. What you doin'?"

"I… I have a cleaning job, too."

"Where at? The pay any good? Maybe they need someone else."

I can't tell her. I don't want her showing up and ruining everything. "The pay sucks. Actually, I don't even get paid. I sleep in a tiny room and get leftover scraps, is all."

"Dayum, if a cute little cracker like you can't get a decent job, ain't no hope for the rest of us."

Aaron emerges from the store, pushing a cart full of supplies. My heart races. He can't see Delta. I open the door. "It's nice to see you again, but I have to help my boss with a pick-up."

"Got you gettin' supplies and shit, too?" she says. "You best stand up for yourself and ask for more money." Aaron's getting closer. "That cowboy your boss? Take some advice, DeeDee—ride that cowboy like he a buckin' bronco, and you be winnin' first prize. You be out of that tiny room in no time."

Sweat soaks my underarms. I have to get her out of here.

"Delta!" a man yells. "The fuck over here."

"Gots ta go," she says and finally leaves.

I try to slow the shaking of my hands as I lower the tailgate for Aaron. "Who was the woman you were talking to?"

"Nobody. She was asking for money."

I'm helping him load things when a beat-up car drives past. Delta sticks her head out the window. "Remember what I said, DeeDee." She laughs as tires burn rubber and a string of profanities comes from the driver.

Aaron looks after them. When they're out of sight, he asks, "What did she mean, remember what she said?"

I reach for the nearest lie. "She was spouting something about Jesus and how we're all going to hell if we don't help each other out. I told her I didn't have any money, but she didn't believe me."

"Yeah, but why in the hell would she call you DeeDee?"

"She's clearly crazy, Aaron."

"Seems strange she would call you that."

I sidle up to him and rub against his hip. "I much prefer Dev."

He smiles, and I can tell all thoughts of the crazy woman are gone. He pulls me into his arms. "What was it you said again about what you wouldn't do for a Chick-fil-A sandwich?"

I stretch up on my toes to give him a kiss. "Take me home, and I'll show you."

CHAPTER NINETEEN

Aaron

I watch her sleep. She's gorgeous without even trying. Maybe that's what I love about her. She's so natural. So raw.

I try not to move. I don't want to wake her. It's the first time we've had a sleepover. Her room at the lodge isn't ideal, but we were up on the roof, and she fell asleep. I carried her downstairs, and when I put her on the bed, she didn't let me go.

I lightly trace the edges of her face. I need to ingrain every inch of her into my memory, because I'm not sure how long she'll be here. I think she's trapped inside a life she doesn't want. She's obviously having fun, and we have this inexplicable connection, but she's at war with herself. She's stuck, unable to get beyond a past that's holding her hostage. Part of me lives in fear that I'll wake up one day and find her gone.

I roll over as quietly as I can, get my phone off the nightstand, and take a picture of her.

Her eyes open. "Did you take a picture of me?"

"I couldn't help it. You looked so peaceful."

She pulls me down next to her. "Take one of both of us."

I snuggle next to her, snap one, then look at it. She didn't bother to push stray hairs off her forehead or straighten her wrinkled T-shirt. It's a beautiful goddamn picture.

When I put my phone back on the nightstand, I see her notebook, a stack of money sticking out of the back. "You really should keep your money in a better place. Don't you have a purse?"

"I don't like to keep it there. It's too tempting if I have it on me. Besides, I'm almost always on the ranch. Speaking of money, do you have any idea when Maddox will need more day laborers? The tips from the guests are great, but I'd like to get more."

"Not until the stable is almost complete. A few weeks, maybe. I could ask around. Wyatt Jenkins is nice. I'm sure he'd hire you if he had a job for you."

"No. I only want to work here."

"If you need money, I'll give it to you." I glance at the thick stack in the back of her notebook. "But it looks like you're set for a while."

"I want to start saving."

"For what?"

"My own place."

"You don't like it here?" When she doesn't answer, I glance around the room that's barely bigger than a large closet and chuckle. "What am I saying? Of course you don't. This place is like a prison cell."

She scoffs. "Hardly."

"As if you'd know." I spoon her. "I like having you close. The nearest rentals are ten minutes away. How will we watch the stars together?" A thought occurs to me, and before I can stop myself, I blurt, "Move into the cabin with me."

She spins to face me. "You're crazy."

"No, I'm not. My cabin isn't huge—it's nothing like Maddox's place—but it's a lot bigger than this room. Hell, I'll add onto it. I built it myself, so it won't be that hard."

"We've only known each other a month."

"That doesn't matter, Dev. It only took me a few days to fall—"

Her fingers cover my lips. "Don't. Please."

"Why not? Don't you feel the same way?"

She moves away and sits up, pulling her knees to her chest and tucking into the corner of the bed where it meets the wall. Making herself small. "Can't we just be happy with the way things are?"

"My mom once told me something Erin used to say. If you want something, don't wait, because you never know what could happen. Live for the day. Don't wait to do the things you dream about."

"Yeah, well, my mom once told me we only get as much as we deserve." She closes her eyes and sighs. A tear rolls down her cheek. "What if I don't deserve you, Aaron?"

I wipe away her tear. "I ask myself that every goddamn day, Dev. It's me who doesn't deserve you, don't you get that?" I pull her down flat on the bed and climb on top of her. "I don't care if you won't let me say it—it's the way I feel, and there's nothing you can do about it."

Her hands sink into my hair, and she pulls my head down until our lips meet. She kisses me like I'm the air she needs to breathe. Like she knows we have an expiration date.

I've never kissed anyone as much as I've kissed Devyn. Kiss, fondle, fuck—that's all I've ever done. And kissing was never important. It was a means to get to the next step. But kissing Devyn is different. I could kiss her all night and not need more. My dick springs to life. Okay—so I'd need more. But it's not the thing I crave the most with her. I crave her lips. The soft curve of her thighs. The intoxicating smell of her.

And when I go down on her, I could set up camp and stay there all day. The sounds she makes, the way her body moves, and how her hands show me exactly what she needs. I've never been with anyone so responsive. And when she touches me, it takes all my control not to explode. Everything she does to me is perfect. I couldn't ask for more, and I can never again settle for less.

I remove her shirt, leaving her naked, and make a mental note to search for her panties on the roof later. She takes off my boxer briefs. We explore each other as if we haven't a dozen times already. She looks at me like it's the first time. I want this forever, for the rest of my life, and it both scares the shit out of me and feels like the best decision I've ever made.

I run a finger through her wetness and rub it on her clit. I know exactly how she likes it. Slow circles at first, then quicker, harder, until she fists the sheets, moaning. I've made a lot of women come in a lot of different ways. None of them compares to the way I feel when she shouts my name. I'm fucking Hercules.

She rolls me over and straddles me, sinking onto me. This is new for us. I didn't know it could get any better. Apparently I was wrong. I sit up and lean against the headboard. I want to watch her face when I'm inside her. She undulates on top of me, working herself in sweet delicious circles, driving me to the brink of ecstasy. I grab her hips, palm her breasts, grip the nape of her neck, run my hands down her back, and squeeze her small ass.

She watches every emotion on my face, absorbing every sweet word I whisper to her. I'm wrapped in her, physically, mentally, emotionally. I'm fucking done. Put a goddamn fork in me. I'm head over heels for this girl. I come gloriously, and she smiles at me, proud of her ability to bring me to my knees.

I lie down and she settles beside me. "Did you really mean what you said yesterday about me helping train horses? Do you think I could ever do something like that?"

A laugh percolates from my belly. "You just gave me the best sex of my life, and you want to talk about horses?"

She blushes.

"I meant it. I've seen the way you are with them. You might be new to horses, but you seem to have a connection with them." I chuckle. "Guess it's not just me."

"So it's okay if I talk to Mickey about watching him and learning? He wouldn't have to pay me, obviously. I want to learn everything I can about horses so maybe one day I could, I don't know, do what he does." She sits up. "It's probably a stupid dream."

"There aren't any stupid dreams, Devyn. Talk to him. I'm sure he'll be happy to show you the ropes."

"So, best sex ever, huh?"

"Every time with you is the best."

She snuggles under my arm and lays her head on my chest. "Every time with you is the best, except I have nothing to compare it to."

I tense. "Say again?" When she's silent, I force her to look at me. "Are you saying you were a virgin?"

"You couldn't tell?"

I try to wrap my mind around it. I'm speechless. How is that possible? She said she'd never had a boyfriend, but that doesn't mean anything. I've slept with dozens of girls, but none of them have been my girlfriend. "Are you serious?"

"I thought for sure you knew. I was so nervous."

I tuck a wisp of hair behind her ear. "You've been incredible. I wasn't lying when I said this has been the best ever."

She giggles. "I'll try not to get a big head."

"All this time, I was sure you were running from an ex. Someone who abused you, maybe."

She picks up her shirt and puts it on, then searches the floor for her panties. When she can't find them, she gets a fresh pair from her drawer. She sits on the chair in front of the sewing machine. "Are you disappointed I'm not?"

I look at her like she's crazy. "Am I mad you weren't raped or abused? No, Devyn, I'm relieved. And you can believe I'm honored as shit to have been your first. But I don't get what you're hiding from."

Her gaze falls to the floor. "This again? We're never going to get past it, are we?"

"We are. I just want to know you. All of you. I swear, whatever it is won't change how I feel."

I can almost see her withdrawing, slipping away. She's practically got one foot out the door. Whatever happened to her is even worse than I imagined, but I'm not going to let it ruin us. I jump off the bed and pull her into my arms. "Tell me, don't tell me. I don't care. I don't want to lose this."

She relaxes against me. "I don't want to lose this either. But nothing lasts forever, Aaron. Nothing."

The way she says it… It's so distinct. So final.

She's wrong. This, what we have, can last. Look at my parents. My aunts and uncles. I'm even more sure than before. I love her, and she loves me. But her past surrounds her like a damn brick wall. I only hope I can break through it before it swallows her whole.

CHAPTER TWENTY

Devyn

The last few weeks have been the best of my life. Being with Aaron is my escape. It's like I'm two different people, living very different lives. The one when I'm with him, where I'm happy housekeeper Devyn Dunlop. The other when I'm former inmate #2356489.

If the two ever converge, my life will implode. It came close when Delta showed up at Home Depot.

Lora comes out of the office. I'm folding dish towels and stuffing them into a drawer. She watches me a lot. She doesn't think I know that. I feel bad for her; she obviously likes Aaron. I wonder if she's had a thing for him since the day she started working here almost a year ago. She's probably not happy that as soon as I showed up, her boss, the former playboy of East Texas, was seemingly off the market.

We don't flaunt our relationship. When we're in public, I'm fairly sure we appear to be coworkers. But she scrutinizes our every move. She sees the way we look at each other, and she's jealous as hell.

I turn. "Hi, Lora."

She leans against the counter. "Who did you work for before coming to DHR?"

"No one in particular. Odd jobs here and there."

"You don't seem the type to do that."

"What type do I seem?"

"I'd say more the sorority-girl type."

I laugh. "You're way off."

"I don't think I am. I get the feeling you'd be one, but somehow you couldn't. Something stood in your way."

"We don't always get what we want."

She grunts. "Was that directed at me?"

I keep quiet. I don't do confrontation well. It's why I learned to stay under the radar. I put away the last of the towels and return to my room.

She follows me and stops in my doorway. "It won't last, whatever you and Aaron have going on. He'll tire of you. Whatever he sees in you will blow away like a summer breeze. You're a lost puppy, and he's taken you in. But puppies grow into unruly dogs— not so cute and playful anymore. When that happens, he'll move on."

"Let me guess, to someone like you?"

"He's college educated and from a well-off family. He'll own a good part of this ranch one day. He needs someone by his side who can support and encourage him, not suck the life out of him."

I get my cowboy hat and walk past her.

"Going riding with *him* again?"

"If you must know, I'm headed to the stables. Mickey is teaching me how to train horses."

She snorts. "I may have underestimated you. You're immersing yourself here. Making friends. You know that will all change when they find out about you, right?"

I tense. "I don't know what you mean."

She laughs cattily. "Sure you don't. Well, enjoy your training. I'll be here with Aaron going over this week's agenda."

She says it to make me jealous, but I don't give her the satisfaction. "Have fun," I say, giving her a smile before I leave.

On my ATV on the way to the stables, I pass Aaron returning from the main ranch. His whole face lights up. "Morning," he says.

He could be remembering last night. It's kind of hard not to. We're getting more and more comfortable with each other, doing things in bed I never dreamed of doing. I still haven't given him an answer to his question about moving in with him. Part of me wants to—the part that's sure what we have is like what I read in books. The other part thinks Lora is right, and he sees me as this helpless pet that needs caring for. I need more time.

"Hi. Did you tell Lora about me? How you found me?"

"Of course not. Why? Is she giving you trouble?"

"Not really. She knows about us, though, and she's jealous."

"It's not our problem."

"Uh-huh."

"Are you meeting with Mickey again?"

I smile. "It's the best part of my day."

He fake grimaces. "Hopefully not the *best* part."

I giggle. "You know what I mean. He's been great. I've already learned so much."

"He likes you. Just don't let him like you too much."

"Who's the jealous one now?"

"I'm kidding. Mickey's happily married. They live in one of the apartments over by the stables. His wife, Sara, is the assistant manager of a diner in town."

"I know. He told me."

"Just how many training sessions have you had?"

"Three."

He laughs. "You're really throwing yourself into this, aren't you?"

"I've got nothing but time now that I've got my routine down at the lodge, and I love being around horses. He's even teaching me more about riding."

His happiness wanes. "*I* was teaching you about riding."

"Yes, but you work a lot."

"I'll always make time for you, Dev."

"Okay. I won't ask him for any more tips on riding, only training. Happy?"

His smile returns. "Extremely."

"Gotta get going. I don't want to be late. Besides, Lora is waiting for you at the lodge."

"See you tonight? How about we do supper at my place?"

My eyebrows shoot up. "You cook?"

"I didn't say I'd cook. I said we'd do supper at my place. I'll rustle up something."

"It's a date, then."

"I like the sound of that. I know you're officially my girl and all, but we've never really been on a date." He laughs. "If you don't count the Chick-fil-A drive-through."

"I hope you don't expect me to put out," I joke. "I usually wait until the fifth date."

"See, now I found out something else about you. You have a sense of humor." With a click of his tongue, Reuben carries him away.

I think of how what he said is proof there are two Devyns. He only sees the fairy tale. The potential to have what Maddox and Andie have. Or his parents. He has no idea he can never have it with me. How long am I going to let him think he can?

The closer I get to the stables, the more excited I become. Lessons with Mickey really are the highlight of my days. Horses make me happy. They're my future, I'm sure of it.

I mostly watch Mickey put his pupils through their paces. Occasionally, he'll pull me into the ring and let me take charge. It's exhilarating. I've never felt this sense of accomplishment before. That maybe I do matter in some small way. I've read how horses can be therapy animals. Maybe they're helping me. Maybe that's why I like being around them so much. They're unassuming and trusting, and most importantly, big enough so I know nothing I do can hurt them.

By the end of this session, Mickey has let me do more than ever. "You're a quick study, Devyn. You have a future in this if you want it enough and work for it."

"Do you really think so?"

"With a few more months of hard work, I'd say you'll be ready to talk to Owen and Maddox about becoming an assistant trainer."

Elation courses through me, until I realize what it would mean. Giving them my name and social security number. My history. "Thank you for the vote of confidence, but I'm happy just tagging along and helping you out from time to time."

"You could do so much more. The horses really take to you."

I walk to the gate. "Thanks, Mickey. See you Tuesday?"

"I'll be here."

Andie catches me before I get to the ATV. "I've been around horses for more than twenty years. Worked with them professionally for ten. I've never seen someone learn as quickly as you have. Are you sure you've never done this before?"

"I'd never been on a horse before last month."

"Incredible." Her phone rings, and she glances at the number, then back at me. "Hold on a sec. I want to talk to you about Sunday."

I sit on the ATV, hearing bits and pieces of her conversation. She's upset when she hangs up. "Everything okay?"

She swallows hard. "No, everything's definitely not okay. Jon—the man who kidnapped me—is up for parole again on Monday. It looks like I'll have to cancel our pool day. I need to prepare."

"What do you mean, you need to prepare?"

"I go to his parole hearings every time he has one. I write down my thoughts, my terrifying experience with him, and read it at the hearing. But this time, I've got more skin in the game. I have Vivian. What if he gets out and terrorizes us? I can't let him do that to my daughter. He's a convict. A killer. People like him shouldn't be allowed loose in society, let alone around children. I plan on spending the next few days drafting a convincing letter saying as much."

My throat is dry. If she only knew who she was talking to.

"Can we do the pool thing next weekend?" she asks. "After all this madness is over?"

"Sure. Go—do your letter thing."

She pulls me in for a hug. "Thanks. You're a real friend, Devyn."

I'm stiff, still not used to being hugged by women. Where I come from, being hugged by a woman meant they owned you. I hop on the ATV and start down the trail to the lodge. When the pressure behind my eyes builds, I pull off the trail, find a tree, and collapse into sobs on the ground, remembering just why we can never be friends.

"Guilty."

Even a week later, at my sentencing hearing, the word rings in my head. I know it's true. But Mr. Craddick was sure the judge would be sympathetic. It's why he talked me into waiving the right to a jury trial. I kept telling him the influence of Ed, my de facto father, ran far and wide, but he just told me to keep my chin up. A few times, he even had me believing I would get off with probation.

The punishment has to fit the crime. It's the way I was raised. If I took an extra cookie, I missed dinner. If I missed curfew, my mother made me stay up all night writing an essay on why curfews are good for teenagers. When I got caught stealing a candy bar when I was seven years old, I was forced to return it and then sweep floors at the convenience store. Even the owner was against it, but my mother stood over me as blisters formed on my small hands.

At least my lawyer was right about the judge. He called Mr. Craddick and the prosecutor into his chambers last week before giving his verdict and told them he wasn't going to find me guilty of manslaughter and send me to prison. He encouraged them to agree on a lesser charge. I think he's a different party affiliation from Ed, which worked in my favor. Although my charge was reduced to criminally negligent homicide, he hands down the maximum sentence—two years in a state jail for the class four felony. My drug charges were also lowered to a class C misdemeanor, resulting in a five-hundred-dollar fine.

Mr. Craddick gathers papers, puts them in a file folder, and stuffs them into his briefcase. "Could have been a lot worse. I doubt you could have worked out a plea for less. Two years is nothing. You'll be out before you're twenty-two, with your whole life ahead of you."

What he doesn't know is that my whole life doesn't matter now. I'd been facing twenty years in prison. I was prepared for that. Even if I'd gotten out when I was forty-one, there would still be one less person on this earth because of me. What kind of life can I have knowing that?

"Stand up," a guard says. "Put your hands behind your back."

I'm handcuffed and led out of the courtroom.

"Good luck, Ms. DeMaggio," Mr. Craddick says, as if I'm going to a job interview and not a dungeon.

The transfer process from the county jail to the state jail is a blur. The bus ride is longer than I expected. A woman two rows up keeps looking back at me. I don't like the way she's staring.

The lady shackled in the seat next to me asks, "Are you even old enough to be on this bus?"

I nod.

"Well, damn. You're the kind of new meat that will make people like her salivate. Keep your head down. This ain't the same as county jail. Even though it's minimum security, it ain't the fuckin' Ritz. Things you could get away with on the outside can literally get you killed where we're goin'. You're nothing and nobody. Your life is worth less than a candy bar. Your days will start at four a.m., and being a first timer, you'll get a shitty job like kitchen cleanup or yard crew. That's after you spend up to two weeks in intake."

"Two weeks?"

"They're gonna poke you, prod you, make you squat and cough. Test you for all kinds of shit. They don't want you bringin' anything in from the outside. You'll be assigned a caseworker. They head-shrink you, too. You get evaluated

by some lame-o with a community college degree who gets to decide what custody level you get and who you bunk with. If you're lucky, you'll get general population. But don't think that's an easy ride. Someone as pretty as you will have loads of inmates wantin' you with them. My advice, find other loners—people not in groups. But don't talk to no one until you see their true colors. Talking can get you into trouble. Do your job well, and maybe in a few months, you can get reassigned to laundry—it's my favorite. You get to walk around and make deliveries. Recreation duty is good, too. Not that you'll get paid a fuckin' penny. Texas is one of the few states that don't pay inmates."

She shakes her head. "When I get out, I swear I'm moving to Oklahoma. Maybe Colorado. Weed is legal there, did you know that? Plus, it's too damn hot here. Best buy yourself a fan pronto. You got money, right?"

I think of the measly two hundred fifty dollars I had left after paying the fine. It's all I'll have in my inmate account for two years. I know it won't last long. There won't be any family or friends bringing me more. "And get a TV if you can. They're small and get terrible reception, but it's better than fighting with sixty other crazy chicks in the rec hall over what to watch."

"Why are you telling me this?"

"Because I was you three years ago. Spent a year here back then. Got out. Did more stupid shit, and now I'm back for another stint—eighteen months this time. It could be worse. Could be the big house. Probably will be next time. How long you here for?"

"Two years."

She makes a face. "Damn, that's tough for your first time. What'd you do? Lemme guess. You fucked your boss, the wife caught you and made him fire you, so you stole her car and smashed it up good."

I gaze out the window.

"It's all good. You don't need to tell me. I'll find out. Sooner or later, everyone will. Sooner or later, everyone in here'll know all your business."

Slumped against a tree, I wonder if the same goes for Devil's Horn Ranch. Will everyone know my business? And if so, what will happen then?

CHAPTER TWENTY-ONE

Aaron

"I'm glad to see we're getting more bookings. You're doing a great job." Lora puts away her iPad and leans on the desk, her blouse opening slightly to reveal cleavage as she bends toward me. "*We're* doing a great job."

I shuffle papers. "I ran into Devyn earlier. She said she talked to you. Seemed a bit upset. Any idea why?"

She shrugs. "Didn't get any good tips this week?"

"That's not it. Are you and her getting along?"

"I get along with everyone."

"She has some great ideas about expanding the business."

Lora covers a laugh. "The housekeeper?"

"You don't need a college degree to be a productive member of society."

She sits down, turning up her nose. "I suppose *she* wants to be the host or something."

"She doesn't want your job. We're talking bigger than that. Maybe offering helicopter tours and VIP flights directly to the ranch and building a smaller stable out here so we don't have to get horses from the main stables. These are all long-term plans, but they're good ideas, don't you think?"

"It must be fun for her, spending all your money."

"What's up with you? Do you have something against Devyn?"

"I've known girls like her my whole life. They swoop in and take what isn't theirs. Watch out for her, Aaron. She's an opportunist. She appears out of nowhere. Says the right things. Acts all innocent and perfect. She gets you to do what she wants, and before you know it, she's running things."

"That is not what's going on here."

She stands, walks around the desk, and perches on it right next to me. "Are you sure? How well could you possibly know her?"

"Well enough."

"Just remember, there are others who are willing to help you achieve everything you want—the safe way. A way that won't bankrupt you or put the ranch in the red."

"Namely you?"

"Of course me. I love this place. I've invested a lot of time and energy in it over the past year. Wouldn't you agree?"

"You've been a great asset. I couldn't have done it without you."

She smiles. "We're a good team." Before I comprehend what's happening, she plops into my lap and puts an arm around me. "We could be so much more." Her thumb runs across my lip.

Lora is attractive. I even hit on her once, because, well, I hit on everyone. But she said she had a boyfriend. Then again, that was almost a year ago.

When her lips brush mine, I realize what the fuck is happening and stand with her in my arms, put her on her feet, and move away. "This isn't going to happen."

"Why not?"

"Because we work together."

She huffs. "The same rule doesn't apply to everyone, though, does it?"

I pinch the bridge of my nose. Devyn and I are a couple, but we don't advertise it. I'm not going to hide it either. "I think we're done here."

She doesn't move. "Are the two of you together? Like seriously *together*?"

"I'm not sure what we are, but if you have to have an answer, then yes."

She laughs. "That sounds promising."

"Lora, I have work to do." I look at the time. "And you're going to be late for your other job."

She picks up her things and goes to the door. "Just don't forget you have options, Aaron."

What the fuck just happened?

I stay in the office and finish up some paperwork, wanting her to be long gone before I leave.

I hear someone come through the back door. If it's Devyn, I'm lucky she didn't show up two minutes ago when Lora was in my lap, or I'd have some major explaining to do.

Quinn pops his head in. "You busy?"

"I'm always busy, but come on in."

He sits down and smacks his lips. "Think I did something stupid."

My eyebrows go up.

"Or maybe I should say some*one*." He glances out the door.

My jaw drops. "You and Lora?"

He rubs his brow.

"But she was literally just in here trying to fuck me."

"That's why it was so stupid. She obviously was with me to try and get to you. We were drunk. She was asking all kinds of questions." He looks guilty as shit. "I may have let it slip that Devyn was homeless."

I get up and pace. "Fuck, Quinn. Are you serious?"

"I know. I screwed up. You asked me not to say anything, and I blew it."

"That explains why Lora has been acting strange. Devyn asked me this morning if I'd said anything to Lora about her." I run my hands through my hair. "What the hell am I going to do?"

"Fire her?"

I shoot him an angry glance. "Devyn?"

"Lora."

"Fire her for what? Sleeping with my best friend? Hitting on me? She's good at her job, man."

"And that's not even the worst thing to happen to me today."

"There's more?"

He puts his feet up on the desk, crossing his ankles. "My uncle is up for parole."

"Oh, shit. Does Andie know?"

"Just came from there. I told her I'd do everything I could to keep him there."

I sit. "I get you want to protect Andie and all, but if you go against Jon, and he gets out anyway, he'll never let you forget it. What will you do then?"

"Avoid him."

"Your uncle isn't someone you simply avoid. He'll go right back to running your grandfather's empire."

"What's left of it."

"What does Karen say about all this?"

"My mom couldn't care less if Jon stays in prison or not. She's happily living off family money."

"She's been living under the radar while he's been locked up. What do you think she'll do if he gets out?"

"She'll do what she's always done—play the devoted sister or daughter. The woman can't think for herself unless she's fucking over some poor bastard like your Uncle Gavin."

"You think she and Jon will go after the ranch again?"

"Who the hell knows. But you can be sure where I stand, brother."

"They'll have a fucking conniption. You know that, right?"

"Their problem, not mine."

"Might be a problem for all of us."

"Let's not worry about something that hasn't happened yet. What are you going to do about Devyn and Lora?"

"I'm going to tell Lora to mind her own fucking business and stay away from Devyn if she wants to keep working at the lodge."

"How do you think that will go over?"

"I don't have a clue."

"Why not just tell Devyn I screwed up? Hell, I'll tell her myself."

"She's already on the edge. Whatever happened to her has her hanging by a thread. If she knew that I told you and you told Lora, the thread might snap."

"And you're sure that's the kind of person you want a relationship with?"

"Remember what I was like after Cam died? Remember how you and Maddox and Andie rallied around me and kept me from slitting my damn wrists? Devyn needs that now. She needs me."

"You think she's suicidal?"

"No, but she's in a dark place. If she can overcome whatever it is, we can have a great future."

"And if she can't?"

I rub my jaw. "One problem at a time, man. One problem at a time."

CHAPTER TWENTY-TWO

Devyn

Aaron sits up, stretches, then leans over and kisses me. "We really do need to sleep at my place more. This bed isn't big enough for the both of us."

"As soon as you stop sneaking over here every time you see me on the roof."

"It's your fault; you climbing out there with just a T-shirt on. You're too damn sexy."

"I'll wear flannel pajamas next time," I tease.

"You'll do no such thing." He stands, pulls on his pants, and eyes my notebook next to the bed. I forgot I left it there. He frowns and pulls the wad of money from the back cover. "Dev, will you please open a bank account?"

I swipe it from him and shove it and the notebook in a drawer.

"Seriously. You're making some good tip money. You shouldn't leave it lying around."

"You think someone will steal it?"

"We have strangers here almost every weekend."

I laugh. "And you think your rich guests are going to come into the tiny bedroom where the help sleeps to see what jewels I might have?"

He buttons his shirt. "You have a point, and please don't call yourself the help."

"Lora calls me the help."

"If you're the help, what is she? She works here, too."

I pull on my shirt. "That is *so* not the same."

"Are you going to hang out with Mickey again today?"

"You know I am. Every chance I get."

"Want a ride?"

"I'll take the ATV."

"But then I won't get to spend more time with you." He sits on the edge of the bed and pulls on his boots. "If you lived with me in the cabin, I wouldn't have to follow you around like a puppy, begging for a few minutes here and there."

"You don't beg."

"Yeah, but you have no idea how much I want to."

I sigh. "I think it's too soon."

He kisses my nose and pops off the bed. "Doesn't mean I won't stop asking."

"Give me twenty minutes to get ready. I think there are some leftover muffins in the kitchen. Take some on your way to shower."

He waggles his eyebrows. "I could shower here."

The man is insatiable. I can hardly blame him, though. I get the same way every time I look at him. "If you think two people in this bed is crowded, I promise you don't want to try the shower. We'd never be ready in twenty minutes."

"My shower is huge," he says on his way out. He gives me a heated glance over his shoulder. "Just sayin', in case you have a list in your notebook of the pros and cons of moving to the cabin."

"I don't. Now go."

His laughter rings in my ears long after he's gone. I love his laugh. I love everything about him. I fall back on the bed and stare at the ceiling, wanting this moment, this feeling, to last forever.

I push away the voice in my head saying it can't work out. That I can't have a future with a man who doesn't even know my name. My past. Maybe I could make one up—a name and a past. I really was Devyn Dunlop once. People change their names all the time. Why not me? But I'd be lying to him, and even Devyn Dunlop would have to have a background check to get a job. I'd never be able to do more than I do right now.

I get up and shower, convincing myself these are problems for another day. Right now, I just want to enjoy him, the horses, and this place for as long as I can.

He holds my hand all the way to the stables. It feels normal, like it's something we've always done.

When we get out of the truck, he jokes, "Have a good day, dear."

I give him crazy eyes.

He laughs. "Would you prefer honey? Baby? Sweetheart?"

Bile rises in my throat when I think of all the times I was called those very names in jail. "None of the above. I prefer Dev, if it's all the same to you."

"All right." He sneaks in a kiss when he's sure nobody is watching. "Have a good day, Dev."

"You too."

Excitement courses through me as I get closer and closer to the training paddock. Mickey sees me coming and waves me through the gate. He seems genuinely happy to see me, which I hope is the case, since I'm spending so much time here.

The mare he's with is not one I recognize. "This is Gypsy. She's an old pro. She's here for a demonstration. Did you do your homework?"

"I did."

"Then tell me, what are the steps in teaching a horse to lie down?"

I remember all the reading I did. "First, teach her to lower her head, then pick up her feet on command, and move her hind feet under herself. I'm missing one. Oh, right, lift her front leg."

"Perfect. You get an *A* on your homework. Now watch as I combine all those steps to get Gypsy to lie down."

I'm in awe at the ease with which he gets her to do it. "That's amazing."

"It's not always this easy. I have to work on some of them for weeks to get them to do it." He waves at Merle, one of his assistant trainers, and he brings another horse into the paddock. Then he takes Gypsy out.

"This is Hammer. You remember him from the other day? I thought he'd be good practice. Today, we'll work on step one. If you've ever watched a horse lie down, you'll notice it will always lower its head and sniff the ground. It'll keep its head down during the entire lying down process. Teaching it to lower its head is a vital clue to your horse that it's time to start thinking of lying down. Pop quiz: how do we teach Hammer this?"

I smile because I know the answer. I've spent hours and hours on my phone, researching how to train horses. "You apply steady downward pressure on the lead rope until he drops his nose."

"For how long?"

"As long as it takes. Minutes, even."

"And when he does it?"

"Reward him by immediately releasing the pressure, even if he's only gone down an inch or two."

He hands me the lead rope. "Want to give it a try?"

I apply the downward pressure. Hammer immediately lowers his head almost all the way to the ground.

I narrow my eyes at Mickey. "You've already taught him this, haven't you?"

"Didn't want you to fail at your first attempt."

"Let me try one he doesn't know."

He laughs. "I do love an eager student. Okay, tell me more about step two."

"You have to be able to control what each foot does. Tap the back of his leg at the pastern or fetlock with a lunge whip. Keep tapping until he picks up his foot, then reward him by stopping."

"Go ahead, give it a try. Even if he only shifts his weight, reward him because he's responding."

I tap repeatedly. I'm glad Hammer doesn't respond right away, because I know he hasn't learned this yet. He eventually shifts his weight, and I stop tapping. I move to the next leg until I've done it on all four, then I start over. After a few minutes of this, he finally lifts one of his legs completely off the ground.

"He's doing it!" I squeal.

"He's got a good trainer."

I'm totally elated by the end of our session. Every minute I spend with Mickey and the horses makes me want more.

"Well done," he says. "How about you brush him down and return him to his stall?"

"Me? Are you sure?"

"I trust you. Do it how I showed you the other day."

I lead Hammer to the gate and turn. "Thank you, Mickey. No one has ever done anything like this for me before. How can I ever repay you?"

"You already have. The way you look at them and your enthusiasm when you work with them is refreshing. It's renewed my love of these magnificent creatures. A few weeks ago, I was actually talking to Sara about retiring and trying my hand at something else. But after watching you, I get that I'm right where I'm supposed to be. So thank *you*."

I lead Hammer away. It's amazing being able to guide a horse ten times my size. He follows without question. I stop in the washroom and brush him down, then give him an apple. "You made me look good today."

"Talking to horses now?" Aaron is leaning up against a wall.

"Were you watching me?"

"For about the last twenty minutes. You're amazing, Devyn."

I pat Hammer's mane. "He's amazing."

"I think you've found your calling."

"Maybe." I take Hammer to his stall and unclip the lead rope.

"What do you mean maybe? Do you see the way they respond to you? I'm telling you, you have to keep doing this."

I latch the horse's gate. "I really want to. It's exhilarating, the feeling I get when I'm with them."

He glances left, then right, then pulls me into an empty stall. "Now you know how I feel every time I'm with you."

He leans me against the wall and kisses me. I'm not normally up for public displays of indecency, but I swear, if he were to lay me down right here in the hay, I'd let him have his way with me.

"Oh, uh, sorry," Luca says when he walks by. He points to the horse in the stall across from us. "I just need to get… You know what, I'll come back."

We laugh as Luca turns red and walks away. Aaron takes my hand. "Let's go get lunch."

I drop off the lead rope in the tack room. Before we get to the truck, he sneaks one more kiss. Andie comes out of her house. Judging by her smile, I can tell we're not fooling anyone.

"You look happy today," I say to her. "Does that mean what I think it does?"

She crosses her arms at the wrist like Wonder Woman. "Parole denied!"

"I'm really happy for you."

Aaron sweeps her into a hug. "That's fantastic. You were so sure this would be the year he got out."

"I was. I pulled out all the stops. Even begged one of our state representatives to help me."

"If anyone could do it, I knew you could," Aaron says. "Which representative?"

"Congressman DeMaggio. He was so nice. He wrote a letter on my behalf…"

She keeps talking, but I don't hear another word. My mouth goes dry. My palms get damp. Blood is pumping loudly in my ears. I feel like I might pass out. I lean over and put my hands on my knees.

"Devyn."

I don't respond. I can't.

"Devyn! What's wrong?" Aaron asks.

"I…"

"You're sweating," Andie says. "Let's get you inside where it's cool."

"I have to go." I walk away. Where I'm going, I have no clue.

Footsteps come up behind me. "Dev, talk to me. What just happened? One minute you were fine, then when she brought up the congressman…" He takes a step back. Anger I've never seen in him crosses his face. "Oh, shit. Is he the one you're running from? Did you work for him or something? Devyn, did he harass you? Is he holding something over your head?"

I keep moving. "I have to go."

"At least let me drive you home."

My throat is thick with tears I don't want him to see fall. "I need to be alone."

"I'm not leaving you alone like this."

"I'll be fine. Please, Aaron. I need to clear my head."

He grabs my hand. "But—"

I jerk away from him. "Drop it, okay? You don't need to fix me. You don't need to help me like I'm some damsel in distress. Just leave me the fuck alone."

I know I've hurt him, but I don't care. He steps back. "Fine. Go."

I make it out to the road without looking back. Part of me wants to go left, in the opposite direction of the lodge. Just keep walking far from here and find a new life. I should. I would if it weren't for him. With every passing day, the odds of him finding out about me grow larger.

But I don't walk away, because one simple fact eclipses all the others: I love him.

CHAPTER TWENTY-THREE

Aaron

"Devyn?"

She doesn't answer.

It's been hours since she stalked off. I'm relieved to see her door open, but it's not Devyn in her room. It's Lora, and she looks like the cat who ate the canary. "What are you doing here?" I ask.

She picks up a new pillow sham Devyn was embroidering. "Admiring her handiwork. I was considering asking her to do something for me."

I take the sham from her, put it down, and motion to the door. "We really shouldn't be in her private space."

"It's your lodge, Aaron."

"But this is *her* room."

Her phone rings. "I need to take this. I'm done here anyway. I'll see you tomorrow." Her voice trails down the hall as she leaves.

I glance around the room. Everything looks the same as we left it this morning. I open the drawer Devyn stuffed her notebook into. It's still there, along with the money.

I sit on her bed and call her again. She doesn't answer. Where the hell could she have gone?

Noise in the kitchen has me jumping off the bed and racing out. It's Joe with the food delivery for the upcoming weekend.

"I can see from your expression you were expectin' someone else," he says. "Sorry to disappoint you. Picked up the food myself today. How about you help an old man unload?"

When I get bags from his truck, I glance in all directions, hoping for a sign of her.

Joe puts the meat in the refrigerator. "You kids really takin' to each other, aren't you?"

I hand him a huge package of bacon. "I don't know. I guess."

He shoves it into the fridge and laughs from deep in his belly. "You ain't foolin' no one." He looks at the steaks in my hand. "Seems they put in a few extras. How about I make supper for you and your lady?"

"I'm not sure she'll be here."

"Lovers' quarrel?"

"I'm not sure what's going on with her."

He points to a chair. "Sit. I'll make you tea, then I'll cook up this extra beef. If Missy comes home, I'll stick a candle on the table and go on my way. If she don't, I'll be your supper companion."

"Thanks, Joe. That sounds good. You know her name is Devyn, right? How come you keep calling her Missy?"

More laughter. "When you're old like me, sometimes rememberin' stuff ain't as easy as it used to be. Makes things easier. Since I've got one foot in the grave, most of 'em let me get away with it."

"You're not that old, Joe. You have a lot of years left in you."

"I may not be dyin' today, but this here body has taken a lot over the years."

My attention goes to his eye patch. "Are you ever going to tell me how it happened?"

He works over the stove and eventually puts down two dinner plates, looks outside—for Devyn, I presume—then sits opposite me and takes his flask from his pocket. He offers it to me. I shake my head.

"You ever gonna tell me why a young'un like you don't like drinkin'?"

I take a bite of steak. It's not that I don't want to tell him about Cameron; it just hurts to talk about it.

"The three of us are quite a trio, aren't we?" he says.

"What do you mean?"

"We all got a past we hide from the world."

Over supper, I tell him about Devyn's ideas for the lodge. Joe sips from his flask when he's done eating.

"You sit," I say. "I'm cleaning up."

He leans back. "You ain't gonna hear me complainin'."

We make small talk until the last dish is dry and put away.

"Got a deck of cards?" he asks.

"I might."

"Up for a friendly game of gin?"

I stare out the window. "I'm up for anything that'll keep me busy right now."

"She'll show up," he says. "Sooner or later."

We play cards for an hour, until the sun starts to set. It's getting harder and harder for me not to worry.

Joe stands. "Go home, boy. Give the woman some space. You don't want to smother her so much that her bright light gets snuffed out, do you?"

We go outside together, and I watch him drive off, listening to the sounds of his truck long after he's gone. I take one last look down the driveway and see someone walking toward the lodge. It has to be her. She stops when she sees me. My heart sinks. She doesn't want to talk. Maybe she's even disappointed I'm here. I think about what Joe said and go to my cabin.

Unable to sleep, I lie in bed wondering what the hell happened to her. She stayed away all day. She never carries money. She doesn't have a credit card. Where did she go and what did she do?

I want to go to her. I get out of bed and watch the roof, hoping she'll emerge. If she does, I know it's an invitation.

I've never seen such a visceral reaction as the one she had earlier. Just the mention of the congressman turned her into an empty shell.

I pick up my phone. There must be something out there if she worked for him and there was a scandal.

I search his name. I get a hundred hits, most of them about his political aspirations to run for senate. I skim them, not sure what I'm looking for. He's been a congressman for two terms. I look at the names of his staff. I search his name and the word "scandal."

When I'm about to give up, I do one more search on Edward DeMaggio Devyn.

Pages and pages come up.

I see words like *manslaughter charges. Child endangerment. Felony drug possession.* "What the fuck?" How can this guy still be in office?

It takes a minute to put it together and realize what I'm reading. Then my heart stops. All those horrible words don't apply to Edward DeMaggio; they apply to his daughter, Devyn.

I feel sick as I read one of the articles.

Devyn DeMaggio, nineteen-year-old adopted daughter of first-time congressman, Ed DeMaggio, was brought up on charges today in the death of DeMaggio's five-year-old biological child, Kasey. Kasey was under the care of Ms. DeMaggio while her parents attended a dinner at the governor's mansion in Austin. The young girl was found lifeless in the family pool after a night of apparent partying by the older sister and her friends. As of now, the two other teenagers present have not been charged and are cooperating with police.

Ms. DeMaggio has been charged with several offenses, the most severe of which is manslaughter. Though sources indicate it's highly unlikely those charges will stick, due to the circumstances and the relationship between suspect and victim, in the state of Texas, serious injury or death of a child through a reckless or negligent act is a second-degree felony punishable by up to twenty years in prison.

The question remains, will the lawyer-turned-congressman use his power to help his eldest daughter or ensure she pays for her grave mistake?

I drop my phone and run to the bathroom, where I hurl my steak dinner.

I spend all night researching what happened. The reduction in charges. The two-year jail sentence. Hell, I read the transcripts of the trial. At four in the morning, I conclude that the reporter's last words were correct; Representative DeMaggio used all his influence to make sure Devyn was punished. He cut off all ties with her, as did her mother, who wasn't her biological parent but *was* Kasey's. In the end, this was a case of parents choosing their blood child over their adopted one. It was a case of a teenager making a terrible mistake that resulted in a horrible outcome.

We're even more alike than I thought. I should tell her. I should go over there right now and make her understand that she's not alone. Mistakes happen—unbelievably bad ones that make us feel like we don't deserve to be alive. Ones that will haunt us until the day we die.

But I stay put. I was in the same place once, and at the time, I wouldn't have been comforted by anyone telling me their own tragic story. She literally just got out of jail and is still processing everything. She needs time to make peace with it. I struggle with whether or not to tell her that I know.

Memories of Cameron flood me. It's only 5:20 a.m. in New York, but it's time I told Mom and Dad. They had no idea why I transferred schools. They were far enough away that I could keep them in the dark. Maddox, Andie, and Quinn are the only ones who know the truth. I understand how that was a mistake. If I ever expect Devyn to open up to me, I have to be willing to own up to my story as well.

I pick up the phone and call home.

CHAPTER TWENTY-FOUR

Devyn

All morning, Aaron looks like he wants to tell me something. As I help Maddox and the rest of the crew paint the last part of the new stable, I can tell something is wrong. Is he done with me? Maybe I pushed him too far, and he's decided he doesn't want to put up with a whiny mess of a girlfriend. We even drove separately to the stable, me on the ATV and him in his truck.

I want to tell him this person isn't me. That I'm a strong, independent woman with dreams and aspirations. But it's not true and hasn't been for almost three years.

"You okay?" Andie asks, handing out bottles of waters. "You look a little pale."

I take one and hold it to my forehead, hoping its coolness will refresh me. It's a sweltering day, even for the end of June. "I haven't been in the sun much."

She narrows her eyes at me. Everyone knows I spend every spare second in the training paddock with Mickey.

"How about you stick to painting the lower areas and let the guys climb the ladders?"

I want to argue, tell her I can earn my twenty dollars an hour just like the rest of them, but I don't because something *is* off. Something's been off for days. Then again, between my late-night excursions with Aaron and not sleeping at all last night, I'm surprised I can even function. "Maybe I will, at least until after lunch. I'm sure food will help."

She goes over and whispers something to Maddox. Great, now Aaron *and* Maddox are both looking at me strangely.

A few hours later, lunch arrives. Maddox always caters meals for his day laborers. I'm ravenous and eat one and a half club sandwiches, a bag of chips, and a pickle.

"Feeling better?" Aaron asks as I'm finishing up.

"Yeah. Sorry about yesterday. I needed to be by myself."

"I get it. Can we talk later?"

"Talk? Is that code for something?"

"It's not code for anything. I just want to talk. You know, have an adult conversation."

"Not if you're going to ask questions I don't want to answer." I throw away my trash.

He follows me to the side of the new stable. "Devyn—"

"What? If it's so important, why wait? Spit it out."

He looks sad. "Not here."

My insides twist. He *is* going to break up with me. I can see the devastation on his face. He probably doesn't want to because the sex is so good, but he can't stand being with such a needy, broken woman.

I pick up a paintbrush. "Mind if I get back to work, then?"

He nods and strolls away.

I'm nauseous, knowing what's coming. No way will I get to stay on the ranch. He'll offer, but it won't work. I can't work this closely with him, live right next to him, and not be with him. If I tell him I love him, will it make a difference? Because I do. I love him so much.

I turn to see where he is. He's up on a ladder, catches me staring, and gives me an unhappy smile. My head spins. My vision blurs. Noises fade. I fall.

My eyes open to a half dozen people standing over me. Aaron and Andie are on their knees.

Aaron takes my hand. "Jesus, Devyn. Are you okay?"

"What happened?"

"You fainted."

"I did?"

My stomach lurches. I quickly turn my head and vomit.

"You must have hit your head," Andie says, handing me a clean rag. "Mind if I check?" She runs her fingers all over my skull. "I don't feel any bumps, but you could still have a concussion. We should take you to the hospital."

"The hospital? No."

Maddox steps forward. "DHR will pay the bill. You were on the clock when it happened."

"But—" I look at Aaron.

He's worried but smiles anyway. It's not the sad smile he had before. It's a reassuring one. "It'll be fine."

"They'll ask for—"

"We've got it covered, Dev. Just let me drive you. Please."

Still dizzy and unfocused, I reluctantly agree. "Okay, but only you."

I don't remember much about the trip. I'm occupied with my impending breakup and an unnecessary hospital bill they'll be forced to pay.

Aaron helps me into the ER and sits me down, then goes to the desk and fills out paperwork. "It shouldn't be long," he says, rejoining me.

"What did you tell them about me?"

"That you fainted and work for DHR. That your name is Devyn Dunlop." He moves closer. "Put your head on my shoulder if you want. God, Devyn, you scared the shit out of me."

"I'm sure it was the paint fumes."

"The paint Maddox bought doesn't have fumes. It's ECOS paint—odorless and environmentally friendly."

"Maybe just the heat, then. I'm sure I'm okay. In fact, I'm feeling better. We should leave."

"We're not leaving until I'm sure you're all right."

"But—"

"We're not leaving. It's fucking settled. I'm not letting the woman I love walk out of here without being cleared by a doctor, got it?"

The woman he loves. Did he really say that? He's alluded to it, but he's never come right out and used the words. "I thought you were going to break up with me."

He takes my hand. "Why the hell would I do that?"

"Just a feeling. You looked at me funny all day, and then you said we needed to talk."

His thumb runs circles around my knuckle in a soothing way. "None of that matters now."

"Devyn Dunlop," a nurse calls.

Aaron stands and helps me up. We walk to the double doors.

"I'm Devyn."

She eyes Aaron. "And you are?"

"Boyfriend."

"Wait out here, please."

He looks upset.

"It's okay," I say. "I'm sure it's nothing."

The nurse escorts me back, takes my history, asks about medications, grills me about what I was doing when I fainted, and takes my blood pressure. Two other people come in. One hooks me up to a machine and does an EKG, and the other draws blood and asks for a urine sample.

I feel like I've been waiting for hours when an actual doctor shows up. He glances through my chart. "I'm Dr. Kallem, and you, Ms. Dunlop, are pregnant."

My heart races. "Wh-what?"

He pulls over a rolling stool and sits next to the bed. "You're pregnant. I've ordered a vaginal ultrasound to see how far along you are. The tech should be in shortly."

"How is that possible?"

"You're sexually active, correct?"

"Well, yes."

"Then it's possible. It says here you're not taking any medications, so I assume you aren't on birth control."

"We used condoms every time."

"It happens more than you think."

"I… I can't be."

"Can I get you anything? A cup of water? Something to eat? It might take a while to sink in, but seeing the ultrasound will help. Is there anyone you'd like to call while you wait?"

I think of Aaron. He'd want to know, but I can't even wrap my head around it. I'm sure there's been some mistake. Dr. Kallem writes something in my chart, and I stiffen. "The people I work for are paying the bill. Will they see the results?"

"We're bound by a law called HIPAA. The only way anyone can find out what's in your records is if you tell them."

I exhale, thankful for small favors.

"So, water?"

"No, thank you."

He leaves, and I spend the next half hour bouncing between feeling sick and sobbing uncontrollably. This cannot be happening.

Someone rolls a cart through the opening in the curtain. "I'm Nicole. I'm here to do your ultrasound." She gets set up. "I need you to lie back and put your feet in the stirrups, like you do at your annual exams." She squirts lube on a long steel rod. "Just relax. This won't hurt."

Relax. Not likely. I've never been so tense.

She works the wand around inside me and keeps hitting buttons and moving a mouse thing on her computer.

"What is all that?"

"I'm taking measurements. They'll tell us how far along you are."

I close my eyes, and my head falls back onto the pillow. "So there really *is* a baby?" I practically choke on the words.

"Look here," she says. I open my eyes as she points to the screen. "This is the heartbeat."

"It's already got a heartbeat? How pregnant am I?"

"I'll finish with this, and the doctor will be back in to talk to you." She does some more typing and moving, then removes the wand thing and hands me a tissue to clean up. Then she gives me a small black-and-white photo. "This is yours to keep."

I turn away. "I don't want it."

"The photo?"

"The photo. The baby. None of it."

"Uh… the doctor will be in shortly."

I've never seen someone leave a room so quickly. The photo is on the table. I lean over and take a look. I can see the outline of its head and abdomen, and there are stubs where its arms and legs are. How can it be so fully formed already? It's surrounded by darkness in the shape of a kidney bean.

Dr. Kallem appears. "Well, Ms. Dunlop, you look to be about nine weeks pregnant. That makes you due on February fourth."

"Nine weeks? That's impossible. I wasn't even having sex then."

"Pregnancies are dated from your last menstrual period, not from the time you had intercourse. Actual conception would have occurred around April twenty-eighth."

That's the night I lost my virginity. I'm speechless.

He hands me some literature. I glance through it. Pregnancy, adoption, abortion. I put the brochures down on top of the photo, feeling sick again.

"Nicole said you were having doubts about the pregnancy. While you should see an obstetrician as soon as possible, I want you to know you have choices. Unplanned pregnancies can be shocking. Take some time to absorb it before making any decisions. Someone will be in with your discharge papers shortly. Do you have any questions?"

My head falls back against the pillow again. "Yeah. How is this my life?"

He touches my shoulder. "This isn't the end of the world. Sometimes these unexpected surprises can turn out to be the best thing that's ever happened."

He has no idea how wrong he is. I'm the last person in the world who should have a baby. With my past, I'm not even sure I'd be allowed to keep it. I don't know why, but I laugh. I laugh until I cry. He pats me again and leaves.

"I need another minute," I say to the nurse with the discharge papers. Aaron is out there waiting for me. I can't let him see me with red eyes and a puffy face. "Can I get some ice, please?"

"Of course."

I hold ice cubes under my eyes for ten minutes, willing myself not to cry anymore. Then I fold the pamphlets and stuff them into my back pocket and slap on my best smile before walking into the waiting room. "All ready."

"You're good? What did they say happened?"

"That the heat got to me. They ran all kinds of tests. Said I'm totally healthy and can go."

He hugs me. "I'm so relieved. I was sure you had a concussion after what Andie said. They had you back there for so long."

"They hooked wires to my chest and took blood and stuff. I had to wait a long time between each test. Can we go now, or do you have to do more paperwork?"

"It's done. Don't worry about it."

"I feel so stupid. Please tell Maddox I'll pay the bill. I probably have enough saved."

"That's your money, Dev. Besides, DHR is a business. They have insurance for things like this. Workers get hurt all the time. You aren't the first one to visit the ER this year, and you won't be the last." He opens the door for me. "Let's get out of here. I hate hospitals." On our way to the truck, he asks, "Are you hungry? Do you want to stop for food?"

"I'd like to go home and relax. Go to bed early. The doctor said with heat exhaustion, I shouldn't push myself to do anything else today. You can just drop me off and finish helping at the stable."

It's a total and complete lie, but I can't be with him right now, knowing I'm carrying his baby—a baby I can't possibly have. What am I going to do?

Back in my room, I hide the pamphlets in the drawer with my journal. I just want to sleep and wake up when this nightmare is over.

CHAPTER TWENTY-FIVE

Aaron

"It's been two days," I say to Andie. "Devyn has barely gotten out of bed. She hasn't even come to see Mickey, and we all know that's one of her favorite things to do."

"I'm telling you, heat exhaustion can take it out of you. Could be she was close to having heat stroke. And with the unseasonably hot weather we're having, could be she's hesitant to have it happen again."

I want to tell her it's more than that. Devyn is pulling away from me. This may have more to do with her past than her fainting. "She seems depressed."

"Let me go see her. Sometimes talking with a girlfriend is easier for women."

"I don't know. Give her a day or two." I hop in my truck.

"Where are you off to?"

"Have an errand to run."

I pull up the address on my phone. Even a congressman's house is easy to find if you dig hard enough. It'll take an hour to get there. That gives me time to figure out what I'm going to do.

I remember the first time I went to see Cameron's parents after he died. It wasn't at the funeral, because I didn't go thinking I'd not be welcome. It wasn't until almost a year later, after they'd tried calling me a hundred times. I never listened to the messages. I couldn't face them. I thought all they wanted was to find out about his last night. His last moments. Was he in pain? Was it fast? Did he know he was dying?

Even after a year, the pain was still raw. And if it still was for me, it would be a thousand times worse for them. But when I finally made myself go to their house in Dallas, what happened was far from what I imagined. I stood in front of the door, sweating, but when they opened it and saw me standing there, they pulled me into their arms. We stood and cried together. When they invited me in, the first thing I saw on their bookshelves was a picture of Cam and me. Me, the guy responsible for their son's death, displayed prominently in their living room.

His mom made coffee. His dad brought out photo albums. We talked and cried and laughed about Cameron's adventures. I begged for their forgiveness. They said there was nothing to forgive. It was a terrible mistake, one they blamed on the culture of the university, not me. They'd heard the stories. Read the testimony from the others who were there. Cam wanted to participate. He wasn't forced into anything. He wanted to join a fraternity so bad, he was willing to drink himself to death. And I was the one handing him the bottle.

They were the ones who begged me to move on and forgive myself, to live a full and happy life. It took a while. I still can't look at a bottle of whiskey without remembering him. However small and insignificant, I have found a way to honor him. That's what Devyn needs—a way to honor her little sister. Something to keep Kasey's memory alive without destroying Devyn's future.

I pull up and wait outside. The development is gated, of course. He's a congressman. I wait forty-five minutes.

A pizza delivery car approaches. I get out of the truck, wave him down, and hold out a hundred-dollar bill. "I'll give you this if you let me deliver the pizza."

He glances at the money. "You're crazy. I could get into a lot of trouble."

"Come on, man. I'm trying to surprise my girl. Gonna ask her to marry me. She thinks I'm away at school."

"I don't know."

I reach into my wallet. "All I've got is another fifty. Take it or leave it."

"If I get caught, I'm going to say you held me at gunpoint."

"Fair enough."

He takes the money, hands me the pizza, and spouts the address.

I get in my truck and pull up to the gate. The security guard calls the homeowner and verifies they have a delivery coming. He pushes a button, and the arm rises.

After making the delivery, I drive through the place. Large Victorian houses occupy huge lots. Some have fences and private gates, some don't. The congressman's house is one that does.

I park between estates and get my tool belt out of the back, then knock on the neighbor's door—one without a gate. No one is home. I go around into the backyard, the tool belt letting me pose as a handyman if anyone should see me. I find a break in the hedges and look from window to window in the congressman's house to try and see anyone. I find a place where I think I can jump the fence.

"What the fuck are you doing?" I say out loud. I'm not going to do Devyn any good if I'm in jail. In fact, I'm certain it would make things worse.

I start back to my truck and hear a child yelling from the congressman's yard, "Mommy, Mommy, you come too. Please? Push me on the swing."

The little girl is five or six. I must have the wrong house. I check my phone. It's the right one. Maybe they have guests. A woman comes out on the back porch, and I immediately know it's Roseanne DeMaggio. I've seen enough pictures of her over the past few days to spot her in a crowd.

I strain to hear her voice. She's at least fifty feet away from where I'm standing.

"Mommy's too tired, but I'll sit here and watch." She drops into a chair under an umbrella and opens a book.

The congressman has another child? In the articles I read, there was no mention of a third daughter.

They've moved on, which is great news. Maybe they're ready to forgive Devyn. I watch for another minute, then return to the street, relieved the neighbors never came home.

I'm smiling as I leave, but my happiness wanes. I can't tell Devyn about this. If I do, she'll know that I know everything. She'll think I've gone behind her back. She may even leave. I stop and bang my head on the steering wheel. Just like me back then, she's going to have to be the one to take the first step. Maddox, Andie, or Quinn couldn't convince me to do it. The Marshalls' incessant calls couldn't make me. This has to be Devyn's decision.

How long can I keep this secret? The woman I love is in pain. She's suffering, and I may be the only one who can understand.

She needs to know what happened to me. Then I have to tell her I know everything about her. But how and when? If I do it at the wrong time, in the wrong way, I may lose her forever.

CHAPTER TWENTY-SIX

Devyn

I finish folding the towels and put them away. When I walk through the kitchen, Joe is busy preparing lunch for the guests. He holds out a cup. "Looks like you can use some tea. Keep an old man company while he slaves away for the paying customers."

I'm in no mood for conversation, but Joe isn't a man you can easily turn down. I sit.

"Did you ever hear the story of how I came to work here?" he says.

I shake my head.

"I was cookin' part time for the rodeo over in the next county. Met Aaron when he come to watch his friend get thrown off mean-ass horses for fun. Aaron told me I made the best grilled street corn he'd ever had and asked if it was a secret recipe. I told him I'd be happy to make it for him again, but he'd have to hire me for an event. I was only kiddin' around, but he told me he might be in the market for a cook and invited me here to show him what I could do."

I smile weakly.

He raises a brow. "Just goes to show you never know when you're gonna meet someone who might change your life."

"Cooking here has changed your life?"

"Best damn job I ever had. Aaron—everyone on this ranch—they treat people right. Don't matter your creed, color, or past. You know how hard that is to find? Once you find it, you best not go messin' with it."

Joe may be one of the wisest men I've ever met, but he has no idea what I'm going through. What I've *been* through. "Thank you for the tea."

"You know I'm good for a cup anytime, Missy."

Back in my bedroom, I lie on my bed and stare at the ceiling. I'm back in prison again, only it's a different kind of confinement. I'm not sure I have any more tears, however. I've cried an ocean over the past few days. I've read all the pamphlets and considered all the possibilities. I know what I have to do. I just don't know if I have the strength to do it.

"Knock, knock!" Andie says from my doorway. She's wearing a bright pink bikini under a white mesh cover-up. "I have margaritas with our names on them back at the pool. I know you're probably afraid of the heat right now, but the pool is a refreshing seventy-eight degrees."

"I don't swim."

"Just dip your legs in to stay cool, then."

"I don't have a suit."

"You can borrow one, or just wear shorts if you don't plan to get in the water."

I wish everyone would leave me alone. "I can't."

She glances around my dark room. "You mean because of your busy schedule? Women know when other women need girlfriend time. I promise I won't make you swim if you really don't want to. Maddox and Vivian went to some "daddy and me" function, and I'm all alone. Christina and Tara are busy."

"So I'm pretty much your last choice."

"I didn't mean it like that. I was just saying if you don't come, I'll be bored and lonely. We don't even have to talk about anything meaningful. We can badmouth men or talk about the weather." She pulls on my arm until I sit up. "Pleeease?"

I've managed to avoid their pool for almost two months. I've managed to avoid *all* pools. If I say I'm sick, she'll want to know why. I've made excuses to everyone for days. I'm all out.

"You really won't try to get me in the water? Because I won't do it, and then I'd be mad at you, and I don't want to be mad at you."

She crosses her heart. "I promise."

I sigh. "Give me a minute to change."

She claps. "Yay. See you outside."

I hear her and Joe have a conversation. He talks with everyone. If it were possible, he would have a conversation with a rock.

I put on a pair of shorts and a tank top. When I button the shorts, I'm reminded of my growing problem. They still fit, but for how long? I examine my profile in the mirror, deciding it's far too soon for anyone to notice.

"Ready?" Andie asks when I emerge from my room.

"Don't forget the sunscreen," Joe calls after us.

I close the door behind us. "I don't have any."

"You can use mine. We stay so covered up on the ranch that we're all white as ghosts."

Ghosts. The word takes me back a few months to a simpler time. I know it's crazy to think it, but I wish I was still living in the attic and the only things I had to worry about were getting food and getting caught. How complicated I thought my life was at the time. I had no idea.

At Andie's house, she pulls around back, and we go through the gate in the fence surrounding the pool. I hesitate. She cocks her head. "Devyn, can you swim?"

"I can. I just don't like to."

"Well, pick a chair, then. The loungers are comfortable. I'll run in and get the margaritas."

I can't even look at the pool. I'm afraid of what I'll see if I do. I turn my chair around. When Andie comes back with drinks, I tell her it's so my face isn't in the sun.

She pours margaritas from a plastic pitcher into plastic glasses. I take mine and sip. Then I remember why I shouldn't and put the glass down. But does it really matter? I take another sip, then feel guilty and put it down again.

I can't have a baby. There are a million reasons why I can't.

But what if Aaron might want it? What if he wants me and the baby, and we can live happily ever after? It's not something I've thought about, because I'm so sure it could never happen, but *what if?*

"You don't like yours?" Andie asks. "You wanted salt?"

"Probably not a good idea to mix sun and alcohol so soon after fainting."

"It's been days. I'm sure you're okay."

I push the drink away, because… *what if?* "I don't want to risk it."

Andie goes back inside and comes out with a bottle of water. She plops onto the lounger next to me. "What should we talk about? Oh, my gosh. Vivian did the most amazing thing yesterday. She pulled herself up on the coffee table. I swear she's going to walk soon." She looks pensively at our surroundings. "I guess Maddox and I need to put in more safety precautions. We have the alarms on the doors, but we should—"

Even as I try to block out everything she says, I can still hear her. I take deep breaths and try to meditate.

"Devyn?"

"Yeah?"

"You were humming. You okay?"

"Oh, sorry. Can you tell me about horses?" It's the only thing I can think of to get her talking about something other than this pool or her daughter. I like Andie, I really do, but all new moms assume everyone wants to hear about their kids.

New moms. My insides clench when I realize I could be one of them.

"What do you want to know?"

"Everything. How you knew you wanted to work with them. Like, what made you decide to become a vet?"

She laughs. "How much time do you have?"

"I want to hear it all." It's not a lie. I've fallen in love with the majestic creatures, and even if I have to leave this place, I vow to end up somewhere with horses.

"It's Maddox's fault," she says. "I knew I wanted to work with animals. My granddad bought me my first horse on my tenth birthday. But it wasn't until I was fifteen and saw Maddox's horse get spooked by a snake and snap his hind leg that I knew I wanted to go into equine medicine."

She goes on and on, telling me about school, not seeing Maddox for a decade, and working for this ranch and others. I think she literally does tell me everything.

"Have I talked your ears off yet?"

"No. You're so passionate about horses. I know it sounds crazy, because I never even rode one until recently, but I am too, and I want to work with them."

"Mickey can't say enough about you. You understand there's a future here for you if you want it, right?"

Future. Another word that scares me to death right now. *Can* I have a future here?

The sliding glass door opens, and Maddox comes out, carrying Vivian. "Hey, babe. Hi, Devyn."

I can't say anything, because Maddox has on swim trunks and Vivian is wearing a little bathing suit with strawberries on it.

"Thought I'd take her for a swim. Want to join me?"

"I will," Andie says. "Devyn just wants to get sun."

My heart pounds uncontrollably. Maddox descends the stairs into the water with Vivian. Andie follows. My mouth goes bone dry, and bile burns my throat as Maddox holds Vivian out and Andie takes her, arms stretched out, zooming her through the water.

My vision blurs, and all I can see is Kasey's lifeless body on the bottom of the pool. I'm helpless. Frozen. The water is still. No ripples at all. How long has she been down there?

"No!" I yell.

Vivian squeals in delight, pulling me from my nightmare. Maddox and Andie stare.

I stand. "B-bathroom." I try to calmly go to the glass door. They think I'm a freak, and why wouldn't they? Running away from a friendly dinner, avoiding them all the time, and now this. When I'm inside, I race to the toilet and throw up.

I sit on the cold tile floor, trembling as the horrors of that night come rushing back.

The doorbell rings. I look through the peephole and see Angelina and Dane. He's carrying a twelve-pack of beer. I open the door. "I told you guys I was babysitting."

"Why do you think we're here?" Angelina says, plowing past me.

"You guys, my parents will kill me."

"They'll never know."

"What if Kasey tells them?"

"Kasey idolizes you, Devyn. She won't say anything." She pulls Kasey's favorite candy bar out of her pocket. "Bribe her with this."

Kasey appears in the kitchen doorway and recognizes Angelina, who's been our next-door neighbor for two years, but not Dane. She stares at him. "Who are you?"

Angelina shoves the candy bar at Dane and whispers, "You give it to her."

He refuses to take it. "Right, because a strange man should give a kid candy."

"Oh, right," she says with a laugh. "Kasey, I brought this especially for you, but it has to be our secret because if your parents know we were here, they'll find out about the candy bar."

Kasey's eyes go wide at the sight of the king-size Reese's Peanut Butter Cups. "That's for me?"

"It is." She gives it to her. "But remember, you'll get into trouble if your parents know you had it, so you can't tell them we were here."

"Okay. Devyn, can I eat it now?"

"Yeah, squirt. We're going out back to listen to music. You can go in my room and play my Xbox, too."

She hugs me. Chocolate and Xbox are the things she loves most. They're also things our parents never let her do. She rips open the Reese's and runs to my room.

"Bring snacks," Dane says, heading out the back door.

I get some Cheetos and popcorn and join them. We drink beer and listen to music. Every once in a while, I check on Kasey, who is happily playing Minecraft, her favorite game.

"Let's go swimming," Angelina says.

"Did you bring suits?"

"Don't need 'em," Dane says, stripping off his clothes.

I'm three beers deep, which makes a hundred-ten-pound girl drunk by anyone's standards, so I agree. I open the baby gate around the pool and shuck my clothes. The three of us jump in.

Usually, when there are three naked nineteen-year-olds, at least two of them are having sex. Not us. We're best friends. Looking at Dane's dick would be like looking at my brother's, if I had one. Besides, he has a girlfriend.

I ask, "What do you think Liz would say if she knew you were naked in the pool with two hotties?"

He laughs. "Have you seen my girlfriend? Sorry, guys, you're attractive and all, but she's got the body of a supermodel and a rack good enough to be a plastic surgeon's poster girl."

Angelina and I attack him, dunking him. He emerges, picks us up one at a time, and throws us as far as he can. He pounds on his chest and does the Tarzan yell. I realize we're being too loud. "Dane, shut up. Kasey will come out here."

"We don't want to scare her off with your little dick," Angelina says. "Might scar her for life if she thinks that's all she'll ever get."

Dane chases her around the pool and then throws her again. I glance up at the light in my bedroom. I'm sure Kasey has my headphones on; she probably won't hear anyway.

An hour later, we're back in our clothes, counting the empty beer cans. "Got any more?" Dane asks.

"I'm not taking booze from the bar. The congressman would have a fucking conniption. He hates me already; I'm not going to give him any more reasons."

"What's up with him?" Dane asks. "Ang told me he's like two different dads, one with you and one with Kasey."

"He's not a dad with me. You know he never would have adopted me if it hadn't helped him politically."

"You'd think after a while, he'd grow to love you, though," Angelina says. "I mean, we have, even though your nose is slightly off-center, and your feet are freakishly small."

I cover my nose defensively. "My nose is not off-center."

She laughs. "Could be my double vision."

"Okay, no more booze," Dane says. "You got a stash?"

"Yaaaaaaas," Angelina says. "You told me you got a ton the other day. You'd been saving for like a month."

"What can I say? It's cheaper in bulk."

Dane chuckles. "So you won't steal a few beers from the congressman, but you'll keep a shitload of weed hidden under his roof? Makes total sense."

I hit his arm. "Shut up."

"Go get it," he says.

"Are you crazy? I'm not smoking pot here. I'm babysitting, and the congressman would throw me in jail if he smelled it anywhere on his property."

Even drunk, Angelina agrees with me. "She's right. He'd kill her and us too." She looks sad for a moment, then smiles. "My parents are gone. Let's just pop next door and smoke a quickie in my backyard."

"I'm babysitting."

"Last time you checked on her, you said she was asleep in your bed. It's late. She's probably down for the night. We'll only be a few minutes."

"You know you want to, Devyn," Dane says. "Maybe we'll call Minton over, and you two can finally do the deed."

"Shut up. We are not calling Billy."

"But we're still getting high, right?" Angelina asks hopefully.

I roll my eyes. "Fine, but only if Kasey is asleep."

The two of them high five.

Up in my bedroom, Kasey is sleeping, my headphones still on and the videogame paused. I tiptoe to my bathroom, open the cabinet under my sink, and pull out the box of tampons I use for my stash. Ed would never find it, and my mom hasn't been in my room in years. She couldn't care less what I do as long as I play the part of the perfect daughter so she can look like the perfect wife of the perfect congressman.

I open the baggie, get a bud, then grab rolling papers and my lighter.

I check on Kasey one more time before leaving the bedroom.

Downstairs, I give everything to Dane. He rolls joints way better than I do. Angelina goes to the back door. "No," I say. "I'm not jumping the fence. Go out the front."

Sometime later, Angelina's sixteen-year-old sister comes home and gives us the once-over. "You guys are so stoned."

I raise my hand off the lounger. "They are, but I'm not. I only took a few hits. I'm babysitting, so I have to be the responsible one." I sit up, and my head spins. "Oh, shit. I'm babysitting. What time is it?"

"Ten thirty," Jen says.

"What time did we come over here?"

"Relax," Dane says. "We've only been here about half an hour."

"I have to go check on her."

"Bring back more weed," Dane calls after me.

I ignore him. I hear the three of them talking loudly on Angelina's back porch as I go through the house and cross the front yard. I have cottonmouth, so when I walk through the door, I stop in the kitchen for a drink of water. Kasey's stool is by the sink. She's not tall enough to reach the faucet, so we keep one under the cabinet for her. She's always forgetting to put it away, but I swear it wasn't out before. "Kasey?"

No answer. Guess she went back to bed. The buzz from the beers is fading, and I did only take a few hits, but I start to feel guilty about leaving the house with Kasey here. What if she had a bad dream? What if she got scared and couldn't find me? I was stupid. I promise myself I won't do it again. Kasey is the best thing in my life. I'd never forgive myself if anything happened to her. Yes, she's the golden child. The wanted child. But she and I have this connection, even though I'm fourteen years older than she is. Sometimes it feels like I'm a mother to her, especially when Mom is having one of her "episodes" and stays in bed for weeks on end.

My bed is empty, the headphones are on the floor, and the TV is still on. She must have gone to her room after getting a drink. I walk to the other end of the hall, to the bedroom next to the master. It's dark except for the nightlight. I enter quietly so as to not wake her, but her bed is perfectly made. "Kase?"

I cross the hall, knowing she likes to climb into bed with my parents sometimes. Mom usually kicks her out, and she ends up climbing into bed with me. Just like I was at that age, I wanted Mom's attention and love, and she didn't give it freely.

I flip on the light in the master. The room is eerily vacant. "Kasey?" Scared now, I race through the house, checking all the bathrooms. I even check the congressman's office—the one place we're not allowed. She's nowhere.

Is she playing a game with me? She likes to play hide-and-seek, but I always know where she is by her laughter. "Kasey, this isn't funny anymore. Where are you?"

I re-visit all the bedrooms, frantically searching every closet and under every bed. Downstairs, I check the garage because she sometimes sits in Mom's convertible and pretends to drive. What do I do? Do I call the police? Is she outside?

Running to the front door, something catches my eye. The pool sliders are open. Did we forget to close them? I push them wider and step through, scanning the dim patio for my sister. "Kasey, are you out here?"

My world implodes when I see it: the baby gate around the pool is open. The baby gate I left open.

I swallow hard and force myself forward through the mesh gate. The pool is illuminated by lights under the water. My heart stops when I see something at the bottom.

It's silent on this side of the fence, but strangely, I hear everything coming from Angelina's house. The three of them are laughing at Dane's impression of Iron Man. He's really good at it. All I want to do is go back over and laugh with them. But I know I'll never laugh again, because I finally grasp that Kasey, my little sister, the light of my life, is four feet under the water, and she's not moving.

"Kasey!" I scream. I jump into the pool, swim down, and grab one of her arms. I pull her to the stairs and drag her onto the deck. "Help! Help!"

By the light of the pool, I see her skin is almost white. I'm shaking. I have no idea what to do. I turn her over and hit her repeatedly on the back. "Help! Dane, call 911! Help!"

My mind runs in circles, like a crazed hamster on a wheel. I think of health class. What did they teach us? I lean down and put my ear over her mouth and nose. "She's not breathing! Help!"

I hear sprinting footsteps on the deck, then screams. I don't know who is screaming or what anyone is saying. I pump her chest with shaking hands, but I have no idea if I'm doing it right. Someone kneels beside me and blows into Kasey's mouth. Sirens blare in the distance.

I'm pulled away, and a man in a fireman's coat puts me on a lounger, holding me back. It's all a blur as half a dozen people help her.

She's okay. She's okay. She's okay. I repeat it over and over and over, leaning into the strong arms around me.

More activity. More sirens and lights and people. Police officers are everywhere. I'm crying. My friends are crying. But when a paramedic stands and sobs, I know my life will never be the same. She looks at the fireman holding me and shakes her head.

I killed her. I'm a murderer. My precious baby sister is gone.

There's a knock on the bathroom door. "Devyn, are you all right?"

"Give me a minute." I stand up, turn on the faucet, and splash cold water on my face. I glare at myself in the mirror, looking at the monster who should never be responsible for another human life. "I can't do this," I whisper to my reflection. I open the door. "I have to go."

Andie follows me. "Devyn?"

I don't turn around. "Thanks for having me. I'll see you later." I cross the driveway and yard and go all the way to the barn that houses the ATVs. I get on the first one I come to and gun it all the way to the lodge.

Joe's truck is still parked out back. I run up the steps and into the kitchen. "Joe, I need a ride."

CHAPTER TWENTY-SEVEN

Aaron

"She ran off? Where'd she go?"

"Took off on an ATV," Andie says. "Looks like she was headed to the lodge."

I pace the living room, then it hits me that Andie is wearing a bathing suit. "Were you guys in the pool?"

"We were sunning on the deck until Maddox brought Vivian out back. One minute she seemed fine and the next, she was sobbing on the bathroom floor. But don't say anything. I don't think she knew I could hear her through the door."

"Fuck." I run my hands through my hair. "Was Vivian in the pool?"

"Of course. She loves the water. Why?"

I shake my head. "I have to find her."

"Aaron, what's going on with her?"

"Not my place to say," I tell her on the way out.

At the lodge, Luca is leading the horses to the path that goes back to the stables. That means the guests are inside. Damn, I was hoping we could be alone.

I knock on Devyn's bedroom door. She doesn't answer, and I open it. It's dark, and she's not here. Could be she's out for more alone time. How long will she be gone this time? On my way out, I notice the drawer to her nightstand is open and things are strewn about, like she was hastily rummaging through it. I know what's in there. Her notebook. Or should I say journal. I badly want to know what she's feeling, but I already know too much that she doesn't want me to know. I can't do anything to further violate her trust.

I reach out to close the drawer, and something catches my eye. I pick up the black-and-white photo, and my heart lodges somewhere in my throat. I know exactly what this is. Andie displayed her ultrasound picture on the refrigerator for months. At the top is a name: Devyn Dunlop.

I sit. Holy shit, she's pregnant.

It explains her fainting and getting sick, pulling away from me, and her highly emotional state.

I can barely wrap my mind around it when I see something else: pamphlets. I open the one on abortion. She wouldn't, would she? I think about what she went through today, having to watch Andie and Maddox in the pool with Vivian. I'm sure she was reminded of her sister's death.

I have to find her. I put the pamphlets and photo back in the drawer, then notice something is missing. The money isn't here. She probably had close to a thousand dollars.

Fuck.

I run out of her room, smack into Joe. "Have you seen Devyn?"

"Just gave her a ride."

"Where?"

"Somewhere in Fort Worth."

"To a doctor's office?"

"Don't know. She had me drop her on a street corner. Said she'd Uber back later. Wanted to do shoppin' or somethin'."

"And you believed her? Did she seem upset?"

"Sure, but ain't that precisely when women go shoppin'?"

"Tell me exactly where you took her."

I've never driven faster in my life. The address he gives me is thirty minutes away. I make it in twenty. I scan both sides of the street, sweat soaking my shirt. What if I'm too late?

I see a women's clinic. I don't even bother finding a parking spot. I pull to the curb, get out, and run inside.

I approach the woman behind the plexiglass. "Is there a Devyn here?"

"I'm sorry, I'm not at liberty to say."

"Devyn Dunlop. I'm her—" I almost say boyfriend, but I wonder if, just like at the hospital, they won't let me in. "Husband."

"I'm still not at liberty to say."

"She's here, isn't she? You have to let me see her."

She motions to someone. A security guard walks over. "Is there a problem here?"

"Yes. She won't let me see my wife."

"You get this is a women's clinic, not couples counseling, right, buddy?"

I go for the door to the back, but the man grabs my arm.

"I have to see her. She can't do this."

"Let's go," he says, pulling me to the front door.

"I'm not leaving."

"Then we'll call the police."

"Devyn!" I scream as loud as I can. "Devyn DeMaggio! Come out here! Please, Devyn!"

"Make the call," the security guard tells the woman.

The door to the back opens, and Devyn sticks her head through. I jerk my arm away from the guard and go to her.

"What did you call me?" she asks.

"I know, Devyn. I know everything."

"Miss," the woman behind the counter says, holding a receiver. "Shall I call the police?"

Devyn shakes her head, and the woman puts down the phone.

Another woman shows up. "Ms. Dunlop, would you and this gentleman like a private room so you can talk?"

Devyn nods, and we're led into a small conference room. "Take all the time you need," she says.

Devyn sits. I can't. There's too much going on in my head. I pace, not knowing where to start. I stop behind her. She doesn't turn around. "Did you do it? Did you get an abortion?"

She sighs. "It's not that easy. You can't simply walk in here and get one. There's a process. How did you know?"

Relief courses through me. I take the seat next to her. "Andie called. She was worried about you. I went looking for you at the lodge. The nightstand drawer was open. I saw the photo and the pamphlets."

"How did you know my name?"

"The other day, when Congressman DeMaggio's name was mentioned, you freaked. I did some digging on the internet."

"He's not my dad. Not my real one, anyway."

"I know that too."

Tears coat her lashes. "Exactly how much do you know?"

"Everything. Jail. Kasey."

Her eyes close. "Then you know I can't have a baby. And if you know all this, why are you here? How can you stand to be in the same room with me?"

"Because I also know it was a huge mistake, Dev. A terrible misjudgment on your part. But that doesn't mean you can't have a baby."

She laughs sadly. "That's exactly what it means. Do you really want the mother of your child to be a murderer?"

"You're not a killer. I read all the transcripts. Even the judge was sympathetic. It's obvious the only reason you went to jail is because Ed made it happen. I wouldn't be surprised to discover he bribed a few people and, at the very least, called in lots of favors. Of course he was devastated, but in his eyes, losing her wasn't punishment enough. He had to make you pay."

"I got exactly what I deserved. Maybe you didn't read everything as well as you think. I got drunk and left the pool gate open. Then I left her alone in the house and got high at the neighbors. Don't you understand that she would be alive today if it weren't for me?"

"There were others there. It's not just on you. I'll bet they threw you under the bus to save themselves."

She points to herself. "*I* was responsible for her. She was only five years old. She was my sister. You couldn't possibly understand."

"You don't know how wrong you are."

She wipes her cheeks and waits for more.

"Four years ago, I was a sophomore in college. I was in a fraternity, and I was stoked to be the one getting to haze the new pledges, because I was hazed the year before. Hazing isn't legal, but it happens all the time. It's a rite of passage. The pledge assigned to me was my best friend. We met my freshman year. He chose not to join a fraternity, but after seeing how much fun I was having, he changed his mind. After eight weeks of crap, it was time for initiation. Just one last party during hell week. One last time for the pledges to show us how tough they were." My throat thickens, and my palms sweat, but I power through. She has to hear it.

"I made sure to get the cheapest, most horrible-tasting rotgut whiskey I could find. Cameron hated whiskey. This was my last chance to be the boss of him, and I was going to make the most of it. It wasn't until the bottle was empty that I realized what was happening to him. He was confused more than a normal drunk, and his skin was pale and cool to the touch. He looked almost blue. I freaked out and made him drink water, then watched him closely. But it wasn't working, and he would stop breathing for like ten seconds at a time. I wanted to call for help, but my frat brothers assured me it would pass. He was piss drunk, and he'd sleep it off.

"But Cam was my best friend. Like my mom, he always fought for the underdog. He loved the environment and made the frat house implement a strict recycling program. He's the one who got me to change my major. I was not about to leave him hanging out to dry if something was wrong, so I called 911, even though my brothers begged me not to. By the time the paramedics arrived, he'd stopped breathing, and I was giving him mouth-to-mouth. They rushed him to the hospital but wouldn't let me go. I didn't know anything until the next day. His parents were called. They drove down from Dallas. I slept in the waiting room. Sat there all the next day until his father told me he was in a coma. He stayed that way for two weeks before they pulled the plug." My voice cracks. "So if you want to talk about murderers, I sure as hell fit the description more than you do. I got him the alcohol. I practically poured it down his throat. He was *my* responsibility. *My* brother."

Devyn's eyes are red. She's shaking. "I... I didn't know. I'm so sorry."

"You want to hear the real kicker? I didn't even get punished. The fraternity was suspended, and we got a slap on the wrist. That's it. I should have gone to jail, Devyn. What I did was far worse than what you did. It's like I took him into the pool and held him under the fucking water."

I don't cry in front of people. Never have. Not even when I lost Cameron. But I'm crying now. I'm sobbing, because I know exactly how she feels, and it guts me.

She takes me in her arms, and we sob on each other's shoulders.

She stutters. "S-so now you k-know why I can't have a b-baby."

"No, I don't know."

"Aaron, I can't be trusted. What if I screw up? I'm not even sure I'm allowed to have a baby. What if the police find out I'm pregnant? With my past, they might take it away."

"Nobody can take your baby away. You served your time. You're not even on parole."

"I can't do this. I know I can't. Every time I would look at him or her, I'd see Kasey. I just can't."

I pace again. "So that's it? You were just going to abort our child without telling me? I thought I knew you better. I thought the connection we had was strong."

"Like I said, it isn't happening today. I was only talking with them. I would have told you before I did anything."

"Well, I'm saying no. No fucking way. We're having this baby."

"It's not your decision to make."

"The hell it's not." I stride over to her and put my hand on her belly. "This is my child. My son or daughter. I fucking love you, Dev. We can do this."

She swallows. "I love you too, but it doesn't change anything."

I choke up. It's the first time she's said she loves me, even though I've known it all along. I want to pull her into my arms and never let her go. But this is my baby we're talking about, and at the moment, I'm the only one fighting for it. "Fine. Don't be a mother. But let me be a father."

"What are you saying?"

"I'm saying I'll raise it alone."

"You want me to have the baby and give it to you? You said you can't even be trusted to take care of a dog."

"This is different, and you know it, and if it's the only way this will work, then yes."

"But then I couldn't… we couldn't. I couldn't be with you if you were raising it."

"I want you both, but it looks like I can't have both. If you abort this baby, I can't be with you. If you can't be a mother, then you can't be with us."

"Aaron." She looks terrified.

"It's a pickle, isn't it?"

"What are we going to do?"

"We're doing nothing right now. We'll go home and get some sleep. You'll think about it. I'll think about it. We'll come up with something that doesn't involve this clinic."

"I don't want to lose you."

I take her hand. "I don't want to lose you either." I kiss her on the forehead. "It's going to work out one way or another."

"Easy for you to say."

"Nothing about this is going to be easy, Dev."

CHAPTER TWENTY-EIGHT

Devyn

I stare up at the stars. Why did I agree to this? How can Aaron and I even be in a relationship if we want totally different things? I spent hours staring at the ultrasound photo tonight. Aaron left me alone, but he didn't leave me. He's sleeping on the couch or in one of the guest rooms. He probably thinks I'm going to run. Honestly, where would I run to?

"Couldn't sleep either?" Aaron asks, climbing through the window and onto the roof.

"You keeping tabs on me? I'm not going to run away, you know. Not right now anyway."

"But you might."

"I might have to leave. You understand that, don't you? How could I stay if I have the baby and hand it over to you?"

He lies down next to me on the blanket. "There's an easy answer, Dev. Stay and be a part of its life. Be a part of *my* life."

"My dad used to call me Dev. He's the only one who did."

He looks confused. "Your dad? But you hate him."

"Ed DeMaggio is not my dad. Never has been. I don't care what the legal papers say. Richard Dunlop is the man I call my father."

"Ah, Dunlop. No wonder you came up with the name so quickly. Tell me about him."

"You already knew Ed wasn't my birth dad, but you probably don't know that Roseanne wasn't my birth mom."

He rises on an elbow. "Actually, I do. I read it in one of the articles I found about you."

"Richard wasn't my birth father either. He and Roseanne adopted me when I was six."

"So Ed was Roseanne's second husband?"

"Yes. I'll get to that. I never knew my birth father, and I have little memory of my birth mother. Roseanne told me my birth mother was addicted to heroin. Apparently, she tried to take care of me, but social services kept getting called, and after being placed in dozens of foster homes, she finally gave up her rights to me when I was five, and I was placed for adoption. All I remember of her is a bunny she gave me. It's the only thing I got to take when I went to live with Richard and Roseanne."

"That's got to be tough on a little kid."

"I don't remember much, but after I was adopted, everything changed. Richard was an amazing dad. He took me to the ballet and soccer games and taught me to play drums. He kept a set in the garage. Mom hated it, but it was his one vice. I think it was how he escaped her."

"Escaped her?"

"She was always sleeping. She'd sleep for days on end. Sometimes weeks, only leaving her bedroom to get a bottle of liquor she called her "soda." Then she'd get a burst of energy that would last a day or two. Those days were my favorite. She'd take me to an amusement park, or we'd ride with the top down on her car, and she'd let me sit in the front seat. But other than that, she didn't pay much attention to me. I got the idea that Richard was the one who wanted a child, not her. She played along when he pushed her, but when he wasn't home, we barely even talked. But I didn't care about all that because he was filling up my life in ways it had never been filled."

"Sounds like your mom was bipolar."

"People assumed she was a moody housewife. But a year later, Richard died. He was flying across the country for work and got some fluke blood clot in his leg that traveled to his heart or something."

"Jesus, Dev. The hand you've been dealt. Are you sure you want me calling you that?"

I smile. "It reminds me of a happy time in my life—one of the few I've had."

"What happened after he died?"

"She stayed in bed *all* the time. I was barely seven, and I had to cook my meals and make my lunch. The bus stop for school was at the end of the block, so I walked. Nobody ever knew she wasn't being a mother to me. After six years in and out of foster care, I was basically used to taking care of myself."

"How does a woman like that end up with a guy like Ed?"

"A teacher called social services when I missed the afternoon bus and Mom didn't show up to get me. After that, she agreed to go on medication. Sometimes she took it, sometimes she didn't. Then she met Ed, and everything changed. She was happier than I'd ever seen her. He doted on her and tolerated me, but they had a good relationship. As a result, she became the mother I needed, and for the first time in years, life was normal again. Until they had

Kasey, their biological child. Mom went back into a depression after having her. Ed hid it from everyone. He was positioning himself for politics, a former district attorney working as chief of staff for some senator. He was afraid if people found out about her, his career would suffer. I'd hear them talking behind closed doors. He begged her to stay on her meds. She would tell him how numb they made her feel. Wanting to please him, she faked taking them, but she wasn't fooling anyone. We could tell by her behavior.

"I was barely fifteen when I became Kasey's primary caretaker. We did everything together. She was more like my daughter than my sister. Even Ed knew it. When he decided to run for congress, he announced he was adopting me. I was young, but I saw right through him. He wanted people to think he was a family man, willing to take on a teenager that wasn't his, and it worked. He was elected."

Aaron looks angry. "He was reelected shortly after Kasey died."

I nod. "According to reporters, it was a tough race, but after she died, nobody felt they could attack his character or badmouth him in any way, so he won."

"He's running for senate now," he says.

"I know. I looked him up when you first gave me the phone."

"Maybe you should go see them."

I sit up. "Are you crazy? No way."

"It might give you some closure."

"One of the first things I did after my release was go by our house. Only it wasn't their house anymore. They'd moved and didn't tell me. They never told me anything. No one even visited me in jail. I thought after enough time had passed, my mom would come. She didn't. Neither did my friends. Two years and not a single visitor. Do you know how pathetic that is?"

"Your friends, what were their names… Angie and Dane? They never visited?"

"Angelina. She hated when people called her Angie. No, they didn't come either. They never talked to me after that night. They told the judge it was my idea to leave Kasey in the house alone. They said it was me who opened the gate and left the slider open."

"But it wasn't, was it?"

"Honestly? I can't be a hundred percent sure. I'd been drinking. I remember telling them I wouldn't smoke pot in the house with Kasey there, and I believe I was the one who opened the pool gate. Everything else is a blur."

"They threw you under the bus to save themselves. You get that, right? If they'd testified about what really went down that night, they would have given the three of you probation or something. Instead, your friends saved themselves."

"I'm sure Ed went to them and their parents. He wanted *me* punished. He didn't care about them. He hated the closeness I had with Kasey. He was always working, and when he came home, he expected her to jump in his lap and love him. But he was never home. He was practically a stranger to her."

"He wanted you punished because *he* was a crappy father?"

"It doesn't really matter, Aaron."

"You didn't deserve two years in jail."

My stomach rolls. "What do you think is the proper trade-off for a little girl's life?"

"Devyn." He reaches for my hand, but I pull away.

He lies back and looks at the stars in silence.

"Don't you understand? I don't want to be my mother. She never wanted kids. She had them for her husbands. Even if I agreed to this, you'd be a doting dad like Richard, and I'd be the pathetic mom like Roseanne. What if something happened to you and I had to do it alone? You really want your kid being raised by someone like me?"

He takes my hand and doesn't let me pull away this time. "You are not your mother, and you are not what happened to you. The mistakes you've made don't define you. I want to take you somewhere tomorrow."

"I'm not going to see them."

"Fair enough, but that's not where I'm taking you."

"Where, then?"

"You'll see."

"Why do I feel like you're trying to trick me?"

"This isn't about you at all. It's about me. Will you go?"

"Under one condition."

"Name it."

"You don't tell anyone about the baby. Not Maddox or Andie or Quinn. Not until we decide what to do."

"Agreed. Now will you lie down and put your head on my chest or something? I've missed the shit out of you this week."

"And my head on your chest will be enough?"

"It will be for now. Because I know you love me."

I move closer and do what he asks, because I've missed him too. The feel of his heartbeat is calming. I just wonder how he can be so calm when I'm sure there's a storm on the way.

CHAPTER TWENTY-NINE

Aaron

"Aren't you scared?" Devyn asks, seated next to me in the truck. "I mean, aren't you freaking out? You're twenty-three years old. There must be a million things you want to do before you have a kid, not to mention how scary it would be to be a single father."

I take her hand. "First of all, I'm going to do everything in my power to make sure I won't be a single dad. I want us to do this together." She turns and looks out the window. I squeeze her hand. "We have how many months before the baby comes?"

"Seven, I guess."

"Seven months is a lot of time to get used to it. Did I set out to be a dad at my age? Of course not. That doesn't mean I don't want it. It's a part of me—of us. And I'm pretty damn fond of us, if you haven't figured that out already."

"What if I can't do it?" she asks. "And you should know, right now, I'm pretty sure I can't."

I give her a tug. "Come here." She moves from the passenger seat to the middle seat. "We have time. Nothing has to be decided today."

"And you haven't told anyone?"

"I promise nobody will know until you're ready, or, you know, it becomes obvious."

She sinks into the seat. "Oh, my god."

"Don't worry, it won't happen for a while. Most women don't start to show until well after twelve weeks. And since you aren't short and you haven't been pregnant before, it'll be more like sixteen, even longer if you don't wear tight clothes."

She pulls back and studies me. "How do you know all this?"

"It's amazing what you can find on the internet. The baby is about the size of a cherry right now."

Even in my peripheral vision, I see her jaw go slack. "How is that possible? It looked so fully formed to be that small."

"It *is* almost fully formed. By the end of the third month, everything is in place, and it simply grows bigger from then on."

"Can we not talk about this anymore? How about you tell me where we're going."

"It's a surprise."

"I don't like surprises."

"Duly noted."

I drive into a modest neighborhood. The houses are close together, and a lot of them look alike. I've been here several times. I know it's the brown house on the corner of the second intersection. I pull into the driveway. On the mailbox is the name Marshall.

"Who are the Marshalls?"

"You're about to find out." I hop out of the truck and run around to open her door.

As we head up the sidewalk to the front door, I admire the tree I helped plant a few years ago. I ring the bell. Devyn is tense. I run a hand down her arm. "Relax."

Mrs. Marshall opens the front door and smiles, then pulls me in for a hug. "Aaron! I'm so glad you came. When you called this morning, I told Jim he had to work from home today so he could see you."

Mr. Marshall appears beside her and extends his hand to me. "Nice to see you, Aaron."

I nod to the yard. "I'm happy to see the tree is getting so big."

"That it is," he says. "Who's this delightful young lady with you?"

"Dottie and Jim Marshall, this is my girlfriend, Devyn. Devyn, these are Cam's parents."

Devyn goes ashen. She whispers to me, "As in *Cameron?*"

Dottie says, "You look like you need to sit. Come inside. I'll make lemonade."

Devyn gives me the stink eye as we go in. Technically, I didn't lie to her. This isn't about her parents. It isn't even about *her.* My hope is that it will help her understand that life after what happened to us is possible.

"What brings you to Dallas?" Jim asks.

"Nothing special. We were out for a drive. Might stop at a bookstore later. It's nice to get off the ranch from time to time."

Dottie pops her head out of the kitchen. "There's a new bookstore on the corner of Fifth, past the Burger King. A friend of Jim's runs it. You should go there."

"Sure thing."

Jim brings his laptop over to the couch, opens it, taps around, and pulls up a picture of a young Asian lady.

"Is that who I think it is?" I ask.

"Yessiree," he says, smiling. "The second official recipient of the Cameron Marshall Memorial Scholarship."

Dottie returns with a tray of drinks and sees what we're looking at. "Isn't she as cute as a button? She's only seventeen. Graduated high school a year early with a perfect GPA. You should read her essay. She doesn't ride in cars unless they're fully electric. Otherwise, she walks or bikes. Her goal is to work on electromagnetic propulsion and reduce the need for diesel-fueled vehicles by having a high-speed network of trains utilizing electrical current and magnetic fields."

"She sounds smart. That's right up Cameron's alley."

Dottie smiles. "He would have loved it."

I know what Dev's thinking. How can I, the person responsible for Cameron's death, be talking to his parents?

Dottie notices Devyn's confusion. "Surely Aaron has told you about the foundation?"

"Actually, no."

"But you're his girlfriend, right?"

I pat Devyn's hand. "It's still new. We don't know everything there is to know about each other yet."

Dottie sits next to Devyn on the couch. "Then let me fill you in. Aaron was generous enough to set up a foundation in Cameron's name. It will pay for people like Suni, who shared Cameron's save-the-world views, to get an education that will help them save the environment."

Devyn puts it together. "Your oil well."

I nod. "All the profits go to the foundation."

"Isn't that kind of ironic, though? Digging for oil isn't good for the environment."

"Not the way most people do it," I say. "I told you, I'm working on a cleaner way to do it."

Devyn looks from Dottie to Jim to me. "I'm sorry. I don't get what's going on here."

"You mean, do we not know how our son died?" Dottie asks. "Of course we know about Cameron. We also know what happened was a terrible, horrific accident. These two were best friends. Cameron brought him home—I don't know how many times. We got to know Aaron, and he became like a second son to us, especially since his parents were halfway across the country. It would be pointless for us to blame him. That wouldn't bring back Cameron. He was nearly twenty years old—plenty old enough to know better. If anyone was to blame, it's Cam. But this foundation is keeping his memory alive. Seeing Aaron does that, too."

Devyn is clearly at a loss for words.

"Jim and Dottie, you should know Devyn has gone through something similar to what I did."

Dottie's arm immediately goes around Devyn. "No wonder you're so pale." Dottie smacks the back of my head. "You blindsided the poor girl, didn't you?"

"I thought if she could see we're okay—"

"Sweetie," Dottie says. "I don't know what happened, and I'm not going to ask. But I will tell you this: forgiveness can't come from anyone else. The only person who absolutely has to forgive you is *you*."

Devyn shakes her head. "I'm not sure I can."

Dottie stands and holds out her hand to help Devyn up. "I'm going to give you a piece of my famous chocolate pie." She tows Devyn to the kitchen, nabbing a photo album along the way. "Then I'm going to introduce you to my son."

An hour later, we're in the truck. Before I back out of the driveway, she says. "Dottie is amazing."

"I know."

"She's nothing like my mother."

"I know that, too."

"My mother won't forgive me like Dottie and Jim forgave you."

"You don't need her forgiveness."

She leans back. "I don't know if I want to thank you or be mad at you."

"I vote for option number one. It has a much better chance of getting me sex."

She looks at her stomach. "You want to have sex with me? Like this?"

I nod vehemently. "Are you kidding? You've never been more beautiful."

"But I haven't agreed to anything."

"You haven't said no either." I throw the gearshift into park and take her hands. "Devyn, I want you. Pregnant or not, you're fucking perfect. I love you. Love doesn't have an on/off switch. I'll love you when you get big. Even if you decide you can't do this, and I have to raise the baby alone, though I may not like you very much, you can be sure as shit I'll still love you."

"You will?"

"I'm twenty-three years old, Dev. I've never said those words to another woman. I'm pretty sure it'll be another twenty-three before it happens again."

For the first time in days, she smiles. "Okay then. I think I'll go with option number one."

My dick swells. I can't wait to get her home. "Fuck the bookstore," I say, backing onto the street.

"What did you need at the bookstore?"

"I wanted to get a book about… things." I glance at her belly. "You know, in case we had any questions."

"Someone once told me that it's amazing what you can find on the internet."

I laugh. "Touché." I want to speed home, but at the same time, I feel the need to inch along and protect my precious cargo.

CHAPTER THIRTY

Devyn

By the time we're home, I'm drenched between my legs. He had his hand on my thigh the entire time, rubbing circles with his thumb, driving me insane. I'm wound like a spring and ready to explode.

There are guests at the lodge, so he takes me to his cabin. We don't go here much, but I like it. It's open and airy. You can see everything except the bathroom from the front door. A wall separates the bedroom but not a door. From the outside, it's a log cabin. On the inside, a trendy urban loft apartment with exposed ductwork in the vaulted ceiling. Makes sense; he lived most of his life in New York City. When he moved here, he was either sleeping in the bunkhouse, one of the small apartments, or in a college dorm. He built the place from the ground up with his bare hands. Andie told me it took him three years of summers, weekends, and holidays.

After Cameron died, he poured himself into this project. Maybe that's why I like working with horses so much—they keep me busy. I haven't been to see Mickey all week, and I miss it.

"Devyn?" I look up. Aaron is completely naked. He didn't waste any time.

I'm sitting on his bed, his penis at eye level. My mouth waters—actually waters. "Where'd you go?" he asks, pulling my shirt off over my head.

"I was thinking about this cabin."

He averts his eyes from my breasts and studies the far wall. "It wouldn't be too hard to open it up, add another room or two."

I grip his erection. "Do you want to talk about your cabin, or do you want to have sex with me?"

He inhales sharply at my touch. "This time, I'll take door number two."

"Thank God, because you almost made me come in the car."

His eyebrows shoot up. "But I barely even touched you." He glances at my stomach. "I think I'm going to like this."

"Like what?"

He chuckles and pushes me down on the bed. "I'm going to try something."

He leans down and takes my nipple in his mouth. Sensations shoot through me right to my center. He might as well be touching my clit. His tongue flicks. His lips suck. His teeth rake. *Oooooh.* His mouth devours one nipple as his fingers fondle the other. I'm well aware I'm bucking under him like the devil in heat, but it feels so good. I almost push him away when it gets to be too much, but then I convulse and shudder, shake, moan, and shout. It lasts forever, and he doesn't ease up until I'm still.

"Hooollllly shit, Dev. That was fucking fantastic."

I pull a pillow over my face, hiding my embarrassment. "I didn't even know it could happen that way," I say, words muffled.

He removes the pillow. "I guess I'm just that good."

I pick up the pillow and hit him with it. "Shut up if you want your turn."

He leans back, erection at full attention, and laces his fingers behind his head. "Consider me mute."

I wrap my hand around him, and he lets out an audible sigh. I pump him softly, then harder. I find the penis utterly amazing. The skin is baby soft, but underneath that is a hard steel rod. I've never been this up close and personal. Usually, we're on the roof in the dark. I take the opportunity to study it. He raises a brow. I know what he's thinking. *Like what you see?* But he won't say it because I might stop.

When I'm done exploring and admiring, I take him in my mouth. He murmurs my name. His hands weave through my hair. He tries to reach every part of me, like he can't help but want more. It's a heady feeling, knowing I have this kind of effect on him. I'm not even sure I'm any good at this, but you wouldn't be able to guess it based on the way he moves under me.

He reaches around to find my clit. "God, Devyn, you're so wet."

Hearing him say it turns me on even more. I had an orgasm not five minutes ago, but I'm already building and nearing the edge. He slides fingers inside me and swirls them around. He pumps them in and out. He crooks them and finds a spot that makes me stiffen and mewl.

"Get on top of me," he says.

It's a command I fully intend to follow. My mouth releases him with a *pop*. I reach for a condom, then remember it's a moot point. Then again, with his past, I hold it up. "Do we need this?"

"I got tested. I'm good." He takes the package and flings it across the room.

I climb over him and slide onto him with incredible ease. He holds my hips as he pumps up into me. "Shit, that feels good," he says.

I watch him closely to see what he does. Will he touch my stomach and break the spell? Will he go easy because he thinks he might hurt something? But neither of those things happen. He pumps hard, then works my clit and nipples. He sends me through cycle after cycle of building and waning. Any second, I'm going to yell at him to let me come. I press my lips together at the intensity.

"I'm going to come, Dev."

That's all I need. Those five words in his low, sexy voice send me over the edge. I grab the headboard and ride him through my orgasm, not caring who or what hears me yell at the ceiling.

I collapse on him. We're sweaty and breathing heavily. When I move, and he slips out of me, embarrassing noises ensue as air and fluid escape me. I roll off next to him, pulling the pillow over my head again. He climbs on top of me and pitches the pillow on the floor so I can't reach it. He traps my hands over my head and leans down to kiss me. Before our lips touch, he declares, "Watching you come has got to be the sexiest thing I've ever seen in my entire life."

I smile as his lips capture mine.

I wake up and catch Aaron staring at me. It's almost dark outside. "Did I fall asleep?"

"You've been out for about an hour. Guess two spectacular orgasms took it out of you." He winks and snuggles into me.

I think about meeting the Marshalls today. I know what he was trying to do. "You get that it's different, don't you? Kasey was my sister. My parents hate me. Even before it happened, they were indifferent."

"Could be enough time has passed that they might feel differently."

"I doubt it. I saw my mother on the street after I got out of jail."

"You did?"

"You know I went by my old house. What I didn't tell you is that I went by the salon where she gets her hair done. I knew she wouldn't have switched unless they moved far away. I went every day for two weeks until she showed up. You know what she did when she saw me? Nothing. Her steps faltered, she stopped and stared, then she went about her day as if I were merely a stranger. That is not someone who is eager to see me."

"If you ever want to go, I'll go with you. I'll do anything for you, Devyn."

I lay my head on his chest. *Almost anything,* I want to say.

"Tell me about jail," he says.

"It's kind of like high school, but without cellphones."

"Really?"

"No."

His chest heaves up and down. "What was it like?"

"It wasn't like the movies, if that's what you're asking. It's not like women go around shanking other women with filed-down plastic spoons. But you did have to watch your back, because some of them were always up for a fight if you even looked at them funny. I was lucky. Some of the older women took me under their wings and showed me the ropes. They didn't expect anything in return, like others would have."

"Were you scared?"

I nod. He leans down and kisses my hair. "My main problem was lack of money. Most people had someone on the outside deposit money into their inmate account. I came in with a few hundred dollars. After I bought a fan and some essentials, it was soon gone."

"What did you do?"

"Used state-issued shampoo and bar soap. Just like on the outside, there is a caste system. Rich and poor. Strong and weak. I was definitely one of the poorest and weakest. I learned to work the system, though. They gave sedatives to unruly inmates, so I became one, and then I pretended to take the pill without taking it. They became my currency. People would trade almost anything for downers."

"My god," he whispers.

I peek up at his face. "Do you want to hear more, or have I totally bummed you out?"

"I want to know everything."

"After a while on kitchen duty, which meant I cleaned what they told me to clean, one of the older ladies got me a job in the laundry. It wasn't glamourous, but it was better than sweeping up roaches and keeping rats out of the pantry. I folded sheets and sewed them when they ripped. I got really good at it. One day, I added my initials onto my favorite shirt so no one would want to steal it. A few people saw it and asked me to do the same to their belongings."

"You didn't have to wear jumpsuits or whatever?"

"For the most part, we could wear approved street clothes. For months, I wore the jail-issued gray uniform with elastic pants until I could afford to buy a few T-shirts from the commissary."

"That's where you learned how to sew."

"Yup."

"And there was a store there?"

"Not like any you're familiar with. Everything was behind a counter, and you had to ask for it. But you could buy things like food, toiletries, certain arts and crafts supplies, envelopes and stamps, stuff like that. We all had an ID we had to carry with us to make purchases. We also used it to go to the gym or participate in programs."

"So it *was* like high school?"

I giggle, and I realize it's the first time I've ever laughed thinking about my life back then.

"Can I ask you something?"

"Okay."

"You said you sewed your initials on your shirt. Your initials are DD. The woman at Home Depot called you DeeDee. Did you know her?"

I sigh. "Her name is Delta Brown. She worked as a food server, one of the better jobs in the kitchen." I look into his eyes. "I'm sorry I lied."

He pushes some hair out of my eyes. "You don't have to anymore. Now you can work here for real. We can add you as an employee, and you'll get paid."

I roll off his chest and gaze at the ceiling. "I don't want anyone else to know, Aaron. They'd hate me."

"They know about me and don't hate me."

"That's different. Plus, you're related. Please don't tell them."

He rises on an elbow. "It looks like we have lots of secrets we have to keep."

"If it's too much—"

"It's not." He pulls me close. "It's all going to work out, Dev."

"I'm glad one of us thinks so."

"Can I ask you another question?"

I close my eyes. "I think I'm about spent."

"This one is easy."

"Okay, what is it?"

"I'm curious. What's the first thing you bought after you got out?"

"Gum."

"That's not the answer I was expecting. Cheeseburger, maybe."

"I always loved gum. It was almost like an addiction for me. But in jail, you can't have it, because it can be used to jam locks. So after I got out, I went to the first convenience store I could find and bought a pack. I would have preferred a cheeseburger, but I couldn't afford one."

"What did you do? Where did you go?"

"You said one more question."

"Right. That's a story for another day. How about we make dinner? For some reason, I'm craving cheeseburgers."

"That sounds great," I say. He moves to get up, and I quickly wrap my arms around his bare chest from behind. "I'm happy for you, Aaron. You and the Marshalls, and everything you're doing in Cameron's memory."

He turns and nods. I'll bet he wishes he could say the same thing about me.

CHAPTER THIRTY-ONE

Aaron

Quinn helps me unload bags of cement mix by my cabin. "You going to tell me why you feel you have to do this *yesterday*?" he asks.

"I want her to move in with me. I figure the cabin will be more appealing if it has more space."

He laughs. "You mean more appealing than the ten-by-ten bedroom she's currently sleeping in? Dude, your place is already like a castle compared to that."

"It's overdue for an upgrade. Thanks for helping me out."

"Don't have anything better to do."

"Nothing better to do, eh? What about flight school? That whole thing blow over?"

"Oh, I'm doing it. It's just that there's a lot of shit to do. You can't just walk up to someone and have them teach you how to fly. Plus, I've been thinking, and I'm not sure it makes sense to get a pilot's license for both planes and helicopters. There's so much more you could do with helicopters, and with a large enough one, you could still offer the VIP transport from the airport. It'll be faster and cheaper to concentrate on that."

I laugh, still not believing a word of it. Quinn has had crazy ideas before. Like taking up bronc riding. I play along, as usual. "Whatever you say."

A Range Rover pulls up the driveway.

"Fuck," he says, slinging the last bag on the pile.

Karen Thompson gets out of the driver's seat and walks over, turning her nose up at the dirt piles that might ruin her white linen pants.

"What are you doing here?" Quinn asks.

"If you'd answer my calls, I wouldn't have to track you down."

"If you weren't such a bitch, I'd answer your calls."

Her jaw goes slack. Then her eyes blaze. "Is that any way to speak to your mother?"

"Maybe if you acted like one occasionally. Listen, is there a point to this little reunion?"

"You've probably heard that your uncle was denied parole."

"Yup. Cracked a beer to celebrate."

She steps forward and jabs a finger in his chest. "You may not like the family you were born into, but we're still your family. You have obligations. Things you need to do to earn your trust fund."

"It doesn't come with strings. It's mine fair and square. I'm of age and have full control over it. You haven't been able to tell me what to do or when to do it for quite a while."

"You're wrong, Quinn. You're a Thompson. That money was made by your grandfather. He expected great things from you."

"And by great things, you mean fucking over other people, like Aaron and his family?"

She eyes me up and down like I'm an inconvenience. "If it weren't for his family, Jon wouldn't be in prison."

Quinn laughs. "If it weren't for Jon, Jon wouldn't be in prison. How obtuse can you be, *Mother*?"

"I'm not going to stand here and argue with you. He wants to see you."

"Who?"

"Uncle Jon."

He shakes his head. "Nuh-uh."

"It's not a request."

"Like I said, you have no control over me. If you want to order someone around, go home and bark commands at your housekeeper."

"He's family."

"No." Quinn points to me. "*He's* family."

"You don't deserve your trust fund. Not one penny of it." She starts back to her car. "You're going to regret this one day."

He waves dismissively. She huffs and drives off in a tizzy.

"What do you think Jon wants?" I ask.

"Same thing he always wants: me to take over running his posse."

I look at him sideways. "He still has a posse?"

"He's got half a dozen guys running things for him. A few years after he went to prison, I went to see him. I wasn't twenty-one yet and didn't control my trust fund." He glances back at the driveway. "She made me go. I never told you because he wanted me to help him get back at you. Said I was in the perfect position because we were friends. He wanted me to immerse myself in your life and become a trusted part of DHR. Then he would take it over from within. I thought if I told you, you wouldn't trust me."

"Damn. I'm glad you didn't say anything. I'm not sure that I wouldn't have been suspicious."

"You know I'd never do anything to hurt you or anyone here. I wasn't lying when I told her you're family."

I pat him on the shoulder. "Same, brother. But why do you think his guys have left us alone all this time if he's hell-bent on getting back at us?"

"Probably wants to do it himself. What would be the fun in ruining DHR if he weren't around to see it?"

"We should tell Maddox and Owen about this."

"I was planning to, but no need to rain on everyone's parade until Jon gets released."

"Hello, boys!" Lora sings across the yard. She's wearing a tight skirt and a low-cut blouse.

I lean toward Quinn. "You're not still sleeping with her, are you?"

"No, but when she comes here dressed like that, I can't make any guarantees."

"You're early," I say as she approaches.

"Thought we could go over my notes. I have an idea I'd like to run past you."

Quinn slaps me on the back. "If we're done here, I'm going to head out."

I lift my chin. "See you, man, and thanks."

Lora eyes my bare chest. Sweat is dripping down my abs. "How about we talk in your cabin?"

Not going to happen. "The office in the lodge is better suited, don't you think? I'll get a fresh shirt and be there in a sec."

She doesn't seem happy, but she covers it with a smile and walks away.

A few minutes later, I join her at the lodge.

"Where's Devyn?" she asks.

"Where she always is. With Mickey."

"Good."

"Why good?" I walk past her and into the office.

"I wouldn't want her overhearing any of my ideas and passing them off as her own."

"Why would she do that?" I ask, turning on the computer.

She sits in the chair on the other side of the desk. "She might be one of those girls who capitalize off the ideas of others."

I'm trying hard not to bite her head off. She's been an asset to the lodge, and I don't need any other problems at the moment. "You don't think the ideas she's had are her own?"

She shrugs. "Seems unlikely from someone with her background."

I give her a punishing stare. "What background would that be?"

"Never mind. I had this idea about getting ATVs for all our guests, keeping them here at the lodge to make things easy, and offering all-terrain tours of the ranch. You could go off-trail to places the horses can't get to. Down the ridge, for instance. It would be something else to offer guests. Might make people want to stay more than just a few days."

I make a note and try not to seem smug. "So you want to use Devyn's idea of offering helicopter tours and housing horses at the lodge, only change horses to ATVs? I'd say that's *you* capitalizing off *her* ideas, wouldn't you?"

She huffs. "Not at all. Nobody has mentioned ATVs before now."

"However it came about, it's still a good idea."

"And not nearly as expensive as building a stable."

I chew on my pencil in thought. "It's something we could start up quickly. I'd have to buy the ATVs, but single-rider ones don't need hauling capabilities and will be cheaper than the ones we already have. We could cover them with tarps until we get a stable built with a large storage room." I smile. "This could work."

She smiles back. "I'm glad you think so. I can get you some prices. We can roll some of the expense into event costs. The more we offer, the more they'll be willing to pay. Pretty soon, we'll be competing with some of the major ranch destinations."

"That would be amazing."

"Maybe there could be a full-time job in it for me? You know, sometime down the road?"

"Let's not get ahead of ourselves. I'm going to have to run the cost by Maddox and my uncle."

"Let me put something together before you do. I'll work up a brochure and do a mock-up of a new website offering the additional tour." She bounces in her seat. "ATVs will make it easier to get guests around faster. We could not only offer an all-terrain tour of the property, but since it only takes fifteen minutes to get to the main ranch by ATV, we could offer excursions there. Say, working with the horse trainers. Or we could put on our own mini rodeo. The possibilities are endless."

"Work something up and get back to me."

She stands and straightens her skirt. "Anything for you. I love it here." She comes around the desk and leans into me. "I mean it, Aaron."

The way she's staring me down tells me she *does* mean *anything*.

"Oh, sorry," I hear from the doorway.

I look over in time to see Devyn scurry away. I go after her. "Hey."

She goes into her room and sits on the bed.

I follow, closing her door behind me. "That wasn't what you think."

"I think Lora wants in your pants, and she was coming on to you."

"Okay, maybe it is what you think, but it was just that second when she came around the desk. The rest of the time, we were talking business."

"I'm not jealous."

"Good, because there's no reason to be. I don't want her. I want you."

She cocks her head. "Why don't you want her? She's pretty, educated, single, and she doesn't come with all the baggage."

"Everyone comes with baggage, Dev. Every person has a past."

"Yeah, but I don't have regular baggage. I come with a whole trunk full of shit."

I sit next to her. "As do I."

"Your trunk doesn't include being an ex-convict or the unwanted quasi-kid of a congressman."

"So yours is more complicated than most." I take her hand. "I don't mind complicated."

She glances down at her stomach and laughs. "Well, you got it."

I think I hear something in the hall and open the door to check, but no one's there. I peek into the office to see Lora typing on her laptop. I must have been imagining things. I return to Devyn.

Back in Devyn's room, I say, "Can I see the photo again?"

When she opens the drawer, it's on top of everything, which makes me think she's been looking at it, too. The thought gives me hope for a future I never even knew I wanted.

CHAPTER THIRTY-TWO

Devyn

Aaron joins me on the roof. It's the first time in a while. I guess he's been giving me time to think.

"It's two o'clock in the morning. I thought pregnant women were supposed to sleep a lot," he jokes.

It's the first time he's mentioned the pregnancy or baby since he asked to see the ultrasound photo a few weeks ago. "You're not funny."

"Sorry. I've been wanting to bring it up. Don't you think we should talk about it?"

"When there's something to talk about, we can."

"Devyn, there *is* something to talk about. And it's growing bigger every day. It's the size of a plum. It's fully formed, with all of its organs, muscles, limbs, and bones in place. Isn't it amazing?"

"Amazing," I say, heavy on the sarcasm. "I meant when I've come to a decision."

"How can you come to a decision if we don't talk about it?"

I point at the sky. "See those stars? If you look closely, you'll see five of them making up kind of an *M* shape."

Frustrated, he lies back on the blanket. "I don't see them."

"Give your eyes a minute to adjust." I take his hand and trace the stars. "That's Cassiopeia. It's most visible in the fall, but you can see it now."

"Why is it named Cassiopeia? She was a Greek god or something, right?"

"She wasn't a god. She was the queen of Aethiopia and very beautiful. You've heard of Andromeda?"

"The one who was chained to the rock and got killed by the sea monster?"

"So you do know a little Greek mythology. But she wasn't eaten. Perseus saved her. Cassiopeia, Andromeda's mother, was incredibly vain. She claimed she and her daughter were more beautiful than Nereus's daughters. He was the sea god. That brought about the wrath of Poseidon, who was going to flood the city or direct the sea monster, Cetus, to destroy it, depending on which version you believe. To save the city, an oracle told Cassiopeia she had to sacrifice her daughter. Andromeda, as you said, was chained and left for Cetus to feast on. But Perseus saved and then married Andromeda. Poseidon thought Cassiopeia should not escape punishment, so he tied her to a chair in the heavens. The constellation is supposed to resemble the chair."

"Interesting. You seem to know a lot about constellations and Greek mythology."

"Not really, but I like the story behind Cassiopeia."

"Why? Because you think you're like her? You think you deserve to be punished for all eternity?"

I sit up. "Do all our conversations have to come back to that?"

"Until you deal with it, you won't be able to deal with *this*." He puts a hand on my stomach.

"What exactly do you want me to do, Aaron? I won't ever forget that Kasey is gone because of me. It's going to be with me my whole life."

"Of course it is. It's the same with me and Cameron. But you have to figure out a way to live with yourself in order to have a life."

"What if I can't?"

"You can. I promise."

I look away. "You want me to go see them, don't you?"

"Not them. Just her. Your mom."

"Even if I wanted to, which I don't, I have no idea where they live."

"I do."

My eyes snap to his. "How?"

"The internet can be a wonderful thing, Devyn."

"Oh, shut up."

"The first step is the hardest. Believe me, I know. I'll go with you. I'll be there every second. I promise I won't let anything happen to you."

"And if she won't see me? Will you let it go then?"

"Yes."

"Fine, but it won't be anything like the Marshalls. Then we'll be right back here."

"On the roof?" he jokes, pushing me down and climbing atop me.

"Aaron, how are we supposed to do this? How can we be together if you want this baby and I don't?"

"Give me a chance to convince you."

"Isn't that what you've been doing the last three weeks?"

He grazes my lips with his. "Move in with me."

I laugh and try to push him off. "Right. Like that's going to solve anything."

"It'll solve the problem of me wanting to have sex with my hot girlfriend and her not being right next to me, so I have to rub one out in the shower just thinking of her incredible eyes." He kisses me. "And her amazing breasts." He kisses me again. "And don't even get me started on her fantastic pus—"

"Aaron!" I cover his mouth.

"What? It's the truth. I love everything about you. And you know what? You love me, too. You may not say it much, but I see it in your eyes when you look at me. I feel it when we make love. Face it, Devyn DeMaggio."

"Ugh. Don't call me that."

He rolls off me, and I snuggle against him. "I'm thinking of changing my name. It's easy, right?"

"I think it's a great idea. Devyn Pearce has a nice ring to it, don't you think?"

My mouth hangs open. "I was talking about changing it to Dunlop."

"Dunlop, Pearce, what's the difference?"

"The difference is one makes me your wife."

"I was going to wait and propose some other time, but as long as you're offering."

"Oh my god. I'm not offering. Why are we even talking about this?"

"Because you're moving in with me and having my baby."

"I haven't agreed to any of that yet."

He pins me to the roof. "You will. I can be very convincing."

He runs his tongue down the edge of my neck. Tingles shoot throughout me. I want to protest, but I can't. I crave this. I crave him.

So I let him try to convince me. Over and over and over.

CHAPTER THIRTY-THREE

Aaron

I'm still wondering how I talked her into this. She's been silent the whole way. She doesn't want me to hold her hand. I didn't dare tell her about the gated community. I thought she might bail if she knew we had to lie our way inside. I had an idea, so I snuck into her room and got her ID, knowing she never brings her purse anywhere.

We approach the neighborhood, and Devyn tenses even more. "It's gated. We came all this way for nothing."

I hold out my hand and show her the ID.

She swipes it from me. "Why do you have this?"

"Because you're a DeMaggio, and they are your parents. I figured with him being who he is and all, they might live somewhere with security and this would come in handy."

"Turn the car around. I've changed my mind."

"We're already here, Dev. What can it hurt? Come on, give it to me."

Reluctantly, she hands it over. I pull the truck up to the guard shack and roll down the window. "We're going to the DeMaggio's," I say and tell him the address. I hand him her ID. "This is Devyn."

He takes her ID inside and looks at something. He returns and hands me the ID. "She's not on the list."

"She's been away at college. Hasn't been here since they moved in."

"If she's not on the list, she doesn't get in."

"Can't you cut her some slack? She wants to surprise her mom."

He looks at me like I'm stupid. "Son, the reason I'm here is because our residents don't like surprises. You can turn around up there before the gate."

I'm running out of ideas. This meeting needs to happen, because I'm not sure I'll ever get her to come back. "Call Mrs. DeMaggio, then."

"What?" Devyn squeals. "No. Do not call her."

"It's okay," I tell her and turn to the guard. "She just doesn't want to ruin the surprise. Call her please."

"Why are you doing this?" she whispers through gritted teeth.

"If she doesn't let us in, we'll go home."

The security guard calls. I can't hear what he's saying, but he eyes me suspiciously as he speaks with her. He hangs up, does something on his computer, and hands me a piece of paper. "Display this on your dashboard." Then he opens the gate.

I try not to smile too much. This is only step one of about a hundred that lead to what Devyn needs, but it's a big first one.

I drive down the street, around the corner, and into the driveway of a house that looks like, well, like a congressman lives here. "Wow," I say, not wanting her to know I've been here before.

"I think I'm going to be sick."

I take her hand. She lets me this time. "This may be the hardest thing you ever do, but you'll feel better after."

"How can you possibly know that? What if she's only seeing me so she can yell at me? You have no idea if she'll forgive me."

"This isn't about that."

"Then why are we here?"

The front door opens, and her mom appears. She looks impatient, like she's waiting for a bus.

I get out and go around to open Devyn's door. "You can do this."

Walking to the front porch feels like escorting Devyn to her version of the fiery pits of hell. She hesitates with every step, pauses on every stair, but eventually, the two women are face-to-face.

Neither of them speak, so I do. "Mrs. DeMaggio, thanks for seeing us. I'm Aaron, Devyn's boyfriend."

"You move fast, don't you? Didn't you just get out of prison?"

"It was jail," I say. "And she's been out for several months."

Roseanne goes back inside but leaves the door open. I take it as an invitation and urge Devyn to follow.

Roseanne sits at the kitchen bar, smoking a cigarette. She doesn't ask us to sit, so we don't. This is the most awkward situation I've ever been a part of. The tension is thick. Maybe it was a mistake to come.

Devyn stares at pictures on the wall. I recognize Kasey in some of them. I also see the other child, who was out in the yard when I was spying. What I don't see are any pictures of Devyn. It's like she's been completely erased from existence.

She plucks a picture of the other girl off the wall. "Who's this?"

"Kasey's sister."

It's not lost on either of us that she doesn't say *your* sister.

"You adopted her?" Devyn asks.

Roseanne takes a drag of her cigarette. "Duh."

"How old is she?"

"Five."

"When did you adopt her?"

"Earlier this year."

"Is she here?"

Roseanne shakes her head. "Day camp."

Devyn swallows. She's the same age Kasey was when she died. Devyn walks to the French doors and peers out back. I don't need to ask what she's looking for. I already know there's no pool.

She takes a deep breath and turns. "Why would you adopt another child if you didn't even want the first two you had?" Roseanne looks at Devyn in disgust.

I step forward. "She's very pretty. What's her name?"

"Julianne."

"I get it," Devyn says. "Ed is running for senate, and that's his MO. He can't win on his own, so he plays the adoption or sympathy card."

"Who are you to judge others, Devyn?" Roseanne gets off her barstool, opens a cabinet, and pours a few fingers of liquor into a heavy crystal glass. It's eleven in the morning.

"I'm just saying, why would you agree to another child? Who's taking care of her? Do you remember all the times Kasey crawled into my bed because you didn't come home on the nights he was away? Wait. Of course you don't remember, because you weren't there. How about all the nights you left me, young and alone, because you couldn't deal with what happened to Richard? I practically raised myself and then I raised Kasey."

"You dare judge me?" she says harshly. "I may be a shitty mother, but at least I never killed any of my children."

Tears well in Devyn's eyes. "I see you've replaced your meds with alcohol."

"One does what one has to do to get through the day."

"You smoke around Julianne?"

"What I do around my daughter is none of your business."

"Why did you let me in here today?"

"Curiosity."

"About what?"

"I wanted to see what prison did to you and if you were remorseful about what you did." She glances at me. "But I can see you're getting along fine. How convenient that you get to live a long and happy life while Kasey rots in her grave."

The tears fall. "Not a day goes by that I don't think of her. Not a second passes when I'm not punishing myself or wondering why I'm here and she isn't. You think I wanted her to die? You think I planned for it to happen? I was young and stupid and irresponsible. Yes, it was my fault. I take full responsibility, but don't think for a second I'm getting along fine, because nothing has ever been further from the truth."

Roseanne throws back her drink and gets another. Then she lights up again. "Well, good then."

"You really hate me, don't you?" Devyn asks.

"If I hated you, do you think I would have begged Dan Forsythe to let you keep your job at the grocery store? I knew when Ed kicked you out and your friends turned on you, you'd have nowhere to go. I even went to the bank once and withdrew a thousand dollars for you, but Ed found out and wouldn't let me give it to you. He wouldn't let me help you or see you. Said it would be bad for him politically."

"I lived in a motel," Devyn says. "Did you know that? I cooked on a hot plate and had roaches as roommates. The only job Dan would let me do was stock shelves overnight. He said people would get mad at him if they saw me cashiering. I spent almost all my paychecks on rent and most of what I had left went toward the fine I had to pay. I went to jail with two hundred fifty dollars. It lasted about two months. You know what I had to do to make money? Because yes, you need money in prison. I sold narcotics."

"Sounds about right. You did like your drugs."

"Pot. It was pot, Mom, and what teenager do you know that isn't smoking weed?"

"I'd prefer you not call me that."

Devyn heads for the door. "This is pointless. We should go."

"I agree," Roseanne says, blowing out smoke. "If Ed knew you were here, he'd probably call the police."

Devyn looks at the pictures on the wall once more. "You really shouldn't smoke in the house. It's bad for Julianne, and I'd hate for anything to happen to her."

Roseanne laughs. "One of my kids is dead and the other is a criminal. How much worse could it get?"

I escort Devyn the rest of the way out. Roseanne stands in the doorway to the kitchen.

Before we leave, Devyn turns. "At least I've learned from my mistakes." She glances at the drink and cigarette in her mother's hands. "It's too bad you haven't learned from yours. Goodbye, Roseanne."

Roseanne strides down the hallway and slams the door after us.

Devyn breaks away from me and runs to the bushes to throw up. I rush over and hold back her hair.

"I'm okay. I just need water."

"I've got a bottle in the truck."

We sit in the driveway for a minute while she drinks. She laughs sadly. "Didn't go exactly how you'd planned, did it? I told you she wouldn't forgive me."

"You think this was about her forgiving you? Didn't you listen to what Mrs. Marshall said? You don't need your mother to forgive you, Dev."

"Then why did you even bring me here?"

"Because there's a process to learning to accept yourself. Tying up loose ends is part of that process. Maybe then you can finally forgive yourself. If you do, you'll find what you're looking for."

"What's that?"

"Peace."

She looks at the house. "Coming here was hardly peaceful."

"Maybe not, but it was necessary."

I back out of the driveway. When we exit the neighborhood, I turn in the opposite direction from home.

"Where are we going now? I'm not in the mood for food."

"We're not going to lunch."

"Then where?"

"You'll see."

"Aaron, just tell me."

"This is the last time I'll do this. I promise."

Twenty minutes later, I pull into a cemetery. Her face softens. "You're going to see Cameron?"

If I can get her there, it might make all the difference.

I park, and we get out. She hooks an arm around my elbow, thinking she's supporting me. I hope she doesn't hate me when she finds out it's the other way around.

We swerve between graves until I find it, then stop. "Not Cameron."

Devyn sees Kasey's name and drops to her knees. She places her palms on the headstone and sobs. I've never seen her like this, heaving and hiccupping. I want to put my arms around her, but she has to go through this. She talks to Kasey, telling her how much she loves her and how sorry she is. When she finally calms, I join her on the ground and take her in my arms.

"I wanted to come see her after my release, but I didn't know where she was. They didn't let me go to the funeral. I didn't know how to find her. How did you?"

"The—"

"Internet is an incredible thing," she says.

We're suddenly laughing. Her mascara is smeared, her eyes are puffy, but she's the most beautiful woman I've ever laid eyes on.

"I apologize. I didn't mean to interrupt," a woman to our right says.

We get up. "You're not," I say.

She's standing on the grave next to Kasey's. "Is she your daughter?"

Devyn shakes her head. "Sister."

The woman looks at the other gravestone. "Timmy's my son."

Both of us read the words on the marker. He was only three when he died. He's been gone about four months. "I'm so sorry," I say.

"The first time I was here after the funeral, I saw Kasey's grave. It's silly, I know, but somehow I feel like she's with him, protecting him, being a big sister to him. I imagine them playing hide-and-seek."

Devyn smiles sadly. "Kasey loved hide-and-seek."

"So did Timmy. I'm Janice, by the way."

"Devyn," she says. "And this is Aaron."

"Will you tell me about Kasey? What does she look like? How did she act? I mean, if it's not too hard for you. I'd like to put a face and a personality to her."

Devyn looks at Kasey's grave and starts talking. "She had blonde hair. It was super curly, and it bounced when she ran. Sometimes I'd twist her curls with my fingers. She loved it when I played with her hair. Her eyes were brown, not dark like chocolate but light like sand. She loved video games. She sometimes crawled into bed with me at night, and we'd play them. I was a teenager then, but she was my best friend, even though I was fourteen years older than her." Devyn smiles. "She squealed when she was happy, like if she saw a butterfly or a puppy licked her face. I swear I can still hear that sound. Oh, and she loved mashed potatoes. She had to have them with everything, even hamburgers."

Janice steps over and hugs Devyn. "Thank you. You have no idea what that means to me."

Devyn says to me, "I'm ready to go now." We're a few steps away when she glances back. "Why did you put that there?" she asks Janice.

A Reese's Peanut Butter Cup is on Timmy's gravestone.

"In my dream, he said he wanted one. That's strange, because he never liked peanut butter."

Tears stream from Devyn's eyes. "Those were Kasey's favorite candy."

"Oh my god," Janice says, her voice cracking.

The women stride toward each other, embrace, and cry. But for the first time today, Devyn's tears might be tears of happiness.

CHAPTER THIRTY-FOUR

Devyn

"Great job today, Devyn," Mickey says. "Really top notch."

"I've got a great teacher."

"Same time tomorrow?"

"There are guests coming to the lodge today. I'll have to clean when they're out with Luca in the morning. Can I squeeze in an hour or so in the afternoon?"

"Sure. Come find me." He starts to leave, then stops. "Don't get too attached to your job at the lodge. I have my eye on you as an assistant trainer. Won't be long before you're qualified."

Excitement courses through me. "Are you serious?"

He winks and walks away.

Aaron swears Maddox and his dad won't have an issue with my record. Although I'm terrified of anyone finding out about me, it's bound to happen sooner or later, and I'll need a job that pays actual money.

"Hey, Devyn," Owen says, exiting one of the stables. "If you're not busy, there's something back here you might want to see."

I cross the yard and follow him into the north stable. He takes me to a vacant stall filled with fresh straw. A few ranch hands are gathered around. Andie runs up behind us. "Did she have them yet?"

I look into the stall, not knowing what the fuss is. "What's going on?"

"Sassy is about to have her litter."

"Sassy?"

Andie pulls me up near the gate and points to a corner where there's a blanket on the straw and a cat on the blanket. A very pregnant cat. "She's a barn cat."

I step next to Owen, suspicious. "Why did you think I'd want to see this?"

"Don't all girls love this shit? Makes you feel all maternal or somethin'?"

He doesn't know. Aaron kept our secret after all.

Andie opens the gate and tugs on my elbow. "Let's get closer. We'll stand against the wall and watch. Have you ever seen an animal give birth?"

I shake my head.

"It's amazing, especially when they have multiples. I'm not sure how many Sassy has in there. She isn't one to let people handle her, but the typical litter is four to six."

"How does she handle them all?"

"Some species are better equipped than others. After having just the one, I have the greatest respect for animals that have litters. I'm not sure what I'd do if I'd had four to six Vivians." She laughs.

"If she won't let people touch her, how did you get her on the blanket?"

"It wasn't hard. I knew she was close by the way she was acting, and this stable is her territory. I laid some blankets in a few empty stalls, and she picked this one. They want a quiet, soft, safe place to have their babies. Look, here comes the first one."

Sassy is on her side. Her stomach is clearly contracting. She keeps licking herself down there, then a yellow blob plops out. Sassy aggressively licks the new kitten.

"She has to break open the sac and stimulate their breathing," she says. "Then she'll chew off the umbilical cord."

Another kitten follows a few minutes later, then three more. Five kittens in all. "Has she had kittens before?"

"This is her first litter."

"So how did she know to lick the sac off them or they wouldn't be able to breathe?"

"Instinct. It's like when I had Vivian. I'd never been around babies much. I was terrified of holding her. I was convinced I'd drop her, and I actually thought she might break. But none of those things happened. I just knew how to hold her. And she had her own instincts. She latched on and fed almost immediately." She glances at Sassy and her kittens. "Isn't nature the most incredible thing?"

An hour later, everyone has long gone, but I'm still here. I can't stop staring at the barn cat and her babies. It's awe-inspiring. It's inspirational. It's—I look down and realize my hand is on my belly. I'm fourteen weeks pregnant, and it's the first time I've unintentionally touched my tiny bump.

My phone pings with a text.

**Aaron: The guests have gone into Fort Worth.
Lots of supper leftover. Join me and Joe?**

Me: At the stable. Be there in twenty. :-)

I sent a smiley face. I don't think I've ever done that. Not since… *before.* I look at Sassy and smile.

Incredible smells bombard me when I enter the lodge kitchen. "What's for supper?" I ask Joe.

"Hope you like beef stew."

I try not to turn up my nose. I don't tell him that I hope it's better than the stew we ate once a week in jail. I doubt what we were served was even real meat. "Sounds good," I say, vowing to choke it down with a smile.

Turns out I don't have to pretend. It's one of the best meals I've eaten. Joe has a way of taking ordinary food and turning it into a masterpiece.

"You look different," he says, pointing his fork at me. "Somethin's changed."

Aaron and I share a glance.

Joe chuckles. "Ah, young love. It's 'bout time you two gave in to it. Been seeing you sneak around for months now. You ain't foolin' no one. But it's more than that, ain't it? Seems a weight has been lifted. This whole damn room feels lighter."

Joe has been a good friend to me. A father, even. I can't believe what I'm going to say, but before I have time to think about it, I blurt, "I had a sister once." Aaron gives my thigh an encouraging squeeze. "She died because of something I did, and I went to jail for a few years. That's how I ended up here."

Joe listens intently as I tell him my story. Then he picks up our dishes, puts them in the sink, and stands with his back to us for a good minute. He's probably wondering what to say to me. Maybe he's wondering if we can still be friends. Aaron and I glance at each other. I shrug.

"Cameron was my best friend," Aaron says. "He's dead because of me."

Joe finally turns, blank-faced. He lets Aaron tell his story as well. Then he leaves the room.

"Do you think he hates us now?" I ask.

"He doesn't hate us. It's just a lot to process. I'm really proud of you, Devyn. That had to be hard for you."

"Same for you. I know you haven't told many people."

"I told my parents last month."

"What did they say?"

"That I should have said something sooner, like back when it happened. They're coming here next week for a visit."

"How come you didn't say anything?"

"I only found out today. They had to move some things around on their schedule."

"Do they know about me?"

"Of course."

I sigh and look at the floor.

"I mean, yeah, they know I have this great girl I'm head over heels in love with, but that's all."

I bite my lip, then smile. "Head over heels?"

He leans over and kisses my cheek. "Since the day you punched me."

Joe returns, sits at the table, pulls out his flask, takes a drink, then swallows. "My platoon died because of me."

I can feel it hit Aaron with the same intensity it hits me. "Oh, Joe," I say.

"Rule number one was don't tell anyone where base camp was. Don't tell no one about where we're goin' or what our mission was. I'd been in Vietnam for about ten months. We were surrounded by our brothers, but it was still lonely. We'd go into town for female companionship. Most of the time, that's all it was. Then I met Mai Le. She was the most exotic beauty. Petite, spunky, and had the most incredible chocolate-brown eyes I'd ever seen." He closes his eyes, and I know he's seeing her. "She wasn't just my Friday night gal. We were in love. I asked her to marry me. When she said yes, I was so excited I brought her back to camp to tell everyone. They gave me shit about it—warned me she could be with the Viet Cong and ridiculed me for being so gullible. But she was the one, I was sure of it. A few days later, she took me to see her parents so I could officially ask for her hand. They agreed, happy Mai was going back to the states with me. Later that night, when I returned to camp, my whole platoon was dead. They'd raided it and shot every single one of my brothers."

"Oh, no," Aaron says. "Mai?"

He shakes his head. "I thought she betrayed me, but shortly after I arrived, she searched me out. As soon as she saw their lifeless bodies scattered around camp, she broke down, confessing she had told her brother about us, but she didn't know he was the enemy until he came home gloating about the American soldiers he and his friends killed. Then…" He clears the frog in his throat. "Then Mai picked up a gun and shot herself in the chest."

My hand flies to my mouth to cover my gasp.

"Jesus, Joe," Aaron says, shaking his head.

"My friends, my brothers, were gone, and so was my love. So I picked up the gun she'd used, turned it on myself, and pulled the trigger. Days later, I woke up in a hospital in Japan. The bullet went clear through my eyeball and out the side of my head, missin' anything that would have killed me. They done gave me an honorable discharge and sent me home." He takes a long drink. "I never told no one it was my fault. Never told a soul I turned the gun on myself. Everyone thought I was the sole survivor of an ambush. The two of you are the only ones who know diff'rent."

"That's a lot to carry around for fifty-something years," Aaron says. "How old were you?"

"Nineteen."

"So was I," Aaron says.

I swallow hard. "Me, too."

Joe takes another drink. "We're quite the trio, ain't we?"

I touch his hand. "Are you okay?"

"All this time, I thought tellin' folks would make me feel worse about it. But you were the right folks to tell, 'cause you could knock me over with a feather, but I feel a sense of relief."

"I'll let you in on a secret," I say. "I do too."

"There's only one thing left to do, then," Joe says.

"What's that?"

He gets up, opens a drawer, and pulls out a deck of cards.

CHAPTER THIRTY-FIVE

Aaron

Mom pulls me close for a hug. "How I've missed you. You know you can tell us anything. *Anything*, Aaron."

"I couldn't talk about Cameron until recently."

"Does a certain someone have something to do with that?"

I smile and toss their bags in the truck.

Dad pats me on the back. "When do we get to meet her?"

"She'll be at the lodge when we get there."

"Tell me how you met," Mom asks.

I should have been expecting this question. This is my mom we're talking about. She's going to want details, but I promised Devyn I'd keep her secrets. "She was down on her luck, needed a job, and the lodge needed a housekeeper. You could say we found each other at a time when we both needed something. But she's so much more than a housekeeper. She's been working with Mickey, our head horse trainer. He thinks she's great. Says he'll even offer her a job as soon as she's ready. And she has great ideas on how to increase business at the lodge."

"Sounds like she's got a good head on her shoulders," Dad says.

"She does, but she's very private. She has a damaged past. Probably best not to bombard her with uncomfortable questions."

For the rest of the drive, I tell them about Devyn's helicopter tour idea and how Quinn says he's going to become a pilot.

When we pull up at the lodge, Dad looks over at my cabin. "Doing some remodeling?"

"I'm adding more rooms."

He grins wryly. "Expecting company?"

"Hopefully."

He laughs. "How about you introduce me to your girl and then take me over to see Maddox?"

I help unload their bags and escort them to our best guest suite. As luck has it (or not), we don't have any guests for the next ten days.

Mom takes it all in as I walk them to their room. "I can't believe what you've done with the place since we saw it last."

Dad grips my shoulder. "It's come a long way since you and I started fixing it up eight years ago."

"Just wait," I say. "In another few years, we'll be one of the premier ranch destinations."

"I don't doubt it for a second."

We're heading back downstairs when Devyn strolls into the grand hall from the kitchen. She sees us and immediately pulls her shirt away from her stomach. She does that a lot lately, but there's nothing to see yet. I'm the only one who knows it's there.

"Hey! How was your morning?"

"Great, as usual."

Mom steps around me. "You must be Devyn. Aaron has told us so much about you. He did fail to tell me how beautiful you are, though."

Devyn blushes. "Thank you, Mrs. Pearce."

"I'm Skylar, and this is Griffin. Please call us by our first names."

"So nice to meet you."

Dad shakes her hand. "And you. Aaron tells us you've taken to the horses and you have great plans for the lodge."

"I don't know about the great plans, but he's right about the horses."

"You'll tell us more over dinner, I hope. Our treat. I thought we'd go to Del Frisco's. We'll bring Maddox and Andie."

"Dad, you have to make a reservation. No way we'll be able to get in."

"You forget Mom is a fellow restaurateur, my boy. Leave it to us."

I might as well let them spoil us. They get to do it so rarely.

"Speaking of food," Devyn says. "I picked up sandwiches. I thought you might be hungry after your flight."

Mom puts an arm around her. "How very thoughtful of you. I'm starving. Lead the way."

In the kitchen, I see the spread Devyn has laid out on the counter and pull her aside. "How did you do all this?"

"Andie let me borrow her truck."

I can't hide my smile. "Trying to impress my parents?" I whisper.

She shrugs. "I'm not *not* trying."

"They're going to love you. Don't worry."

Dad asks Devyn about the horses. She happily tells him what Mickey has been teaching her. He probably has no idea what she's talking about, as he doesn't know one end of a horse from the other, but he hangs on her every word.

It's nice to see her so excited about things. Joe was right last week when he said something was different about her.

After lunch, I clean up and put away the leftovers. "Devyn, I'm going to run Dad over to the main ranch. Would you mind giving Mom a tour of the lodge? I'm sure she's going to want to see the new prints I had made for some of the guest rooms. Oh, and Mom, be sure to look at the towels and pillows—you'll see Devyn's handiwork."

"I'll be glad to give you a tour," Devyn says.

Mom locks elbows with her. "Where should we begin?" They stroll away.

Dad elbows me. "So she's the one, huh?"

I nod. "She's the one."

CHAPTER THIRTY-SIX

Devyn

Skylar looks at one of the pillows I embroidered. "This is fabulous. Where did you learn how to do this?"

"I, uh… taught myself."

"It appears you have many talents."

"Thank you." We leave the last guest suite. "That does it for up here."

She stops at a door. "What's in here?"

"The attic."

"Is it big?"

"Very."

"Show me. Attics sometimes have the most character of any building."

"Okay." I open the door and lead her up, trying to remember if I left any evidence of my having lived up there.

At the top of the stairs, she glances around. "This is amazing." She runs a finger along the top edge of one of the large portraits stored here. "I'm glad Aaron didn't throw these away. I'll bet this man was the original owner or something. There's probably a lot of history up here."

She has no idea just how much.

She strolls around, peering out each window, taking it all in. "You can see Aaron's cabin from this one."

I peek around her as if this is news to me. "I guess you can."

"Oh, wow, this window is fabulous," she says. "If I'd lived here as a kid, you can bet I would have sneaked out this one to lay under the stars."

I have to bite my tongue and hide my smile. Then something on the floor catches my attention. It's an old condom wrapper. I nonchalantly shuffle over and kick it behind the bookshelf. Skylar pretends she doesn't see, but I catch her grin.

"You two should do something with this. There's so much space."

"I'm not sure what we'd do with it."

"You'll think of something, I'm sure."

I catch my foot on the edge of the bookcase and almost fall. Might not be as embarrassing as the condom wrapper, but I don't need Skylar thinking I'm a slut *and* a klutz.

We go back downstairs and tour the grand hall, the sitting room, the living room, and the office. Back in the kitchen, she asks, "What's down this hall?"

"My room. Do you want to see it?"

"The tour wouldn't be complete without it."

Thankful I made my bed and tidied up this morning, I step into my room, and she follows. She glances at a string of lights I recently hung. "I like it." She admires the old sewing machine and then goes to my nightstand and picks up the book on constellations. "You're a fellow admirer of stars. You've been out the window, haven't you?"

I nod. "It's why I hung the lights. Makes it seem like I'm outside when I can't be."

"Speaking of outside, how about you show me the grounds? We have time before the guys return."

"We don't have any horses here."

She laughs. "Oh, Lord. I don't think I could even get up on one. I meant let's go for a short walk, if that's okay with you."

We go outside, past Aaron's cabin to the start of one of the trails. She tells me about her restaurant and her daughter, Gracie, who's nineteen years old and going to NYU. *Nineteen.* I think of all the horrible things that happened when Aaron, Joe, and I were that age. I pray Gracie has a much better year.

I find it interesting, however, that Skylar doesn't ask me many personal questions. No prodding me about what my parents do or if I have any siblings. No quizzing me about my childhood or where I grew up. Not a single question about what I did before I set foot on the ranch, other than asking about my sewing skills.

Aaron must have told them something to keep her from asking; but what and how much?

We stop at a place where we can see one of the pastures, where a few mares graze while their new foals play.

"Look at that," she says. "How old are those baby horses?"

I point. "That one is a month old. His name is Coconut. And the filly over there is Milly Mouse."

"Funny names for horses."

"Those are their nicknames. Their papered names are Sir Coco Del Naught and Millisandra Mousilini."

"Papered?" She laughs. "I won't even pretend to know what that means. It must be amazing to see them give birth. Have you been able to watch?"

I shake my head.

She leans against the fence post. "You haven't had the opportunity? Or you haven't wanted to, considering your condition?"

I tense. "My… what?"

She glances at my belly. "When are you due?"

My heart lodges in my throat. "I, uh—"

An arm goes around me. "Don't worry. Aaron didn't spill the beans, but I can tell."

"H-how?"

"Subtle things. The way you keep tugging at your shirt because you think someone will notice your bump. The three extra pickles you had with your sandwich. The way you protectively held your belly when you tripped over the rug upstairs."

I don't know what to say.

"Your secret is safe with me, Devyn. You're not telling people. I get it. You want to wait until you're further along."

"You must think I'm a terrible person."

"Ha! Like I'm one to judge."

"Then can I tell you something?"

"Anything."

"I'm not one hundred percent sure I can do this. I'm not ready. I'm only twenty-two, and there are other reasons I shouldn't be a mom."

"Has Aaron told you the story of how he was conceived? And about his guardian angel, Erin?"

"He has."

"Then you know I didn't want to be a mother. I was a party girl. A businesswoman. I had no desire or inclination to have a child. I didn't know one thing about it. I only wanted to do something good for someone. Heck, it was practically a dare from my friends."

"So how did you know you could handle it?"

"One day, my sister, Baylor, came over and told me she was in a bind, and I had to watch her newborn, Jordan. It was only for a little while, she said. The big fat liar left Jordan with me for the entire day." She laughs. "I didn't know a baby could eat and poop so much. It was horrible. I was sure I was going to drop her or step on her or feed her too much or too little, or put her on her stomach when she was supposed to be on her back. I'd never been so exhausted or so mad at anyone before."

"Uh… okay."

"I thanked her later, but it took me a while to bond with my unborn child. I went months thinking I was just the incubator, and then I had to start seeing him as mine. It was a huge adjustment." She scans our surroundings. "And now look at him. He's living here, loving life. Loving *you*—I can tell. This may not be how you planned it, but sometimes life's best surprises come when you're least expecting them."

"Can I tell you something else?"

"Yes."

I take a deep breath and tell her about Kasey. For the second time in as many weeks, I'm letting someone see into the depths of my hell, this time a virtual stranger.

She takes me in her arms. "Don't you see? The two of you are meant for each other. You and Aaron are both hurting. You're both healing. This little one might be the key to all your future happiness."

I glance down. "How could it be? How can this not be some twisted cosmic joke?"

"Babies have a magical way of making your other problems disappear. Don't take this the wrong way. Having Aaron didn't make it okay that Erin died, and the sorrow of what happened to Kasey will never truly leave you, but someday, when you least expect it, this little one will smile or laugh or babble a word that will remind you of your sister. You'll realize it's a good memory, not a bad one. Life sometimes comes from death. I honor my friend, Erin, every day by loving my son. While this child will in no way replace the void in your life or the hole in your heart, he or she might make it smaller."

I wipe away a tear. "It's so nice to talk to someone. I'd never be able to talk to my mother about this."

She squeezes my hand. "You can talk to me anytime. I'm only a phone call away."

"Thank you for being so understanding and not hating me."

"How could I ever hate the woman my son loves? Not to mention the mother of my grandbaby. I'm not afraid to tell you that Griffin and I will spoil the hell out of him or her." She pauses. "Will you find out if it's a boy or girl?"

"Tomorrow, actually."

"Come on." She pulls me in the direction of the lodge. "I'll tell you about the day we found out Aaron was a boy."

Twenty minutes later, we're back at the lodge. Skylar gazes at a large arrangement of flowers in the grand foyer, then pulls two from the bouquet. She extends her arms, holding a rose in one hand and a lily in the other. "Pick one."

I go for the lily. It was the first flower Aaron ever bought me. Actually, they are the only flowers he ever buys me.

Skylar smiles. She smiles big.

"What?" I ask. "Is this supposed to mean something?"

"Go look it up," she says and walks away humming.

CHAPTER THIRTY-SEVEN

Aaron

"Are you nervous?" I ask on the way into the doctor's office.

"Stupid question, Aaron. Yes, I'm nervous."

"Why?"

"Because there's this thing growing inside me that you think I'm going to immediately fall in love with when I see it on the computer screen, but I won't and then you'll be disappointed and have to ask yourself what kind of woman isn't happy about having a baby and if I'm who you want to be with if I can't get on board with it."

"Wow. You've really thought about this a lot. I was thinking you'd be nervous to see if the kid has the appropriate number of limbs and stuff."

We check in and take a seat. I pick up a parenting magazine and flip through it.

"Your mom thinks it's a boy," she whispers in the crowded room.

"She does?"

"Something about flowers and an old wives' tale."

"I still can't believe you told her."

"I didn't tell her, she guessed."

"Yeah, but you could have denied it."

She laughs quietly. "I get the feeling your mom isn't easily denied."

"She does have that way about her."

"She was so understanding about everything."

"Everything?"

"I told her about Kasey. Jail. All of it."

I close the magazine and stare at her in utter surprise. "You did?"

"Uh-huh."

"I'm happy you felt comfortable enough with her to share your story. How did she take it?"

"She talked about Erin and not wanting a child. It's nothing you hadn't told me before, but it was different coming from her."

"You're bonding over the whole 'I don't want a baby' thing."

She leans back. "It's not that I don't want a baby, Aaron. It's that I question my ability to be a good mother."

I put my arm around her. "I don't question it at all. I see the way you are with the horses. You're patient and gentle and kind."

"They're horses. It's different."

"I don't think it is. You're a nurturer. You have been your whole life."

"Dunlop," a lady calls from the doorway.

I lean over. "She could be calling Pearce. Just sayin'."

Devyn rolls her eyes and stands. "Can he come?" she asks.

"Is he the father?"

"Yes."

Father. It's the first time I've heard it said out loud. For almost two months, I've thought it. I've dreamed about it. Setting up a swing set behind the cabin and pushing my little boy as he squeals, "Higher, Daddy!" Teaching my little girl how to ride a horse. I can hear a sweet voice in my head: "Giddyup, horsey." A father is never something I thought I'd be at twenty-three, but now I can't imagine any other scenario. I follow Devyn through the door—I definitely can't imagine a scenario without her.

I stand aside while they take her weight and blood pressure, then we're led to a room. "No need to undress," the woman says. "You can lie down here." She hands Devyn a blue paper sheet. "Unbutton your pants and tuck this in the waistband so you won't get any gel on your clothes. The ultrasound tech will be in shortly."

I pace the room while we wait. Maybe I'm nervous after all. I look at all the tech equipment. I see something and laugh. I pick up a steel dildo on a cord. "What the hell is this?"

She giggles as I examine it. "They used that for the first ultrasound. The baby was too small to see any other way."

"This was inside you?"

"Not this one, but one like it."

I shift my stance. "I gotta say, I'm turned on a little thinking about it."

"You're terrible."

"I'm sorry if the thought of my girl using a dildo makes me hard."

She glances at my crotch. "You can't be serious."

I shrug. "A little bit."

She blushes. "Aaron, think of something else."

"You're lying down, pants unbuttoned, shirt pulled up. Fat chance."

There's a knock on the door and someone opens it. "Oh, shit." I quickly pull over a chair and sit down next to Devyn. She's trying not to laugh.

"Hello," the tech says. "You must be Mr. and Mrs.—" She glances at the chart.

"Not Mr. and Mrs.," I say. I take Devyn's hand. "Not yet anyway."

"Let's get started," she says, holding up a bottle of gel. "This might be a bit cold." She squirts it on Devyn's lower tummy and then puts a flat wand on it, moving it around and doing things on her keyboard at the same time.

"What exactly are you looking for?" I ask.

"I'm examining all the organs and taking measurements."

"Does everything seem okay?"

"So far, so good. No visible heart defects. Looks to be around twelve centimeters. That's about the size of an—"

"Orange," I say.

"You're right. But they grow quickly. This little one will double in size in three more weeks."

"Double?" Devyn says, rising on her elbows. "I'll be huge."

"Have you felt any movement yet?" the tech asks.

"No," Devyn says. "Is that bad?"

"You're about seventeen weeks. First-time moms usually feel them later than women who've been pregnant before. It will be any day now." She hits a button on the computer and sound comes through a speaker.

Emotions I've never felt before bombard me as I hear my baby's heartbeat for the first time. "That's… oh my god, that's incredible."

The tech nods. "It is. Nothing short of a miracle."

Devyn is shaking. Is she freaking out? She looks at me, crying. I lean down and kiss her forehead. "Everything is going to be okay."

She shakes her head. "It's not that. I'm good. I was just thinking. If… if it's a girl, would it be morbid to call her Kasey?"

For the second time in a minute, my heart swells so big, I fear it will burst from my chest. Suddenly I'm crying right along with her. "That would be a great way to honor her." I sniff. "You know the name works for a boy, too."

"Oh, gosh, you're right, just like they named you after Erin."

"Casey with a *C*," I say. "Or with a *K* for a girl."

The tech clears her throat. I imagine she's used to emotional outbreaks like ours. "I take it you'd like to find out the sex, then?"

Devyn's eyes light up. "You know it?"

She smiles. "I do."

Devyn and I look at each other and nod excitedly. "Yes, please," I say to the tech.

"Well then, congratulations. It appears you're going to have a Casey with a *C*."

My throat clogs with more emotions. "It's a boy?"

She points to the screen. "Here's the evidence."

I squeeze Devyn's hand tightly. "It's a boy."

She nods, eyes closed, tears rolling down her cheeks.

"Are you okay?"

She sniffs. "I was hoping for a boy."

Of course she was. A girl would be too much of a reminder. "Are you sure you want to name him Casey?"

"Not just Casey," she says. "Casey Cameron."

Now I'm crying like a baby. I kiss her. "Do you know how much I fucking love you right now?"

"I love you, too."

It's only the second time she's said the words, but it's the first time I let them sink in, even though we have an audience. I glance at the screen, wondering if we just became a family.

The tech grins and points. "It looks like he's sucking his thumb."

I grab my phone and take a picture.

"No need," she says. "I have a shot of it, and I'll print it out for you. The whole ultrasound will be on a flash drive. You can take it with you and watch it anytime. Sit tight, and we'll be done in a sec."

Devyn's eyes are glued to the monitor. The baby moves, and she takes a breath. Then she squeezes my hand. "You were right. I'm in love with him. And I'm in love with you."

This might be the single best moment of my entire life. I stroke her hair. "How soon can you move in?"

On the drive home, Devyn can't stop staring at the pictures. She traces his tiny head. "I can do this, right?"

"*We* can do this."

"Are you excited?"

"I've never been happier."

"I never thought I would be joyful again, but now…" She sighs and gazes out the window. "Do you think it's okay for us to feel like this?"

"They would have wanted it. I know it."

"Are you really okay with calling him Casey?"

"I wouldn't have it any other way. Are you okay with giving him my last name?"

She studies the photo. "Casey Cameron Pearce." She smiles. "I like it."

"And how are you feeling about me giving *you* my last name?"

"One thing at a time, cowboy. I haven't even moved in yet."

"Yet? Does that mean you will?"

"We are having a baby and all." She laughs. "But it occurs to me we should probably go on an actual date."

"We went to dinner with my parents last night."

"Doesn't count."

"Hm. It can't be any old date. It has to be epic. Give me some time to put something together."

"You don't have to wine and dine me. I'm pretty much a sure thing."

I reach over and rub her bump, something I haven't done until today but that I plan on doing as often as possible. "Can we tell people now? You can't hide this much longer."

"Okay."

I'm surprised. "For real?"

She nods.

At a stoplight, I pick up my phone and call Maddox. "Dude, get Andie and meet us at the lodge in ten. Make sure my parents are there. It's really important." I hang up and dial again. "Quinn, go to the lodge pronto. See you shortly."

"You meant right *now*?" Devyn asks.

"I'm bursting at the seams, Dev. I'm going to be a father. I want to scream it from the rooftop."

Quinn and Maddox's trucks are there when we arrive. I run around and help Devyn out. We hold hands as we enter the lodge. Everyone is standing around in the kitchen. Mom is the only one with a smile. Nobody else knows anything about anything.

I look at Devyn. "Do you want to?"

"You do it."

I put my hand on her belly. "We're having a baby, and it's a boy!"

Jaws hit the floor. Mom hugs us, then Dad. Finally, Quinn, Maddox, and Andie join in the jubilation, and congratulations are offered by all.

"Let's see the bump," Andie says.

Devyn flattens her shirt against her body. She looks proud. What a change from just twenty-four hours ago.

"Eeeek!" Andie squeals. "When's the big day?"

"February fourth."

The women fawn over the ultrasound photos.

Dad pats me on the back. "You know, Griffin is a strong name for a boy."

I laugh. "Maybe the next one." When Devyn turns green at my remark, I wink at her. "We've already picked a name. Everyone"—I put an arm around her and place my other hand on her abdomen—"meet Casey Cameron."

Dad raises his eyebrows at Devyn. "A family name?"

We share a look. "Yes."

Mom touches Devyn's arm. I have a feeling she's taken it upon herself to be a stand-in for Roseanne.

"What a lovely way to honor your friend, son. He would like that."

"I hope so."

The back door opens, and Lora comes in. She looks at all the beaming faces. "Did I miss the party?"

"Kind of," Andie says. She holds out one of the ultrasound pictures to Lora.

Lora takes it and smiles. "Oh, you're having another baby?"

"Not me. Devyn. They just found out it's a boy."

Lora pales. It's like she got hit by a stun gun. She quickly tries to recover. "Uh, well, congratulations." She shoves the picture at Andie and turns to leave. "I forgot something in the car."

"What was that about?" Mom asks. "The woman looked utterly shaken."

"That was about her hopes and dreams being crushed," Quinn says. "Lora has been after Aaron since the day she set foot on Devil's Horn Ranch."

"Oh, the poor girl."

I wave it off. "She'll get over it."

"I don't know," Dad says. "We Pearce men are kind of unforgettable."

Mom swats him on the back of the head, and we all laugh and then they kiss. "Okay, your father may have a point."

I pull Devyn into my arms. "What about you? Do you think we're unforgettable?"

"Definitely. What was your name again?"

CHAPTER THIRTY-EIGHT

Devyn

I wake up feeling strange. The slight queasiness I felt early on has long since gone. In fact, for being twenty weeks pregnant, I feel I've done pretty well. I've only gained eight pounds. I never really had morning sickness. I'm just now to the point of needing new clothes. The main side effect of all this is how horny I've been. Like all the time horny. When I ride a horse—horny. When I go over bumpy roads in the truck—horny. I turn and stare at Aaron— you guessed it.

I love watching him sleep. Usually, he's up before I am—at the crack of dawn. But since I moved in, he's been sleeping better. There's a calmness about him I've never seen. It gives me hope that everything really will be all right.

I feel strange again, like I'm having gas bubbles or a nervous twitch. I gasp when I realize what's happening. Casey must be moving. I still completely, hand on stomach, not wanting to speak or move a muscle, and wait for it to happen again. When it does, I can't help shedding happy tears. I lie here and revel in the amazing feeling of my child tumbling inside me.

"I've never seen you look more beautiful," Aaron says.

"He's moving. Casey is moving."

"I know. I've been watching you." He sidles up next to me and puts his hand over mine. "Where is it?"

"It's hard to say really. Just an allover feeling. It's so subtle that I almost didn't feel it."

He moves his hand from place to place, stopping and waiting.

"Can you feel anything?"

"No."

"I'm sure you will soon. The book says it will take other people longer to feel it."

His eyebrows shoot up. "The book?"

"I may have started reading *What to Expect When You're Expecting*."

He traps me underneath him. "Enjoying your reading cave, huh?"

My old bedroom in the lodge has become my private getaway until the addition in the cabin is finished. I read there. I sew. Occasionally, I even nap. I keep an ultrasound picture in a frame on the nightstand and sometimes stare at it for hours.

I wiggle my hips. "I'm enjoying *everything*."

My alarm sounds, and I silence it.

"Don't you have to meet Andie?"

"I do. I also have to pick up something from the lodge first." I giggle. "Guess I'll be a few minutes late."

He smiles as his lips claim mine.

"I'm jealous," Andie says, perusing a rack of maternity clothes. "I needed these way earlier than you do."

"I've been living in elastic-waisted pants for three weeks. Either that, or I can't do up the buttons."

She pulls a cute top out and holds it up to me. "This will be so much fun." She adds it to the amassing pile I'm supposed to try on.

"I'm not going to need much; I'll only wear them for twenty more weeks. Seems like a waste of money."

"You'll probably have to wear them longer."

"Longer?"

She nods. "I hate to be the bearer of bad news, but your body won't deflate as soon as the baby comes out. If you're lucky, you'll be able to ditch the maternity clothes a month after he's born."

I swallow a bitter pill. "I'm still going to look pregnant?"

"And don't be surprised if strangers ask when you're due. That's the worst."

"Ew."

"It may not happen to you. You might fit into your clothes sooner than most. Don't worry about that now." She adds a pack of maternity underwear to the pile.

"I need underwear? Can't I just wear what I have? They can sit low under my belly."

She snickers. "Watching you get bigger is going to be entertaining." She holds up a pair of jeans with an elastic panel on the front. "These will fit in no time."

"Those must be for women much larger than I am."

She checks the tag. "These are exactly your size."

My mouth drops open. No way will I ever fit into those.

We pass a rack of bathing suits. Andie looks at me with sad eyes. "You have no idea how bad I feel about forcing you to go to the pool."

"It's my fault. I should have told you sooner."

"You were brave to tell us at all. Thank you for trusting Maddox and me."

"Thanks for not judging me."

Her arms come around me. "Like I said, we're family now."

"Technically, what will Casey be to you and Maddox. Second cousin?"

"He'll be Maddox's first cousin once removed. I googled it. But most people just call them a niece or nephew, and he'll call us aunt and uncle. Casey and Vivian will be second cousins."

"I think I have enough to try on now. I'll have to weed some out to fit my budget."

Andie pulls a credit card out of her pocket. "No, you won't. Aaron gave me this. Said he'd disown me if I let you pay. He wants you to get everything you need."

"But I have a bank account now."

She pushes me toward the dressing room. "Will you let the man spoil you? It's one of the perks of being pregnant."

"I get the idea he would spoil me even if I weren't."

She smiles. "That's because he's one of the good ones."

The associate unlocks a dressing room. I step inside and look around. "Someone left something in here."

"Those are padded bellies." She picks one up. "It says the size of the pads here. We have six through nine months. It helps you see how the clothes will fit."

When the lady leaves, Andie picks up the big one and straps it on. She admires herself in the mirror. "I miss being pregnant."

"Really? But Vivian is barely a year old."

She shrugs. "That's the perfect time to start on another one, don't you think? They'd be less than two years apart. The perfect age for playmates."

"What does Maddox think?"

"Are you kidding? He tossed the condoms two months ago. He'd have ten kids if I agreed to it. I could be pregnant right this second."

"I envy you. It must be nice to fall in love and marry and then plan to have a baby—one you were excited about from day one." I sit on the bench and sulk. "We've done everything completely out of order."

"Aaron would marry you tomorrow if you'd let him."

"I know. He tells me every day. I just want to make sure Casey isn't the only reason."

"Devyn, you're blind if you don't think he's crazy in love with you."

"I feel the same way about him." I strap one of the pads on. "But this in a wedding dress? No, thank you."

"We'll plan it for a few months after Casey comes. You'll have your rockin' body back then. We can do it in the indoor arena, like Maddox and I did. We'll hang lights and order flooring to cover the dirt. It'll be amazing."

I catch her eyes in the mirror. "You'll be my maid of honor?"

"Matron," she says. "Yes, I'd be honored."

"Don't be," I joke. "You're kind of my only friend."

We share a laugh.

"Before long, you'll have lots of friends. Remind me later, and I'll give you the name of the yoga place I go to. They have great pregnancy classes. You'll meet a ton of women there."

I check the time. "I should hurry. We have a full house at the lodge this week."

She exits the room and stands outside. "When are you going to let Aaron hire another housekeeper?"

"As soon as Mickey hires me as an assistant trainer. I'm not going to be dead weight around the ranch." I try on a shirt and am amused at the way it fits over the pregnancy pad. I open the door and show Andie.

Hands steeple over her nose and mouth. "You're glowing."

"Andie, please don't tell anyone what we talked about as far as the wedding and matron of honor stuff, okay?"

"It'll be our secret. You'll do it when the time is right."

"Devyn?"

I turn and see Jill Benson staring at my belly. "Uh, this isn't… It's a pillow… I mean, I am, but not this big." I'm not sure why I fumble my words. She was one of the few people at the jail who didn't intimidate me.

"My word, look at you." She comes closer and takes my hands, holding them out as she appraises me.

I pull a hand free and reach under the shirt to unstrap the pillow. "I'm not this big yet."

"You're having a baby? You look positively amazing."

I run a hand down my shirt so it outlines my small bump. "It's a boy." I turn to Andie. "Jill, this is my friend, Andie. Andie, this is Jill Benson. She was my caseworker."

Jill's eyes go wide. She's surprised I revealed our relationship.

"Nice to meet you, Jill."

"And you. I'm trying to find something for my granddaughter. She's expecting my first great-grandchild."

I'm surprised. "No way are you old enough to have a pregnant granddaughter."

"I'm flattered you would say so, but I'm seventy-one."

I admire her rich brown skin that shows signs of aging, but I'd have guessed she was pushing sixty. "Well, you're beautiful."

She brings my left hand up to examine it. "No ring. It may be none of my business, but I hope your little one's father isn't hanging you out to dry."

"He isn't. He wants to marry me."

Her eyes water. "Oh, sweet Lord above. I've thought about you a lot these past months. Of all my cases, yours hit me square in the pit of my stomach. You were so young when you were assigned to me, and what happened to you—simply heartbreaking. I thought you might self-destruct after leaving. Even after your call, I would lay awake some nights, wondering what became of you. The Lord is at work today, bringing me peace of mind by showing me that you're okay."

"I'm more than okay, Jill. How about you? How are you doing? Is there anyone special in your life?"

"When you're my age, you're lucky to get a spam caller to keep you company." She laughs. "Don't you worry about me. I got plenty of memories of my Gregory."

During one of our first meetings, she told me how hard it was after her husband passed away ten years prior. She was trying to make me feel better, and she was the only person who ever did. Not about what I'd done, or what I deserved, but she didn't treat me like a criminal.

"I can see you're busy," Jill says. "I'll go about my business. You still have my number?"

"I do."

"Please call me after the baby comes. I'd be most grateful to know how you and the little one are doing."

"Of course."

"And you'll come to the wedding?" Andie says. I elbow her.

"With bells on," Jill says. "Just tell me when." She kisses my cheek and goes on her way.

I smile. She was the first friend I made after I'd lost everything else. She was my only friend for two years. She made me feel something nobody else in jail ever did: human.

When we pull up to the cabin, there are two police cars parked to the side of the lodge.

"Oh, gosh. I hope one of the guests didn't have an accident."

"Let's go inside and see," Andie says, parking her truck. "Then I'll help you take your bags to the cabin."

We enter through the back door. Three police officers and Lora are standing by the kitchen table.

"Devyn DeMaggio?" one asks.

Lora points at me. "That's her."

An officer steps toward me. "Ms. DeMaggio, you're under arrest for grand larceny. Turn around, please."

My heart sinks. Larceny—that's stealing. I'm finally being punished for living in the attic and stealing food.

"What's going on here?" Andie says, clearly shaken. "You can't arrest her. She didn't do anything."

Another officer strides over and stands between Andie and me. "Miss, step back and let us do our job."

"I'm calling Aaron," she says. "This is all one big misunderstanding. We'll figure it out."

I shake my head. "I did it. He knows I did. There's nothing he can do."

Out of the corner of my eye, I see Lora's jaw drop. "She admitted it. Did you hear her?"

"Ma'am, I need to read your rights. If I were you, I wouldn't say anything until you hear them. You have the right to remain silent…"

Those are the same words I heard three years ago, spoken by a man wearing the same uniform. I want to fight, tell them I'm different now, but my mother's words keep echoing through my mind: *We only get as much as we deserve.*

CHAPTER THIRTY-NINE

Aaron

The past few weeks have been the best we've had. Living with Devyn is more rewarding than I imagined. Waking up to her every day is something I never knew I wanted and something I never again want to go without. Seeing her smile, watching her become the woman I knew she could be—it's wonderful.

"A little help," Quinn says, lugging plywood into the back of my truck. "This is kind of your gig."

I get out of my head and lend him a hand. I'm working double time to get the addition on the cabin done, and I have a surprise for her. I just don't know how I can pull it off without her knowing.

Quinn chuckles. "Your face is going to crack if you keep smiling like that."

"Can't help it," I say, grabbing another piece. "Wait and see. It'll happen to you one day."

"What will?"

"The moment when you can see your future and realize it's everything you ever wanted."

"Damn." He shakes his head. "Guess I've permanently lost my wingman."

We're laughing when my phone rings. It's Andie. I sit on the tailgate. "What's up?"

"You need to come home now."

The concern in her voice sets off alarms in my head. "Is it the baby? Has something happened?"

"Devyn has been arrested."

I jump off the back of the truck. "What?"

"We came home from shopping, and the police were here. They're taking her away now."

"Did they say why?"

"Something about larceny. Aaron, I don't understand. They won't tell me anything. We have to do something."

"I'm on my way." I hang up and stash my phone. "Leave the rest. I have to go."

Quinn glances at the pile of plywood on the dolly. "Leave it?"

I run around and hop into the truck. "Will you get in the goddamn truck?"

"What's going on?"

"Devyn's been arrested. Call Maddox. Have him meet us at the lodge. Find out the name of the lawyer DHR uses."

"What the fuck?"

"Do it, man."

I drive like a bat out of hell while Quinn speaks with Maddox. When we get to the lodge, I see a police car, park next to it, and look in back. It's empty. I race through the back door and see someone in Devyn's room. An officer restrains me when I try to go in.

"What are you doing in there? Where is Devyn?"

"And you are?" he asks.

"Aaron Pearce. I run this place. Why are you in her room? And will someone please tell me where the fuck Devyn is?"

Andie and Lora come in from the front hall. I hear the buzz of guests talking in the other room. Lora says, "They're fine. Pissed but fine. I've scheduled a limo to pick them up and take them to dinner—on us."

"What am I missing?" I say. "What the hell is going on?"

"Sir," the officer says. "Your housekeeper has been taken into custody."

"Why?" I ask while someone comes out of Devyn's room with plastic bags. "Why are you taking her things?"

"Those aren't hers," he says. "They're things stolen from your guests."

I'm confused. "Impossible. She was with me this morning, and then she went shopping with Andie."

Lora steps forward. "One of the guests saw her here this morning."

"So? She said she had to stop here for something."

"Shut up," Quinn says behind me. I turn and narrow my eyes at him. "Dude, don't say a word. Anything you say might be held against her."

Maddox barges in, and Andie tells him everything. I listen, trying to make sense of things. Why in the hell would she steal from the guests?

Maddox hands me his phone. "Jason Truly is on the line. The ranch has used him for legal help in the past."

"Mr. Truly, can you meet me at the police station?"

"Won't do you any good. They'll be processing her. You won't be able to see her until tomorrow."

"She has to stay overnight?"

"Given the late hour, yes."

My stomach turns. "She's pregnant. Maybe they'll make an exception."

"Unless she's in active labor or has an imminent medical need, it won't matter. Listen, I don't deal in criminal law, but I know people who do. I'll make a few calls. I assume you're willing to pay top dollar?"

"Whatever it takes."

"I'll get back to you in a few hours."

"Is there anything I can do right now?"

"Just sit tight and try not to worry. She'll be out on bail before you know it."

I hand Maddox his phone. "I don't get it."

Andie sits. "This must be a big misunderstanding."

"Seems pretty cut and dried to me," Lora says. "The guests saw her this morning. They reported items missing from their rooms after their ride, the police were called, and they found their things in her room."

My head is reeling. Criminal law. Larceny. Stealing. Bail. "No way would she have done it."

"She admitted she did," Lora says.

My eyes snap to hers. "What?"

She nods. "Said she did it, and there's nothing anyone can do."

I grope for the nearest chair and sit, my head in a fog and my stomach in knots, until the police leave with the evidence. I thought we were happy, that *she* was happy. Did she do this because she doesn't think she deserves to be?

"It's a mistake," I say. "Even if she did it, she didn't mean to. She's dealing with a lot of shit. She must be confused."

"We'll figure it out," Andie says.

I turn to Lora. "Comp their stays. We need to do whatever we can to keep this from ruining the business."

"Already done."

I nod. I've never felt so helpless in my entire life. She's locked in a jail cell, and there's not a damn thing I can do about it. I go to the bar and pick up a bottle of vodka. As I leave via the back door, I hear Maddox say, "Don't leave him alone."

"Not on your life," Quinn says and follows me.

I wake with a pounding skull and eventually notice the empty bottle on the kitchen table. Quinn is sleeping on my couch. I sit up and my stomach heaves; I'm just not sure it's from the alcohol or the reason I drank it. I run to the bathroom and throw up.

Quinn appears in the doorway.

"Why'd you let me do it?" I ask, then rinse my mouth.

"You think I was about to take the bottle from you? Hell no, man. You'd have ripped my head off. But I'm not afraid to tell you I poured some down the drain every time you took a whiz. I wasn't about to let you drink the whole damn thing."

I knew he'd have my back. "I have to see her."

"Check your phone. Maddox texted you all the info. The lawyer will meet you there at nine."

"That's in less than an hour."

"Figured you could use the sleep. It was better than watching you pace all morning."

I splash water on my face, brush my teeth, and change clothes. I throw my keys to Quinn. "You're driving."

Justin Kalvin is waiting for us outside the police station. Maddox included his picture in the text. He's writing something in a notebook.

"Mr. Kalvin?"

He extends a hand. "Justin. You must be Aaron."

"What do you know?"

"Nothing yet. I'm going in now for the court hearing. It's a hearing via video with a judge who will determine if there's probable cause. If there isn't, she'll be released. If there is, he will determine bond."

"Bond? As in bail? I'll pay it."

He checks his watch. "I need to get in there. I'd like to have a few minutes with her before the hearing."

"Let's go."

"You can't go with me. The only people allowed in the hearing are Devyn, her counsel, and the prosecuting attorney."

"Shit."

"I'm not going to sugarcoat this, Aaron. Maddox told me about Devyn's history. She's a convicted felon recently released from a state jail. If the judge finds probable cause, she may have a hefty bail."

"I don't care what it takes, I'll find the money."

"I'll meet you here when we're done. Hopefully Devyn will be with me."

"Thanks for taking this on with such short notice."

"Jason's a good friend of mine. We were fraternity brothers. If he says y'all are good people, I believe him."

"Tell Devyn I'm here, and I'll do everything in my power to help her fight this."

"I'll let her know."

He walks inside, and I lean against the building. Ninety minutes go by. I'm ready to march inside and ask what the holdup is when Justin exits the building alone. I can tell from the look on his face that he doesn't have good news.

"I'm sorry," he says.

"She's not getting out?"

He shakes his head. "But it's a good thing you didn't go with a public defender on this one. Apparently Devyn thought she was being charged with stealing food from the lodge."

"That's not what the police said last night."

"The DA told the judge she confessed to the police before she was read her rights. But Devyn thought she was confessing to stealing food, not money, jewelry, and the laptop they found in her room."

"I'm confused. So did she do it or not?"

"Devyn says she didn't do it. Said she was with you in the morning and then with Maddox's wife all day. She did visit the lodge to pick up thread or something she wanted to take into town and match at a store."

"If she said she didn't do it, then she didn't. Believe me. If she had done it, she'd accept the punishment."

"I'm her attorney, I have no choice but to take your word and hers. But the judge is faced with a tough decision. All evidence points to Devyn. She was homeless after her recent release. She stole food and slept in the attic without permission until you offered her a job that gave her direct access to the valuables of the guests, which were found in a room only being used by Devyn."

"What about fingerprints?"

"They haven't been analyzed yet, but don't get too excited. A lack of her fingerprints would not exonerate her."

"But she'll get out on bail until she has to go to court, right? How much do I have to come up with?"

"Maybe we should have this conversation elsewhere."

Fuck. More bad news is coming. "Just tell me, Justin."

"Every person arrested gets a PSA score. That's a public safety assessment. Some people who have no record and have a proven job and means to support themselves might be released on presumption of personal bond before they're even booked. Especially on a non-violent charge like this one. The PSA score determines how likely a person is to show up for their court appearance. Given Devyn's prior conviction, her lack of employment, and no known address, she's considered a flight risk."

"But she has a job, and she lives with me."

"Neither of those things are documented."

"So she has to stay in jail?"

"There's more."

"For Christ's sake, what?"

"The judge was contacted by Devyn's father, Congressman DeMaggio. He said Devyn came to his house and harassed his wife and daughter last month."

"What the fuck?" I kick the wall. "That's bullshit. Roseanne voluntarily let us through the gate and into her house, and her daughter wasn't even home."

"Be that as it may, he has a lot of influence."

Something occurs to me. "How the hell did DeMaggio even know she was arrested?"

"Beats me."

"The whole goddamn system is corrupt."

"Right now, things don't look good for her. With Devyn in custody, there is no incentive for police to look at anyone else."

"What's our worst-case scenario?"

"This could go to trial as a state jail felony, which means the goods stolen were worth more than fifteen hundred dollars but less than twenty thousand. A state jail felony could put her away for up to two years. I'm going to try to get the DA to lower the charges to multiple misdemeanors, as in each item was worth less than fifteen hundred. If I'm successful, she may not get any jail time at all, just probation or community service and retribution."

"What about DeMaggio? Can he influence the DA?"

"Yeah. I'm going to try and find out if they have a social relationship. Maybe we'll get lucky and they don't."

I stare at the ground. "Devyn's never been particularly lucky."

"That's not true. She has you. I'd say she's very lucky."

"Can I do anything?"

"Legally, no. But if Devyn is telling the truth, and she didn't steal those things, who did?"

Oh, shit. All this time, I've been thinking maybe she did it because she wanted to be punished somehow. But she doesn't want to go back to jail. She wants to be with me. She wants to have Casey. "I swear to God, I'm going to get to the bottom of this. I'll question every guest until I figure this out."

"Don't go out of bounds, Aaron. You'll only make things worse for her."

"When can I see her?"

"She'll be transferred to the county jail today. She'll have her first court appearance in three or four days. I'll keep you posted, but you should be able to see her tomorrow."

Tomorrow. He might as well have said next year, because at this point, tomorrow seems like a fucking lifetime away.

CHAPTER FORTY

Devyn

For the second time in my life, I'm locked up in the county jail awaiting a court appearance. But this time is nothing like the last time. I'm innocent. I don't deserve to be here. I rub my belly. He doesn't deserve to be here.

I try not to fall into the dark place I went to years ago. I try not to look at the ceiling tiles. I block out the smell coming from the plastic mattress with rips in it. I close my eyes and think of Aaron. Will he hate me for this? My lawyer, Justin, said Aaron hired him and would do anything to get me out, but I have to wonder if it's for me or for Casey. Justin said all the evidence was in my old room, which I use for reading and sewing. I'm a convicted felon. Will anyone truly believe me when I claim innocence?

County jail is different from state jail. We have zero choices here. There's one outfit: an orange jumpsuit. One thing we can do other than sleep: go to the rec room, and that's only for a few hours a day. It's boring. Sitting around all day with nothing to do is hard, much harder than working my ass off in the laundry or sweeping rodent droppings out of the pantry.

It's isolating. We all have our own cells. Small concrete cells that have a steel door with a slot in it. There's a thick window beside the door, but it's frosted.

My door only opens for three things: food, bathroom time, or recreation. I follow the other inmates down a long hall into the large open room with tables much like a high school cafeteria. Old televisions are bolted to the wall in several locations. Women are already fighting over what to watch. One gets punched. Blood spatters close to me, and I jump back. A guard intervenes but doesn't punish the one who took a swing.

It's loud. Women fight, yell obscenities, put each other down. I try to keep to myself, but there are few places to sit alone. I choose the corner far from the televisions. A slender woman with discolored teeth sits next to me. She looks at my stomach. "When you due?"

I'd hoped no one would notice. "February."

"They won't let you keep it. I had my kid, Bennie, in lockup two years ago. His foster parents send me pictures. I was hoping to get him back until my punk-ass boyfriend got me mixed up in selling drugs again. You got someone on the outside to raise the kid for you?"

"Yes, but I won't be staying long. I didn't do what I was accused of."

She laughs, and I try not to cringe at the smell of her horrid breath. "You keep telling yourself that."

Several other women join the conversation and say similar things. They are all mothers. Their kids are being raised by strangers or estranged exes. Terror crawls up my spine. What if nobody believes me, and I go back to state jail or prison? What if Casey has to spend his first years never knowing his mom? What if Aaron meets someone else, and she takes my place in the baby's life?

What if all of the hopes and dreams I finally allowed myself to realize are swept away?

Maybe two years wasn't long enough, and I'm still being punished.

I can't think like that. I don't belong here. I get up and move to an empty table, leaving the women to talk about the kids who don't know them. I stare at the large clock encased in bars. *What do they think we would do with a clock?* I watch the secondhand tick. I try to calculate how many seconds have to pass until my court appearance. Unlike last time, I will hold my head high when I tell the judge I'm not guilty.

I'm not guilty.

I say it over and over in my mind until I'm interrupted by a guard calling my name. "Devyn DeMaggio!"

I stand. "That's me."

"Visitor," he says. "Come with me."

My heart soars. Justin said Aaron would come see me as soon as he could. I practically run over the guard's heels to reach the visitor's room. He directs me to sit on the third stool. This room has ten of them. Each has a phone where we can talk to the person on the other side of the glass wall. There isn't much privacy here, not even partitions between prisoners. I'm sad I won't be in a private room with him, like I was with my lawyer.

I sit for a few minutes and wonder if they got it wrong. Maybe nobody is here for me. Then my stomach twists in knots and dread consumes me when I see who appears on the other side of the window. It's my father.

He almost smirks as he sits and picks up the phone. "Well, well, well. Looks like you're right back where you belong."

"I'm not guilty."

"The hell you aren't."

"I didn't do this."

"Doesn't matter in my book."

"Why are you here, Ed? Won't it ruin your precious reputation if you're caught seeing the daughter you disowned?"

"Oh, quite the opposite. There are cameras outside the jail. Somehow the press found out I would be here. When I leave, I'll look forlorn. They'll be sympathetic. I'll tell them I wish you no ill will. I came here to forgive you. You paid your debt. I'll tell them I came here to see if I could help."

His words sink in. He's even worse than I remember. "Help? Is that what you were doing when you contacted the judge and told him I was harassing Mom? You used me once to get elected. Now you're using me again."

"People love a hero, and that's what I am, Devyn. Someone they can look up to. Someone they can empathize with. An ordinary person who's been through hell but can find it in his heart to forgive."

"It's all a lie. You'll do anything to further your career, including capitalizing on Kasey's death."

He runs his tongue across his upper teeth, saying nothing.

"Do you even miss her?" I ask, my heart filled with rage. "Do you care that she's gone? Would you bat an eye if anything happened to Julianne?"

"She was my daughter. Of course I care. And don't go sticking your nose in where you don't belong. If you ever get out of here, stay away from my wife. Stay away from my house. Stay away from my family."

"You mean *my* family."

"Not anymore."

"I was your daughter too. Did you stop for one second to think about what I was going through? Do you think I meant for any of it to happen? That I don't punish myself every single day? I loved her a lot more than you ever did." I stand. "We're done now." I hang the phone on the wall.

Ed locks eyes with a guard and shakes his head. The guard comes over and pushes me back on the stool. "Pick it up. Time's not done yet."

"But I don't want to talk to him anymore."

He says harshly, "Pick it up."

I do what he says. "Did you bribe him or something?" I ask Ed.

He laughs. "I don't need to do that. I'm a congressman. Soon to be a senator if all goes well. That position comes with a lot of power, more than you'll ever know."

I stare at the counter. He doesn't talk. He's stalling. He needs the press to see he spent time with me.

"How did you know I was here?"

"Like I said, I'm powerful."

A horrible thought takes residence in my head. "Are you responsible for this? Did you set me up?"

His expression doesn't change. He doesn't even flinch. "I'm glad you're finally realizing just how influential I can be, but no, Devyn, I didn't do this."

"I don't believe you."

He's amused. "Do you think I care what you believe? You're a convicted felon. You can't even vote."

"You're wrong. I can. After my release, I wasn't on parole or even probation. My voting rights were restored."

"Until now," he says, smirking. "And touché for knowing the law. I can't get one over on you now, can I?" He glances at his watch and straightens his tie. "I think I've been here long enough. People are waiting for me outside. Have a nice life, Devyn." He looks at the orange jumpsuits and the sterile concrete walls. "I hope you're very happy here."

He puts down the phone and walks away, not looking back.

The guard comes over. "Follow me."

He takes me back to my cell. I'm relieved. I didn't want to go to the rec room and listen to anyone else tell me I can't keep my baby. I close my eyes and try to nap, wanting Casey to move so I can feel him inside me. I lie here for hours and nothing. Is the stress of this affecting him? What if something's wrong? What if he died inside me? I'm almost sick with fear at the thought. Then finally, I feel it: a flutter, a soft swipe, a roll.

A few weeks ago, I couldn't imagine my life with a baby. Now I can't imagine my life without him.

My cell door opens. "DeMaggio," the guard says. "You got a visitor."

It has to be Aaron. It *has* to be.

When we enter the visitor room, I see him, and my heart lurches. I love him so much. I sit and gaze into his eyes. Neither of us goes for the phone right away; we just look at each other for the longest time.

He picks up the phone at last, then I do.

"How are you holding up?" he asks.

"As good as can be expected."

"I'm so sorry you're in here."

"I can't imagine what you must be thinking, Aaron. Are you wondering if I really did it?"

He shakes his head. "Not even for a second, Dev. I know you didn't."

"How?"

"Because you said you didn't, and I believe you."

I look down. "You're probably the only one who does."

"I'm not."

"Even so, you might be raising this baby by yourself after all."

He swallows. "It won't come to that."

"If I tell you something, you can't call me crazy."

"I'd never call you crazy."

"Ed was here earlier."

"The congressman was *here*? And you talked to him?"

"It was a publicity stunt. He played the father struggling to cope with the loss of his daughter while at the same time pretending to forgive the child responsible for her death."

"You're fucking kidding me."

"He admitted it, Aaron. Here's the crazy part. What if he set me up? What if he knew where I was all along? What if he had someone come to the lodge, steal those things, and frame me?"

His eyebrows go up, and he rubs his jaw. "Shit. That makes sense. He knew you were arrested. He convinced the judge not to set bail."

"He denied it when I asked."

"He may be a low-life politician, but he's not stupid."

"There would be no way to prove it. Like he told me, he's a powerful man."

"Maybe fingerprints."

"You think anyone he hired wouldn't have worn gloves?"

"Right. But someone must have seen something. A ranch hand. One of the guests. If anyone was there and out of place, someone would have noticed."

"Like someone noticed me the weeks I was living in the attic? Like you said, I was a ghost."

His jaw drops. "Say that again."

"I was a ghost."

"I would fucking kiss you right now if it weren't for the two inches of glass between us."

"What do you mean?"

"I have to go, Dev. I don't want to cut this short, but there's something I have to do."

"You'll come back, though?"

"No. I'll see you when you get out of here, free and clear." He hangs up the phone and walks away. But unlike the congressman, he looks back. He looks back and smiles.

CHAPTER FORTY-ONE

Aaron

The truck is barely in park when I open the door, jump out, and run to the lodge. At my computer in the office, I pull up the footage on the camera I installed months ago when I was trying to find the ghost. I'd forgotten all about it. *Stupid, stupid, stupid.*

I pray the footage from Thursday is still there. It overwrites itself when the file reaches capacity.

I open the file dated Wednesday night, just before midnight. I breathe a small sigh of relief. It had to have happened after that. The guests arrived Wednesday afternoon but didn't notice anything missing until Thursday, after their trail ride with Luca.

"What had you running in here like your pants were on fire?" Quinn asks from the doorway.

"Come here. I have video of the lodge."

His eyebrows scrunch together. "Since when do you have surveillance cameras?"

"It's just the one. I installed it back when—" I stop. I never told him Devyn was sleeping in the attic and stealing food. "You know what, it doesn't matter." I sit back and lace my fingers behind my neck. "If whoever did this went down the back stairway, I'm screwed. And by that, I mean Devyn is screwed." I tell him about Ed DeMaggio's visit to the county jail.

"This is seriously fucked up," he says. "You think he'd go this far to get publicity for his election?"

"He's done it before. When Kasey died, he milked it like crazy. I've seen campaign videos. The guy is pathetic. Now he's playing the I'm-a-forgiving-father card."

He pulls up a chair, and we browse the footage.

A guest comes down the stairs after midnight and goes back up a minute later with a bottle of water.

"He had enough time to stash the goods," he says.

"A laptop was taken. We'd have seen him carrying it. It's a 4K Ultra HD camera. We could zoom in on a fly on the wall if we wanted to."

We move forward slowly, watching the shadows of night disappear as daybreak shines through the windows. More guests appear, going in the direction of the kitchen. Most of them are laughing or talking. No one acts the least bit suspicious.

"What about this one?" Quinn says when an angry looking dude comes down the stairs.

I shake my head. "He's a grumpy old guy. He's the boss who arranged the stay. Rich fucker. I had a talk with him yesterday. Doesn't seem like he'd have a reason to steal from anyone."

People come and go up and down the stairs for another hour, then Luca appears, waiting for the guests to gather in the grand foyer so he can take them out. I count them and watch them leave.

There's at least forty-five minutes of nothing. I fast forward, then stop the video when I see someone. It's Lora, and I start forwarding again.

"Stop," Quinn says. "Go back. Watch closely."

I do what he says.

"She has a laptop."

"She owns one, Quinn."

"Yeah, but is it an Apple? And why was she upstairs when all the guests were gone?"

I zoom in. "What the hell? No, she doesn't own an iMac, and she sure as hell doesn't own one with a sticker of a rock band on it. It matches the description of the one they found in Devyn's room."

"And see how she's looking at the front door? Dude, I can practically see the sweat on her brow. She's the goddamn thief. Holy shit, Aaron, she framed your girlfriend. I knew she was obsessed with you."

I stand up so forcefully, my chair falls over.

"Hold on," he says. "Let's watch the rest of it."

"Fuck this shit. She wanted to destroy her, Quinn, and she almost succeeded."

"You have to watch the rest. Don't you want to see it all?"

I right my chair, sit, and start playback again. There's no sound. I had it set to record video only. My insides are shaking as Lora drops something, a piece of jewelry. "Holy crap. There, right there; this proves it. We fucking caught her red-handed."

"How did she not know about the camera?" he asks. "Doesn't she do the bookkeeping? Wouldn't she have noticed the purchase?"

"I borrowed the camera from Maddox when guests were complaining about strange noises. Anyway, forget that. The point is, Lora didn't know about it."

She disappears off the video, and I fast forward two hours to when the guests come back. They go to the kitchen for lunch, then some of them go upstairs. One comes back down, clearly angry. He says something to the others, and they follow him up the stairs. They don't come down for a while, not until Lora shows up.

"*Humph*," Quinn mumbles. "Convenient."

The angry guests file downstairs. Some of them appear to be yelling. One woman rubs her wrist as she talks to Lora. "A bracelet was missing," I say to Quinn. "An expensive one."

Lora puts her phone to her ear. "Holy shit," Quinn says. "She's calling the police, isn't she?"

"Well, she didn't call me."

"Don't you think she would have? If she wasn't trying to frame Devyn, wouldn't you be her first call?"

We watch as they all mill about, going in and out of view for an hour until the police arrive. Lora takes them upstairs. A while later, they come out of the kitchen; she took them down the back stairs. She says something to some of the guests who try to go back in. The police block their way.

"They just found the stuff," I say. "She led them right to it. Can she even do that? Let them search the property?"

"She does work here." Quinn turns to me, looking pensive. "Why do you think she didn't take the back stairs when she had the stuff?"

"I have no idea, but thank God for small favors."

Two more officers show up. Guests are questioned by police with notepads. Suddenly everyone looks toward the kitchen. Lora and the police walk out of frame.

"Devyn just arrived," I say, pinching my brows knowing she's about to get arrested.

A while later, we watch her being escorted by a cop through the foyer and out the front door. At least they didn't put her in handcuffs.

I pick up my phone.

"Calling the police?"

"Calling Lora."

He takes the phone and hangs up. "Don't. You have to do what's best for Devyn. If you confront Lora, she'll deny it, maybe even run away. You need the element of surprise."

I look at him like he's crazy. "I need *what?*"

"Give Devyn's lawyer the video. The iMac and the necklace prove she's innocent. Did you see Lora wearing gloves? Nope. Her fingerprints will be all over that shit. Don't jump the gun here. Do it by the book."

"How in the hell do you even know what that means?"

"I watch a lot of *CSI*."

I call Justin and upload it using a link he provides. Thirty minutes later, he calls back, and I put him on speaker. "You've definitely got something here. I'll need the original footage to have it authenticated, and then I'll present it to the judge at Devyn's first appearance, day after tomorrow. I'll ask for a full dismissal of all charges. The DA is bound to agree, and then he'll issue an arrest for Ms. Belmont."

"The day after tomorrow? Can't you go to the judge sooner?"

"We have to respect the process, Aaron. It's thirty-six hours. Don't say anything to Devyn. Although I'm fairly sure this is in the bag, I don't want to get her hopes up and then dash them."

"She knows something's up. I ran out of there today when I remembered the camera."

"You told her about the video?"

"No."

"Good. Let me work on this. I have every reason to believe she'll be home with you by Monday afternoon."

"And Lora?"

"Definitely don't let her know what you found. It may be hard for you, but it'll be better this way."

"Promise me something. Find out when they're going to arrest Lora. I want to be there."

"I'm buddies with the police sergeant. I'll see what I can do."

"Thanks for all your help."

"I didn't do anything. You're the one who's clearing her name. I don't mind telling you now that I was sure she'd be convicted. Anyway, sit tight. I'll call you with any developments."

I hang up and smack my hand on the desk. "What the fuck am I supposed to do for the next two days while she's locked in a cell?"

"We've got a shitload of Sheetrock over at your place."

"That's not what I want to work on. I have another project. Can you help?"

"You know it, bro."

"Good. Round up the troops. I'm going to need everyone to pull this off."

"Knock, knock!" Lora says from the kitchen.

Quinn and I look at each other, wondering how long she's been here.

She stands in the doorway, holding up her phone. "I saw you tried to call. I was in the car on the phone with my other boss. What's up?"

"Uh, sorry," I say, trying to hold myself back from jumping over the desk and tackling her. "Butt dial."

She laughs. "You can butt dial me anytime. As long as I'm here, I may as well do some bookkeeping."

She approaches the desk, and I quickly close the camera software. I don't want her on the computer. She could find it. Hell, I don't want her in the lodge. "Not now. Quinn and I were discussing your ideas about the ATVs. Your proposal impressed Maddox. We were putting some spreadsheets together."

Her smile is a mile wide. "I'm glad."

I want to puke. I want to puke on *her*. "We'll be in here crunching numbers all day. You can go back to enjoying your weekend."

"If you're sure."

"Oh, I'm sure. You deserve it, Lora. You deserve everything that's going to happen."

Quinn kicks me behind the desk.

"Thank you," she says, miming a curtsey as if she's some kind of royalty. She turns to leave. "Call if you need me."

She has no fucking idea her world is going to implode in thirty-six hours

CHAPTER FORTY-TWO

Devyn

It's like a bad movie playing over and over in my head. I'm handcuffed, taken to a van with other inmates, and driven to the courthouse. I wait in a room with guards until it's my turn. I look at all the other people in orange jumpsuits.

It's so unfair. If you get out on bail, you can wear your own clothes to the preliminary hearing. If you don't, you have to show up in these hideous jumpsuits. Will wearing it somehow sway the judge's opinion of me?

The first time this happened, the judge agreed there was enough evidence to go to trial, although he did allow me to leave jail until then. Ed hated it. He didn't let me back in the house. He made my mother pack my clothes in plastic bags and leave them on the curb. It was the day I became homeless. It wasn't until Aaron offered me a room and a job that I started to feel anywhere near normal again.

"DeMaggio."

I get off the bench and follow a guard. They don't take off my handcuffs. When I enter the courtroom through the side door, I immediately scan the public seating area. As soon as I see Aaron, I feel a sense of relief. Even though I may be going back to jail, he'll be there for me. He smiles so brightly that it's hard for me not to smile back.

Justin, my lawyer, clears his throat, reminding me we've got things to do. He pulls out a chair for me at the table, and I sit. He leans over. "Hang in there. I think you'll be pleased with how this day turns out."

"Really?" I try not to get too excited. What could he have done? I peek at Aaron, who's still smiling.

When the judge calls my case, Justin stands. "I'd like to enter a motion to dismiss all charges."

"On what grounds?" the judge asks.

"On the grounds that we have video evidence proving Ms. DeMaggio did not commit the crime she's been charged with."

The DA stands. "I object. We haven't been made aware of this evidence."

"It's only recently come into my possession," Justin says.

"This is a preliminary hearing," the judge says. "I'm going to allow it."

Justin explains how he got the video. Aaron's name comes up. I sneak another look at him. He nods gleefully and appears ready to burst from his seat.

A television in the corner is turned on, a video starts, and we see the inside of the lodge. The view of the foyer and the stairs is crystal clear. I am glued to my seat, heart pounding, wondering who or what I'm about to see. Is it someone Ed hired?

Something totally unexpected happens. Lora walks down the stairs. She appears to be extremely nervous. Justin pauses the video and zooms in on the laptop. "The woman in the video is Lora Belmont, employee of Devil's Horn Ranch Lodge. She is holding the laptop that was described by the guest from whom it was stolen. We've also verified through this woman's employer that she does not own an Apple computer." He starts the video again, and Lora drops something on the stairs. Justin pauses and zooms in again. "She is holding a necklace belonging to one of the other guests." He pulls a picture out of his folder. "I'd like to introduce this photo as evidence. It's a picture of a lodge guest wearing the same necklace Lora Belmont dropped on the floor. This necklace, along with the laptop and various other pieces of jewelry, were found in my defendant's personal space in the lodge and are currently in an evidence locker at the police station."

The bailiff takes the photo from Justin and gives it to the judge.

"You'll notice that Ms. Belmont keeps looking off in one direction—that's the front door. She knew the guests would be out of the lodge for hours. She also had a key to the guest rooms and Ms. DeMaggio's reading room. As you can see, she's not wearing gloves. Her fingerprints could be on the laptop and the other—"

"I've seen enough," the judge says. He turns to the DA. "Mr. Hunter, how would you like to proceed?"

"The prosecution does not see probable cause to move forward, and as such, moves to dismiss all charges, Your Honor. We also request an arrest warrant for Ms. Belmont."

"Granted." The judge turns to me. "Young lady, you're free to go."

I turn to Justin. "I can leave? That's it?"

"That's it," he says.

The guard takes off my handcuffs, and I hug Justin. "Thank you so much."

"I'm not the one you should be thanking." He glances at Aaron.

Aaron moves toward me, arms outstretched. I fall into them, and he pulls me over the half wall separating us.

"I love you," I whisper into his hair.

"I'll bet you say that to all the guys who break you out of jail." I laugh.

"Let's get you out of this jumpsuit."

"Orange is definitely not my color."

On the drive back to the county jail to collect my things, he tells me what happened. "It was you, Dev. When we were talking the other day, you said something about finding a ghost. I had forgotten all about the camera I installed when I was trying to catch you. If we'd waited one more day, or even ten hours, the footage would have been overwritten."

I swallow. "I was lucky, huh?"

He takes my hand. "You were overdue for a little good fortune."

"I can't believe she did it."

"I had no idea how deep her obsession went, Dev, or I'd never have kept her on. I can't believe I didn't see it. You did, though, and Quinn warned me. I honestly thought it was only a crush."

"This is on her, not you. I assume you fired her after you saw it. What did she say?"

He smiles. "This brings us to my second surprise. She doesn't know we have the tape. She doesn't know anything. I've arranged for her to be at the lodge when the police show up. My gift to you—watching the bitch go down."

"Is it terrible that I'm giddy over this?"

"She tried to ruin you. Watching her arrest will be the highlight of my year." He puts a hand on my belly. "One of them anyway. Oh, and I've got another surprise. I've arranged a news conference at the lodge tonight. You can tell everyone about Ed and how he's putting on an act to get reelected. How he used you and Kasey to get where he is today."

"Can you cancel it?"

"Why?"

I gaze out the window at the beautiful blue sky and the green trees that will soon turn to the colors of the fall. I've never felt so free. "Despite what he's done to me, he still lost a child. I haven't even met Casey yet, and already I can't imagine life without him. I want to leave everything else behind and move on. Ed can't hurt me anymore because I won't let him."

We stop at a light. He turns. "Are you forgiving him?"

"Maybe I am. But in a way, I'm forgiving myself."

He raises my hand to his lips and kisses it. "You're amazing."

"*You're* amazing."

At the lodge, Aaron parks out front, which is strange. He never does that. We get out, and he says, "Go up to guest suite four. Take a long bath and wash off the jail grime. I'll get you some clothes."

"Why here and not the cabin?"

"You know, the renovations. I wanted you to be able to relax. All the guests are gone. We can even stay here tonight."

"Suite four?" I never told him, but I've always wanted to stay there. Sometimes when I was living in the attic and there were no guests around, I'd lie on that bed and pretend I was someone I wasn't.

"Only the best for my two favorite people in the world."

"What about Lora?"

"Justin has contacts in the police department. He'll give me a heads-up when they're on the way. Should be at least an hour or two. Now go. There are more surprises."

In suite four, there are flower petals on the bed. I'm usually the one who places them there when we have a wedding party or an anniversary couple. I put rose petals in the shape of a heart on the bed. But these are lilies. There are several vases of them around the room. I touch my bump. "Who knew your daddy was so romantic?"

In the bathroom, soothing music is playing. A bath has been drawn. I stick my hand in the water—it's warm. More lilies in vases surround the tub. I strip out of the clothes I got back from the county jail and sink into the water. It's heavenly. I lay my head back on the bath pillow and relax. Casey must like the warmth; he's moving. I rest my hand on him and enjoy this quiet moment with my son, and for the first time in forever, I am at peace.

After my bath, I find a dress in the bedroom, the kind I'd wear for a party. Not fancy, just pretty. He knows me well, better than anyone ever has. I put it on and go downstairs.

Aaron is sitting on the bench in the foyer. He looks up, and I feel like Cinderella going to the ball. The way he's looking at me is like he just won the lottery, but *I'm* the one who hit the jackpot.

He's wearing khakis and a blue button-down, a far cry from the jeans and T-shirts he usually throws on.

"What's the special occasion?" I ask.

"You. You're the special occasion."

"Are we going on a date?"

"We are, but not how you might think. It's a surprise."

"Another one? I thought you said the police were coming."

"They are." People join us from the kitchen. Maddox, Andie, Owen, Quinn, Joe. I question Aaron with my eyes. "You had an audience at your arrest," he says. "It's only fitting she have one at hers."

"Is she here yet?"

"Any second now."

"What'll you say?"

"To be honest, I don't know."

As if on cue, Lora appears. "What's with all the stuff up on the—" She sees me and stops talking. Heck, I'm fairly sure she stops breathing. "What are you doing here? Did they let you out on bail?" She turns to Aaron. "Why would you invite her back here?"

Aaron crosses the foyer, reaches inside a large artificial flower arrangement, and pulls out a video camera. "Man, you gotta love technology. These things can pick up everything, right down to the Reckless Alibi sticker Ms. Jones had on the cover of her iMac."

The blood drains from Lora's face.

Aaron laughs. "This is ironic. I installed this camera to catch a ghost, but it captured something much more important."

Lora turns to leave, but Joe blocks her escape, arms crossed.

"You can't keep me here," she says. "Besides, videotaping me without my consent means it can't be used in court."

"Even if it can't," Aaron says, "fingerprints can. You weren't wearing gloves. Did you know that with today's technology, unless you use certain chemicals, you can recover fingerprints even if they've been wiped? Or maybe you didn't even do that. After all, what more evidence would they need after finding stolen goods in an ex-con's room?" He cringes. "Sorry, Dev. Trying to make a point."

"You deserve someone better than her," Lora says. "She's a criminal."

Aaron laughs. "Says the pot about the kettle."

"I'm not anything like her. I have a college degree. I come from a good family. I'm certainly not a murderer."

"No, you're worse. What happened to her was a tragic accident. What you did was intentional. You'd have had her locked away for years for something she didn't do."

"I'm standing right here," I say. "How about letting me handle this?"

Aaron moves aside. "Gladly."

She has nowhere to go and is surrounded by the enemy. "I've met a lot of lowlifes, believe me, but framing someone so, what, you can sleep with their boyfriend? He told you repeatedly he wasn't into you. Only a crazy person wouldn't take the hint. Earlier, when I was sitting in the tub, washing off the grime put on me by *you*, I did a lot of thinking. Everything makes sense now. The time Aaron caught you in my room, you said you were admiring my work. You found my journal, didn't you? You read about my past. Discovered my name." Something occurs to me. "Oh my god, you called my father. You knew he'd make it even harder for me to get out. For the life of me, I couldn't figure out how he knew I was there in time to get to the judge."

Aaron rushes forward, looking like he wants to deck her. "You called the fucking congressman?"

Quinn holds him back. "Don't. She'll get what's coming to her."

"Who do you think you are?" I say to her. "Who are you to mess with someone's life like that? You're pathetic. Lower than the scum I dealt with for two years. How can you even look at yourself in the mirror? I almost feel sorry for you, because I know what kind of life you're facing, but I can't. You brought this all on yourself. Someone once told me people get what they deserve. Well, you're about to get dished up a whole heaping serving of it."

"I don't have to put up with this. I'm leaving." Lora tries to duck around Joe.

A police officer comes through the kitchen. Owen must have let him inside. "Lora Belmont?"

She shakes her head and closes her eyes in defeat. I see it. This is the moment she knows she's lost.

The officer reads her rights to her and leads her away. I follow them to the door and say, "One more thing?" He stops. I stride right up to her. "You're fucking fired."

After they leave, I sit at the table. Everyone gathers around and claps.

"Damn, girl," Andie says. "Way to stand up for yourself. I've never seen you like that before."

Aaron leans close. "I am so fucking turned on right now."

My eyes go wide. "Really?"

"Oh, yeah."

I giggle, then heave the largest sigh of relief. I look at my friends. No, they're more than friends—they're family. I know it's cliché, but I can't help but think this is the first day of the rest of my life. My new life.

CHAPTER FORTY-THREE

Aaron

"You kicked ass," I tell Devyn after everyone leaves. "I've never seen you stand up for yourself like that before. I think I like this new you."

She smiles seductively. "You didn't like the old one?"

"I *loved* the old one." I pull her close. "I love all of you."

"What do you think will happen to Lora?"

"She'll get out on bail; she might even get probation. But if they can prove she did it to frame someone, they can press more charges. I'd love to see her locked up, even if it's only for a few months."

Devyn shudders. "She'll probably do better in jail than I did."

"Why's that?"

"Because she's a bitch. They get by easier."

I laugh. "Then maybe it'll be a breeze."

She twirls, and the bottom of her dress floats up. "What's with this?"

"I told you, we're going on a date."

"I'll need different shoes," she says, glancing at her flats.

"We're not leaving the lodge."

"We're going on a date here?"

"Joe's already in the kitchen. He's been working on something all afternoon. Should be about ready."

She frowns. "If this is our first official date, I'd like to put on some jewelry."

"You have jewelry?" I ask. "I've never seen you wear anything but earrings."

"I picked up a few things at Target a few weeks ago. Nothing special."

"Tell me where it is, and I'll run to the cabin and get it."

"I can do it."

"Devyn, just tell me."

"Is there some reason you don't want me to see the cabin? Did you take down the wall? Is that why you had me shower here?"

"The cabin is fine."

She looks at me warily. "Then why all the cloak and dagger?"

I kiss her forehead. "Play along, okay?"

"Fine. I guess I don't need any jewelry. It wouldn't have gone with this dress anyway. Where did you get it, by the way?"

"Andie picked it out. She knew your size from the other day."

"It's very pretty."

"You're very pretty."

She touches my chin. "So are you. You shaved."

"Did you just call me pretty?"

She laughs. "Not how a cowboy wants to hear himself described, huh?"

"You can call me anything you want, Dev, as long as you keep undressing me with your eyes."

Joe clears his throat. "Ready for supper?"

I lean forward to whisper, "I'm ready to eat. I don't know about supper."

Joe snickers. He may have heard me.

We relocate to the dining room. The table seats twenty-four, but Joe has set us up at one end. Candles, lilies, sparkling water. The whole nine yards. Devyn's favorite snack, crab cakes, is waiting for her.

"Aw," she says. "You remembered."

"You've been craving these for a month. How could I forget?"

I hold out a chair for her. Joe brings her a small bowl of ketchup. "No rémoulade for you," he says. "Makes you nauseous."

"How did I get so fortunate to have two amazing men in my life?"

"If we could find Joe a lady, everything would be perfect," I say.

"I'm too old to be goin' on any dates."

"You are not," she says. "You don't even look your age." Devyn stands. "Excuse me. I'll be right back." I follow her back to her reading/sewing room and contemplate stopping her, but it appears she's on a mission. The room has been cleared out. Everything is gone, including the framed picture of the ultrasound. "What happened to all my things? Did the police take them?"

"They didn't take anything. I moved them."

"To the cabin?"

"You'll find out sooner or later."

"But there were things in here I need."

"And you'll have them."

"But there's something I need *now*."

"Like what?"

"Jill's phone number."

"Jill, your caseworker?"

"She'd be perfect for Joe. They're the same age. I didn't realize it until I ran into her last week. And they're both alone. It was with my things."

"Is it okay if we get it later?"

"Don't let me forget. Aaron, I thought we said I could use this room until the cabin expansion was done."

"All part of the surprise."

She cocks her head. "I know you're good and all, but no way did you complete the addition in the four days I was gone."

"Nope."

"You're not going to tell me? Not even a hint?"

"Supper's getting cold."

She rolls her eyes and returns to the table. During dinner, we whisper about Joe and Jill. She's excited about introducing them. "Even their names sound good together," she says. "Joe has lived his life in the shadow of his mistake. I know how that feels, and so do you. I promised myself after the night of our confessions that I wouldn't end up a seventy-year-old spinster who'd wasted her life, sulking about a past she couldn't change. Kasey wouldn't have wanted that for me."

"Do you know how happy I am to hear you say those things?"

"We all did a lot of growing that night," she says, then rubs her stomach. "And some since then."

I chuckle.

"Thank you for tonight, and for the bath and the dress. Everything."

"You thought it was over?" I stand and offer her my hand. She takes it, and I lead her up the stairs. She probably thinks we're going to the room to have sex, but I turn to the attic door. "Go ahead."

She smiles. "You want to go out on the roof?"

"My night wouldn't be complete without it."

She goes first. I wait at the bottom of the stairs. When she reaches the top, I flip on the light, then run up to join her. She turns a slow circle and appraises the room illuminated by string lights similar to what she had in her old bedroom.

I had the attic cleared, cleaned, drywalled, and painted. At one end is a large table, and on it is her sewing machine. Next to it is a large, extraordinarily comfy chair beside a bookshelf lined with books. Along the far wall is a playroom. It contains a play pen, baby swing, various mats and toys, a small changing table, rocking chair, and a mini fridge.

"You made me a woman cave?" She goes to the playpen. "And a baby cave? Aaron. This is incredible. How did you do all this?"

"With a whole lot of help from the guys at DHR."

Her hand goes to her heart when she sees the pictures on top of the bookshelf. Her framed picture of the ultrasound is there, along with two others. One is a picture of the two of us. The other I took from her wallet and had blown up—a picture of Devyn and Kasey. "This is perfect. Kasey would have loved it here."

"I know. Her favorite game was hide-and-seek."

"It's the first game I'm going to teach him."

"There's more."

"More? But this is so much already."

I flip off the lights from the top of the stairs, wait a second for our eyes to adjust, then lead her to the window. "I wanted to make this a door, but it would have taken too much time."

"I love it the way it is. We've always climbed out the window. A door just wouldn't feel the same."

I raise the window open, and she climbs through. I grab a blanket from the new cabinet and follow her out. She looks around, awestruck. The guys and I built a platform on the roof and surrounded it with a railing. I bought a large lounger that reclines all the way back for optimal viewing and comfort.

"Why did you do this?"

"I thought we could—"

"Bring Casey out here and teach him about the stars?"

"Yeah."

A tear falls. I catch it with my thumb.

"I dreamed of this," she says. "Of watching the stars with him. It's like you read my mind."

I breathe a sigh of relief. "You like it then?"

She throws her arms around me. "I love it. All of it. How did I get so lucky?"

"I'm the lucky one, Dev." I motion to the seat. "Want to hang out up here for a while?"

She giggles. "Hang out, huh?"

"Or something."

"Nice touch with the lounger. No more sore knees and scraped backs." She lies on it.

I lie next to her and tuck a wisp of hair behind her ear. "I can see us up here, just like this, with Casey between us."

She smiles. "And when he falls asleep, we can put him inside."

"Now you're talking. Let's practice that part now, the part after we put him inside."

"I thought you'd never ask."

"I'll always ask, Dev." I remove her flats and lift her dress up and over her head. She's wearing the matching bra and panties

Andie picked for her. I'll thank her later. I never thought a pregnant woman could look so sexy. "You're beautiful."

She runs her hand across her tummy. "I'm getting so big."

"That will just make you more beautiful."

I kiss her. The taste of her is intoxicating. I didn't know I couldn't live without her just a few months ago, and I hope I never have to. She's this superhuman force that draws me in, and I doubt I'll ever be able to get enough of her.

I trace the edge of her jaw with my lips, then move to her neck, her collarbone, and the soft skin between her breasts. I push the cups of her bra down and lick her sensitive nipples. She arches against me and weaves her hands into my hair.

"I haven't been afraid of many things in my life," I say, "but I'm terrified of losing you."

It's dark, but I can almost see light radiating from her eyes. She touches my face. "That won't ever happen. I'm afraid you're stuck with me. Us."

I bury my head between her breasts, her words reverberating through my head. She was a gift from God or maybe my guardian angel, and I vow to make every day, every moment, every touch worth living for.

I reach into her panties and between her legs to find her drenched. She moans as I slide my fingers in and out of her, working her wetness up and around her hard little clit. The noises she makes get me rock hard. "I have to taste you."

She swiftly removes her underwear and lets her legs fall open. I gaze down at her, naked, breasts pushed up by her lowered bra cups, her pussy glistening in the moonlight, and I'm sure I've died and gone to fucking heaven.

I hastily strip off my clothes, then she pushes me down and climbs on top of me in the sixty-nine position. Yup—heaven.

She takes me in her mouth as I feast on her. It takes everything I have not to come. Because when I do, I want to be looking into her eyes. I concentrate on her—I lick, suck, hum, and nibble. My hands grip the soft globes of her ass. She's close, I can tell, so I slip a hand between us and pinch one of her nipples. It takes her over the edge. She releases me from her mouth and shouts, riding my face like she's astride a wild bronc. I've never felt more powerful.

When she stops pulsating, I move her off me and climb on top of her. "I was the first man inside you, and I want to be the last."

She guides me inside her with a single word. "Yes."

She's so damn gorgeous, with her satiated eyes. It's like I'm an adolescent in heat. I pump once, twice, three times, then I come. She wraps me in her arms when I collapse on top of her. As I recover, I realize I could be squishing the baby and roll off.

"I'm not sure if Casey liked that or not, but he's really moving around."

I rise on an elbow. "Where?" She takes my hand and places it below and a little right of her belly button. I feel a faint flutter. "Holy shit, that's him?"

She nods.

I keep my hand there and close my eyes. More flutters and then something that feels like a kick.

"Did you feel it? That was a good one."

"I did. It's… it's fucking incredible. If sex makes him move around like this, we need to have it all the time."

She laughs.

This might be the best moment of my life, but there's one thing that might make it better.

I pull a small black velvet box out of the pocket of my pants. "Your outfit needs one more accessory." I show her the box.

Her eyes sparkle. "Is that what I think it is?"

"That depends. If you say yes, then it's what you think it is. If you say no, it's just a box I'll stick back into my pocket while trying not to feel totally emasculated because I look like a complete idiot."

She opens the box. The ring is in the shape of a star. I had it made right after I found out about the baby. She wasn't ready back then. I hope she is now.

"So?" I wait. Not moving. Not breathing.

She bites her bottom lip and raises her brows. "I wouldn't want you to look like an idiot."

"Jesus, Dev. Is that a yes?"

"That's a yes."

I stand and pick her up and twirl her around.

"Uh… Aaron?"

"Yeah?"

"We're naked. If someone walks by—"

"They'll see the silhouettes of two deliriously happy people." I put her down. "You are deliriously happy, aren't you?"

"For the first time in my life, I am."

I take the ring out of the box and slip it onto her finger. "This means you're mine forever. You and Casey. It's a binding agreement. No takebacks, okay?"

"No takebacks. But, Aaron, I want to wait until after he's born. If this is going to be my one-and-only wedding, I don't want to have to wear a maternity dress."

"Whatever you want. Because you can bet your ass this will be the one and only for us."

"Thank you."

"For what?"

"For not pushing me to get married before he comes. For wanting to marry me in the first place. For pulling a gun on me the day we met so I couldn't leave. For giving me a place to sleep and work. For being my best friend. For… everything."

"I can't wait to tell everyone. My parents will be so happy. Oh, that reminds me, I have something else to show you."

"Another surprise?"

"Not a surprise so much. I thought I'd introduce you to my guardian angel."

"Erin?"

I pick up her dress and help her into it, then put my clothes on. "Let's go inside." I get the letter out of a drawer in the changing table and hand it over.

She examines it. "It's sealed."

"I thought we could read it together."

She reads the writing on the envelope: *For Aaron when he finds out he's going to be a father.*

"It's amazing how she left you so many notes."

"Some I'll never read."

"Why not?"

"Say I didn't have kids—I'd have never known about this one."

"So your aunt and uncle have a vault of these letters somewhere, waiting for certain things to happen? That is so cool. I wish I could have met her. She sounds like someone I'd want to know."

"Me, too." I gesture to the envelope. "Go ahead."

She opens it like it's a priceless piece of art. I read over her shoulder.

Aaron,

You're going to be a daddy! I may not know what it feels like to become a man and do things men do. I may not know what it feels like to do a lot of things I write about in these letters. But one thing I do know is how it feels to find out you're going to be a parent. It's indescribable. It's scary. It's miraculous.

I hope this news makes you happy. But even if it was unexpected, that doesn't mean it's wrong. However it happened, remember to trust in fate. There is a plan for you, sweet boy, and you don't always know what that plan is.

Have faith it will take you where you are destined to go. This child, planned or not, will change your life in ways you never thought he would. Even before he or she is born, you will look at the world differently. Trees will seem greener. The moon will be brighter. At the same time, the world will become more frightening because now you have someone to protect. Someone you would give your life for.

I hope with all my heart that you are reading this with her—the one you've chosen to spend your life with. Reassure her often. Compliment her daily. Be her sunshine when she's weathering a storm. And don't be afraid to let her be yours.

Life doesn't always go the way we want it to, so embrace every day. Live to the fullest. Don't be afraid to take your baby in the snow. He may be cold for a few minutes, but the snow angels you make with him will last a lifetime. Don't be afraid to run along the shore. She may slip and fall, but the sandcastles you build together will heal her more than a Band-Aid. Take him to Disney World, even if you don't think you can afford it. He may catch a cold, but the pictures of him with Mickey Mouse will be something you'll always treasure.

Remember this: Storms pass. Wounds heal. Scars fade.

And if all else fails, there's always chocolate. Especially peanut butter cups—those are my favorite.

Your guardian angel,
Erin

EPILOGUE

Deryn

Four months later…

I'm up before dawn again. I can't sleep… again. Having a stubborn seven-pound cowboy sitting on my bladder twenty-four seven isn't helping. He's gotten so big, and my back has been in almost constant pain these past few days. I pad through the cabin, taking in the expansion. He added two bedrooms, a sitting room, and a loft. There's a huge porch around back. I heard him telling Quinn once that it would be easy to expand further in the future. I know he eventually wants more kids. Me—I just need to get *this* one here.

I sit in the rocking chair and look at the date circled on the calendar. It came and went three days ago. I've been ready for weeks. The bassinet is by our bed. Baby clothes are arranged in the drawers. Diapers are stacked by the changing table. Everyone is ready for Casey to come into the world except Casey.

Part of me can't blame him. This world can be ugly, cruel, and unforgiving. Where he is right now is safe and quiet. If I didn't look like a whale and feel like a punching bag, I'd want him to stay inside, too.

I hum a song to him. One of Kasey's favorites.

Arms wrap around me from behind. "How are my two favorite people today?"

"Miserable. I'm as big as a house, and he barely has any room to move."

"We've done everything the midwife recommended to help move things along. He just likes where he is. Who can blame him?" He kisses my head, then cups my breasts. "We could do it again if you want."

"Ugh. I love you, Aaron, but if we have sex one more time, I may start to think of it as not such a good thing."

"All right. No sex. Eggs with tabasco it is."

"I'm sick of that, too." I hunch over. "Will you please come out already?"

I feel a pop, then a gush and stiffen.

"Dev?"

"I think my water just broke." I feel between my legs. "Oh god, it did."

He laughs. "Let's pray our kid always listens to you that well."

"Stop laughing. We have to call Suzy." I freeze with fear. "I thought I wanted this, but suddenly I'm terrified."

"We *do* want this. Look around; we're ready." He kneels down and holds my stare. "Now let's do this and meet our son."

He calls Suzy, our midwife. Everyone thought I was crazy for not wanting to have him in a hospital, but I know how much Aaron hates hospitals. Waiting there for days to see if his best friend would live or die. Seeing him lifeless on a ventilator. I wasn't about to do anything to bring up those memories on a day that should be happy.

He pulls the phone away from his ear. "Are you having contractions?"

I shake my head. He relays the information.

"She wants to know if the water is clear." With his help, I stand, and we assess the wet cushion. "Looks clear," he tells her. He listens and nods. "Okay. Yes, all right. We'll talk later, then." He hangs up.

"Later? What do you mean later?"

"She said if you haven't had any contractions, and you're not in any distress, you probably have a while. We're to call back if you start bleeding or when your contractions are five minutes apart."

"What the heck am I supposed to do until then?"

"We talked about this, Dev. Take a warm shower. Play cards. Walk around."

"Easy for you to say."

"First, let's change you out of those clothes. Then I'm going to let everyone know."

"You can call them, but I don't want anyone coming over here and watching every move I make."

"Understood."

While I change, he calls Maddox, Quinn, Joe, Owen, and his parents. "Don't forget to call Shannon."

"Oh, right."

Shannon is someone I met at prenatal yoga. We hit it off from the beginning. Although I'm very selective about who I let into my circle of friends, knowing not everyone would accept me as they have, she didn't judge me, and we've become close. She'll be one of my bridesmaids in May. She's going to be a single mom. The father didn't want anything to do with her. I wanted to introduce her to

Quinn, but he laughed, saying a baby was the last thing a helicopter-flying, bronc-riding cowboy needed.

Aaron is walking me around the house from room to room by my elbow. "I don't need an escort," I say. "I'm having a baby, not a hip replacement."

He holds up his hands. "Sorry."

A contraction hits me, and I clutch his arm, feeling like my body is going to rip apart. It's like a huge muscle cramp combined with the worst indigestion combined with being kicked in the back—all at once. When it's over, I need his help to sit. I glare at him.

"What?" he says. "I didn't say anything."

"But you were thinking it."

He chuckles. "This is going to be a long day."

"Ya think?"

"I'm here for you. Whatever you want, whatever you need, just ask." He puts both hands on my stomach. "Today is his birthday. It's going to be one of the best days of our lives."

"Says the guy who doesn't have to push something the size of a watermelon out of his nostril."

He laughs again.

"This isn't funny, Aaron."

"You're right. What can I get you? Water? Tea?"

"Tea sounds good." He gets up to leave, but I grab his arm hard. I'm having another contraction. "Ahhh, oh god." I grit my teeth and press a hand to the side of my tummy.

"Um…" He checks the time. "I don't think that was five minutes. More like two."

"I feel something down there."

His eyes go wide with fear. "What do you mean, you feel something?"

"I think I should lie down." As soon as he gets me to the bed, another contraction hits. I bite my lip so hard, blood trickles down my chin. "It hurts. I feel like I have to push."

"What?"

"Look down there."

He removes my yoga pants and undies and checks between my legs. His face loses all color. "I think I see the top of his head."

"Oh my god!"

He pulls out his phone, calls Suzy, and throws it on the bed. When she answers, he yells, "The baby is coming. I can see his head."

"I'm on my way. I'll be there in thirty minutes."

"What if she doesn't have that long?" He glances at me, clearly worried. "Wait, maybe Andie can help. Where's your phone?"

I point to the kitchen. He runs to get it while Suzy asks me questions. When he returns, he says Andie is coming over.

"She births foals, Aaron, not babies."

"She can help," Suzy says.

"Suzy thinks I've been in labor for at least a day," I tell him. "My indigestion and back pain."

"That's labor?"

"It can be," Suzy said. "Apparently it was. First babies never come this quickly."

"I really have to push."

"Go ahead," Suzy says. "Your body knows what to do." She gives Aaron instructions about feeling for the cord and turning the baby's head, but I'm so focused on getting him out, I can't think of anything else.

"His head is out," he says. "Oh, Jesus."

"And the cord?" Suzy asks.

"I don't feel it."

"That's good. Devyn, with the next contraction, give it everything you have. That will get his shoulders free, and then he'll slip right out. Be ready, Aaron."

"Oh shit," he says, looking at me. "We're really doing this."

"Be careful," I say. "Don't drop him."

"Not on your fucking life."

"Ahhhhhh!" I scream as I'm torn in two.

"That's right," Suzy says. "Push hard. Keep pushing."

"Ahhhhhh!" I feel like my insides are coming out. Then suddenly it's over.

"Oh my god, oh my god, oh my god," Aaron chants.

I rise on my elbows. He's holding our son. The door flies open, and Andie runs over. She doesn't take the baby. She instructs Aaron to rub his back. "Don't be afraid to rub it firmly. You need to get him breathing."

"He's not breathing?" I cry.

"Don't we need to cut the cord?" Aaron asks frantically.

"Give him a minute," she says calmy, like the world didn't just shift on its axis. "The placenta gives him oxygen until he can breathe. Keep rubbing him." She tickles Casey's feet.

A loud, angry cry fills the room, and we all sob in relief.

"Put him on her chest," Andie says. "Pull up your shirt, Devyn. He needs to be on your skin, where it's warm."

Aaron places Casey on me. "Hi there." I wrap my arms around his tiny, slick body. "I'm your mom," I say. I can't hold back tears, because saying it feels so unreal. I look at Aaron. "I'm a mom."

I have another small contraction. It's not nearly as bad as the others. I peek at Andie.

"It's the placenta being expelled. Not to worry."

Aaron comes up by my head as Andie works below. "Hey, buddy," he says to Casey. "Just so you know, the woman holding you is the best thing that ever happened to me, and you're the best thing that has happened to *us*. We love you so much."

"Aaron, do you want to cut the cord?" Andie asks.

"I can do that now?"

She nods and hands him the scissors. "You're the father."

His eyes get misty. "I am. I'm the father."

He cuts the cord and then lies down next to us, wrapping us in his arms.

Andie puts a blanket on top of Casey. "The placenta looks complete. I think you're all good, but you may need a few stitches. I'm going to step outside to wait for Suzy."

We can't even acknowledge her. We're mesmerized by our son. The door closes, and we're alone. We're a family.

I kiss the top of my son's head. Then I kiss my fiancé. "How did I not know this was going to be everything I ever wanted?"

He brushes a wet piece of hair off my forehead. "You've never been more beautiful. I love you, Devyn."

"I love you, too."

Our son is sleeping on my chest. I put my hand on his back, needing to feel his every breath. "Do you think they're here?"

"I'm sure everyone is waiting outside, except my parents, but they're catching the first flight out."

"Not them." I lift my chin. "*Them.*"

He understands what I'm asking, because he's the only person who's ever understood me. He nods. "Yeah, I do."

I look at my son and then at the ceiling. "Everyone, meet Casey Cameron Pearce."

ACKNOWLEDGMENTS

20 BOOKS! Wow—I never thought I'd be an author of so many.

If Texas Lilies was the first book you've read of mine, you'll want to go back and read about Maddox in Texas Orchids, or better yet, start from the very beginning with Baylor and Gavin's incredibly sexy story, Purple Orchids.

Thank you to my incredible beta readers, Laura Conley, Joelle Yates, Shauna Salley, and Jen Meador. You all have special talents you bring to beta reading.

To my alpha reader and quasi-editor, Ann Peters, I appreciate your continued dedication.

As always, my editing team at Murphy Rae Solutions deserves a shout out. And also my proofreader, Amanda Cuff.

Last but not least, I have to thank my super-awesome assistant, Julie Collier, who not only does beta reading, but helps me in all things.

It's been so much fun writing the Mitchell Sisters' next generation, and I can't wait for you to read the final (and hottest) book of the series, Texas Roses. Readers have been begging for Amber's story since Black Roses came out years ago. And boy, will you get a story!

ABOUT THE AUTHOR

Samantha Christy's passion for writing started long before her first novel was published. Graduating from the University of Nebraska with a degree in Criminal Justice, she held the title of Computer Systems Analyst for The Supreme Court of Wisconsin and several major universities around the United States. Raised mainly in Indianapolis, she holds the Midwest and its homegrown values dear to her heart and upon the birth of her third child devoted herself to raising her family full time. While it took time to get from there to here, writing has remained her utmost passion and being a stay-at-home mom facilitated her ability to follow that dream. When she is not writing, she keeps busy cruising to every Caribbean island where ships sail. Samantha Christy currently resides in St. Augustine, Florida with her husband and four children.

You can reach Samantha Christy at any of these wonderful places:

Website: www.samanthachristy.com

Facebook: https://www.facebook.com/SamanthaChristyAuthor

Instagram: https://www.instagram.com/authorsamanthachristy

E-mail: samanthachristy@comcast.net

www.ingramcontent.com/pod-product-compliance
Lightning Source LLC
Chambersburg PA
CBHW031511010826
48973CB00012B/200